The Croesus Tithe

F.W. Lane

Order this book online at www.trafford.com
or email orders@trafford.com

Most Trafford titles are also available at major online book retailers.

Printed in the United States of America.

ISBN: 978-1-4269-4365-2 (sc)
ISBN: 978-1-4269-4366-9 (hc)
ISBN: 978-1-4269-4367-6 (e)

Library of Congress Control Number: 2010913883

*Our mission is to efficiently provide the world's finest, most comprehensive book publishing
service, enabling every author to experience success. To find out how to publish your book,
your way, and have it available worldwide, visit us online at www.trafford.com*

Trafford rev. 10/23/2010

 www.trafford.com

North America & international
toll-free: 1 888 232 4444 (USA & Canada)
phone: 250 383 6864 ♦ fax: 812 355 4082

About the Book

The Island of Jersey is the largest of the Channel Islands group and great wealth resides there.

Paradoxically, it is virtually defenceless, even in today's world of heightened security, against terrorist attack.

In this story, I have endeavoured to highlight the vulnerability both as a warning to those living there and also to the politicians who govern it.

Complacency can be very costly, especially in this day and age. Those who enjoy the privilege of residency need to be mindful of the need to invest in protecting themselves and their beautiful Island, while the going is good.

I hope this book helps to bring this about, while there's still time; better to do so through choice, rather than desperation, quite obviously.

After working there for over six years, my love for the place and the Islanders continues and this warmth inspired me to write this book for their wellbeing as much as anything.

About the Author

This is my third book and although all of them have a connection with Jersey, this work specifically centres upon this small and extraordinarily wealthy island.

I lived there for over six years, (1986 - 1992) during my tenure in the Channel Islands, as the Head of the offshore subsidiary of a major London financial organisation.

The people, both native and the wealthy 'tax exiles' in residence, were very welcoming and I made and still have, many friends on Jersey.

Now retired, after more than forty years in the finance industry, I remain fascinated by the allure of this beautiful and quaint place, its relaxed lifestyle and relative defencelessness.

I was and still am, very aware of the vulnerability of the Island to an assault upon it, given the exceptional wealth held there.

The Croesus Tithe

Synopsis

A modern day, Robin Hood, hijacks the Island of
Jersey and gets away with it.
The wealthy enclave pays up.
Only the innocent benefit; not the perpetrator.

Acknowledgements

I have to thank many friends and supporters for their encouragement in my writing this third book but especially so, Julie and Clare, who have again spent a lot of time and effort in bringing this about.

As previously, their tireless contributions, on the graphic design work involved and editing processes, are genuinely appreciated. Without them, the finished article would have remained an unread manuscript.

Contents

THE CROESUS TITHE

Chapter One

An Eye for an Eye......

It was just past 3.15 am that morning and everything was at rest, as it should be, two hours before daybreak. From the top of the hill overlooking Managua, Nicaragua's capital city, the urban sprawl was lit like a giant diadem enclosing the metropolis which squatted along the shore of the lake which bears its name. The city was more brightly lit than its surroundings, like a huge diamond occupying the centrepiece of the tiara of shimmering neon light.

There was a bright, full moon, with only a few clouds to be seen; otherwise the pale lit, night sky, comprised solely a myriad of twinkling stars from a billion or more miles away, making for a heavenly backdrop to the tranquility below.

Nothing stirred. Well, almost nothing; a solitary pair of tiny lights were on the move, along the road, heading south, out of the city towards Diriamba. The car was travelling along within the speed limit for that part of the town; well below the 80 kmph restriction, in fact.

The vehicle was motoring along at a steady 50kmph, as if the driver was lost or looking for something. To the casual observer, it could be construed the subdued pace was attention - worthy, suspicious even, especially at that time of the morning, with no other road users around.

The car ambled its way up the slight gradient, maintaining the same speed, almost certainly governed by a cruise control fitment and when it got to the top of the hill, its lights were extinguished and the engine switched off. The dark coloured saloon ran silently alongside the kerb for a few more yards and came to a stop between a couple of street lights, some one hundred yards apart. The time was now 3.25am. Nothing further occurred for a full five minutes: very suspicious!

Then, at precisely 3.30am, the driver got out, closing the door quietly and went to the rear of the vehicle. He looked around furtively, and then opened the boot, depositing a few things onto the pavement.

The man was dressed all in black, wearing a sort of jump suit, with a tight fitting hood attached. He looked around again and then picked up a large backpack, pulled it on and slung a couple of smaller items over his shoulder. He closed the boot lid, again quietly and after a final look-see, he jogged away from the vehicle towards a metal fence bordering the road.

He was up and over it in a couple of swift movements and then started a quick walk up the hillside beyond. Two minutes more and he was out of sight of the road. A few clouds passed across the face of the moon, temporarily obscuring the pale lunar light but soon the moon-glow was restored.

The lone figure moved stealthily up to the top of the hill and, after a brief look back from whence he came, he moved beyond the crest of it and was gone. He walked purposefully down part of the far slope of the hill and, finding a flat piece of ground overlooking a large property some one hundred feet below his vantage point, he stopped. He man-handled the heavy rucksack off his shoulders and put it down, along with the other items he was carrying. He stooped towards the edge of the hillside, took out a small telescope from the breast pocket of his jump suit, squatted down and surveyed the scene below him.

Through his spyglass, equipped with 'night-site' optics, the isolated property he was interested in was lit up in green 'daylight,' as he slowly traversed the target area. The building was a ranch-style, two storey, eight bedroomed, house he'd been told beforehand by his boss, Ernesto Alvarez. He concentrated on the flat roof area towards the rear of the substantial construction and its proximity to the walled garden surrounding the place. It was clearly well guarded, with a few figures walking about, some with dogs, even at that time of the morning.

He counted three security guards slowly patrolling the outside of the premises, all with dogs on leashes, those that he could see, at any rate and two more standing either side of the large front door.

His scan revealed an inner fence, some twenty five yards back from the garden wall and he counted half a dozen dogs wandering around or lying down in the space between the fence and the wall.

"Hopping over the garden wall is no option with this place," he whispered to himself, as he continued to consider the scene. A few moments later, he lowered his spyglass, collapsed it into a quarter of its viewing size and put it back into his breast pocket. He looked at his watch, just as the moon clouded over again but the luminous dial clearly showed it was 3.42am.

He left his observation position and returned to the flat area where his equipment was located. He opened the large rucksack and pulled out the contents; an assembly kit for a paraglide. It took Manuel Cortez, Ernesto's Guatemalan 'retributionist,' (he hated the term 'assassin', considering it to be a cowardly description of him and his work) about fifteen minutes to erect the triangular gliding apparatus.

Having satisfied himself that all the fittings were firmly secured, he picked up the smaller satchel he had with him, slung it over his shoulder and moved, with the glider, back to his reconnaissance point.

Taking out his spyglass once more, he re-surveyed the scene below him. All seemed set; everything appeared as tranquil as before and even the clouds obliged him. A large expanse of darker clouds was following behind the pale clouds now passing in front of the lunar body.

"Time to go, I think - I won't get a better opportunity for it," he said to himself, as he held up the black linen apparatus above his head, adjusted his grip on the paraglide and, having taken a few backward steps, ran towards the observation point with it. Within a foot of the edge of the hillside, he launched himself into the air and was immediately aloft, with little noise from the 'lift off,' he determined.

A few seconds later, he'd steadied himself into a comfortable position, as the craft glided silently in a circle, while he got his bearings. Everything seemed set for a noiseless landing onto that flat roof which he was aiming for.

There was only a mild breeze that morning and he'd calculated he was downwind of it anyway, so any slight noise he might make on his approach to the flat roof shouldn't betray his presence. With a slight adjustment to the glider's rudder and a gentle downwards pressure on his 'handlebar' he began to descend to his dropping zone.

Like the dinner jacketed suitor of a gal who adored a particular brand of chocolates by a famous manufacturer featured in the TV ads of the early nineties, Manuel approached the roof of the building. He wasn't carrying a box of scrumptious chocolates with him, though; six sticks of gelignite were his 'present' for the owner of this property!

A few feet above his chosen landing spot, he jerked up the 'handlebar' of his glider, which instantly 'killed' his modest speed and he stepped onto the roof, taking only two forward steps on the asphalt to stop himself.

His light footfall seemed as unobtrusive as his flight thus far, which encouraged him to gently lay his glider alongside one of the large chimneys near him. With little wind and the moonlight still subdued by the dark clouds obscuring the moon, he took off his small backpack and took out the 'present' for the householder.

On the top landing of the house, however, a snoozing Doberman pricked up its ears, making a muffled grunt, as it got up to listen intently for any further sound. It wandered along the landing, back and forth, straining to hear any further tell-tale noise of a possible intruder.

Cortez, although unaware of the dog's alertness some fifteen feet below him, was a thorough practitioner of his craft and had left little to chance. He'd put on some socks over his trainers before he'd set off with his glider, knowing that these would soften his footsteps all the more on the rooftop. He was right and this small safeguard could well have prevented the animal giving his presence away. It slumped down again to slumber once more but remained alert.

The Guatemalan 'retributionist' worked quickly but quietly. He stuck an I.C. timer, set to detonate at 6.30am, into one of the sticks of explosive, attached a nylon cord to the bundle of them and lowered it down the lounge chimney to within eight feet of the fireplace floor. He used a laser measuring device to determine the precise distance it was from it and then tied off the bundle around the chimney stack to suspend it at that point.

He knew the owner of the house, Ronaldo Martin, was a creature of habit and he always liked his lounge log fire to be lit when he was at home. His housemaid, having cleared the grate the night before and set up the kindling for the next morning's lighting up, would attend to it around six o'clock, later that morning.

He'd arranged for the 'gelly' to explode some thirty minutes after the fire was lit as Ronaldo, being an early riser, was most likely to be drinking his early morning coffee in the lounge at that time.

Having attended to his 'suspended present' for the unsuspecting Ronaldo, a feared drug baron operating in and around Managua, he satisfied himself everything was set up properly. He then, deftly, put on his empty rucksack and picked up the paraglide once more.

A slight breeze got up, though and he almost lost control of it, with the right wing strut scraping the glass on a nearby skylight, making a light screeching noise. At this, the dog was up again and barked loudly, looking up towards the loft trap door and Manuel heard the bark and cussed under his breath.

As he prepared to leap off the roof to make his escape, the two guards by the front door burst into the hall and the Doberman looked down at them, barking again. The security guys bounded up the stairs, pistols drawn and proceeded to search all the upstairs rooms. Sadly, for them, neither took any notice of the dog, which resumed its upward stare but didn't bark any more, probably confused by all the sudden, lateral, activity around it.

Unbeknown to Cortez, this was a stroke of luck for him, since his exit trajectory was not as lofty as he'd hoped for and his flight path could have been spotted from the front of the house, had the door guards still been in position there. Fortunately, the moonlight remained dimmed by dark clouds and he was swiftly over the boundary of the property, looking to land near his parked car.

The street below him was still deserted at that time of the early morning, so he made a beeline for his vehicle, in case the dog bark had prompted a full scale alert and search for an intruder back at the hillside property.

It hadn't, since nothing untoward was found back at the house, no forced windows or broken glass indicating an entry, were evident and the dog was chastised verbally for waking up the household! It slunk off to the far end of the landing and slumped down again to snooze with a rather dejected expression on its face!

Meanwhile, the black-clad 'retributionist' landed safely and quietly next to his car. He quickly wrestled the rucksack off his back and stowed it in the boot and then only took a minute or so more to collapse his flying apparatus and stuffed it in there, too.

He got into the car, taking off his Velcro attached hood, as he started the engine and then drew smoothly away from the kerb, turned around and drove back down the hill towards the City. It was 4.10 am by his watch, as he settled down for the twenty minute ride back into town.

He arrived at his small flat around 4.30am and once inside, telephoned his boss, Ernesto Alvarez, the leader of 'The Enlightened Way,' to tell him that everything had gone according to plan.

"That's good, Manuel, very good. Call around later and we'll have breakfast together and watch the early morning TV news, eh? There should be something worth watching, I hope, if there's any justice in this world. I hate that man's activities and he deserves all he gets, especially after killing some of our people, too!"

Ernesto's reputation was rather akin to a modern day 'Robin Hood' - robbing the rich to give to the poor; ninety per cent of his haul from them, anyway.

He'd long harboured a grudge against the very wealthy who'd refused to give to the poor, even a smidgen of what they had, after he'd requested a 'donation' from them.

He'd only failed twice on their behalf; the first time, because a millionaire ship-owner simply sailed away with his family, after Ernesto threatened to foreshorten their lives on this planet, if they didn't accede to his request for a donation and they didn't. And then this guy, Ronaldo Martin. He was something quite different!

Because of Ernesto's growing reputation, with a private army behind him of some one hundred fighters, the drug lord seemed genuinely agreeable to a discussion about matters, or so he'd thought. However, Ernesto's emissaries had been ambushed by Martin's men on their way to see him and their bodies returned to him in pieces. A note pinned to the chest of one of them, stating that:-

"No-one threatens Ronaldo Martin in this City - so beware of upsetting me again!" hadn't really impressed Ernesto Alvarez in the way it was intended to. Quite the opposite, in fact; it had spurred him on to vengeful thoughts, before the drug dealer really moved against him.

A demonstration of who Ernesto was and what he could do, was clearly called for; hence Manuel's retaliatory visit to the man's house, early that morning.

Manuel called around to his boss's flat, as invited, just after 6.40am for breakfast and to watch the early morning news on TV with him. He was sure he'd heard a distant rumble on the way over to him and hoped the news bulletin they were anticipating would confirm a successful operation for them.

They sat down to watch an outside reporter interviewing the infamous drug baron, though, with a smouldering house in the background. Ronaldo Martin was putting the explosion down to a freak gas leak at the property which had, unfortunately, led to the death of his housekeeper, Maria Sanchez.

Apparently, she'd started the fire in the lounge, as usual but as the wood for it was a little damp that morning, she'd applied the gas poker to the kindling, to get it going in time for him. Before she'd finished tidying the room, as usual, the fireplace exploded and she died a few minutes later. The blast must have been due to a build up of gas, he suggested, since it took out two supporting walls, as well as destroying the lounge, dining room and most of the hall area.

Ernesto, however, looked at the expression on the man's face and turned to his 'retributionist' and said, flatly, to him,

"He knows, Manuel, he knows it was us. Don't believe all the rubbish about him thinking it was a gas explosion; once the reporters have gone away, he'll send a squad after us. Come on, we'd better go, back to our village, while we've still got time."

Cortez didn't argue with his boss. They packed up while the interviews were still going on and they got away from the City and headed for their homes in Guatemala, a few hundred miles away.

On the way there, Ernesto realised he'd made the classic mistake of underestimating his adversary, albeit through a lucky break for Ronaldo; he should have ensured he'd finish him off in one go. Now, he had a 'wounded tiger' to contend with and an injured one is a far more dangerous animal to confront!

It was, indeed, a lucky break for Ronaldo Martin that morning. He'd completed his ablutions by 6.25am, rather later than usual and was straightening his tie, when Maria was downstairs trying to get the lounge fire going with the poker.

He was combing his moustache and admiring himself in the full-length mirror a few minutes later when she wiggled the poker, quite vigorously, to get the fire really going this time. Although her effort sent a mass of sparks and flame up the chimney, it was 6.30am. The detonation shook the building with devastating results.

Ronaldo was thrown against the wall of his bedroom and was temporarily stunned by the blast but he finally got up and once the dust had cleared somewhat, he gingerly went downstairs. His lounge looked as if a bomb had hit it and, of course, one had! He tried to revive poor Maria but she passed away in his arms, having suffered terrible lacerations to her face and torso.

One of his security guards, who was passing the room at the time, was lying unconscious in the hall; the explosion having propelled him twenty feet backwards into the atrium.

By the time Ronaldo had picked up his dead housekeeper in his arms and wandered out into the hall, he was surrounded by most of his security people. He handed the corpse to one of his men and went back upstairs to change out of his dust covered suit.

Having showered once more, dried himself off and put on another, hand tailored, suit, he was in front of the mirror again. After going through the same dressing routine to ensure his dapper appearance was maintained, he looked at himself and vowed, in a low voice, conveying both determination and menace,

"This was the work of that, so-called, 'Robin Hood,' Ernesto Alvarez, I'm sure of it! He will pay very dearly for this." The suavely dressed, sixty year old, drug baron, moved closer to the mirror and affirmed to his reflection,

"He will pay the ultimate price!"

He continued to stare at the stern expression he exhibited and wondered whether this and his penetrating black eyes, would be sufficiently intimidating to a foe. He thought it would be and with a haughty 'humph' to the figure looking back at him, he turned away.

One of his bodyguards knocked on the open bedroom door to tell the gang boss that some press people were on their way and,

"Would you be prepared to give them a statement, sir?" his acolyte enquired.

"Yes, certainly….I'll,…eh….be down directly." The man nodded in acknowledgement of his employer's response and turned away, saying he'd tell the media, accordingly.

Having composed himself and brushed back his hair, once more, Ronaldo Martin walked downstairs into the large hallway and then out onto the driveway to address the crowd assembled there. It was 6.45am as he was getting into his stride addressing the throng of reporters; just the moment Ernesto and his 'retributionist,' Manuel Cortez, tuned in to see the TV news.

Upon returning to their village of San Luis, in the foothills of the Maya Mountains, in Guatemala, Ernesto told Manuel Cortez that even here wasn't far enough away from a man like Ronaldo Martin. He would, therefore, move out of the Country for a while and only return when things had died down and then he'd properly 'take care of' the notorious drug baron. Permanently, next time!

"As he doesn't know who you are, Manuel, you stay here and keep me informed of things, okay?" His 'retributionist' nodded and said he would.

Chapter Two

An unholy Alliance comes together.

Ernesto Alvarez had escaped from Guatemala, via the Maya Mountains in the east of the country, the terrain he knew very well, unlike his pursuers. They were no match for his agility across the barren slopes and since the mountains straddled the border with Belize, he was soon over the other side, heading for the port of Belize City, the capital of the erstwhile British colony.

The journey of some one hundred and twenty miles from San Luis in the foothills of the Maya Mountains to Belize City took a fortnight to complete: he had to make several detours initially to throw his pursuers off the scent but after a few days into the trek, he realised they must have abandoned the hunt for him.

He stayed in Belize City for three weeks, arranging for most of his 'loot' in his bank account in Guatemala to be transferred to the National Bank of Belize. He'd opened a new account there, under the name of 'Ernest Ravel,' purporting to be a wealthy land agent from Managua, Nicaragua.

He had a few contacts in that City, chiefly an American ex-pat by the name of Arnold Fleischer, who'd made quite a name for himself in New York as an alleged fraudster. He'd jumped bail in 1997 and escaped to Managua in the summer of that year, and since there's no extradition treaty between Nicaragua and the United States, he'd resumed his illegal activities, operating from his home in Managua, without difficulty.

The American continued his unsavoury practices from there, becoming heavily involved in 'Pyramid selling' to the gullible Latinos who were not too conversant with this particular scam, unfortunately for them.

One of Ernesto's 'fences' had recommended Arnold Fleischer to him in early '99 as a discreet 'laundryman' in Managua, should he ever require such services. He did in January 2000, initially as a 'reference' for his new bank account opening in Belize, under the name of Ernest Ravel and later on for more tangible business between them. Arnold would be happy to oblige on both counts!

Ernesto's money transfer of some $9 million into his new account in Belize took just under three weeks to come through. Once in credit there, he was hoping to go down and visit Arnold to meet the man who'd so impressed him over the telephone but without a passport, that wouldn't be easy. Moreover, he received word that a couple of British security agents were asking some 'locals' where they might be able to find him. Fearing his whereabouts might soon be discovered, he decided to move elsewhere. Any business with Arnold would have to wait.

He wandered down to the port area of the City and found a trawler about to sail for Havana. The absence of a passport wasn't a problem when $500 was proffered in lieu and he was no sooner aboard, than the ship cast off and headed towards the open sea.

The voyage to Castro's Cuba took three days and after disembarkation, Ernesto found himself in Havana harbour, drinking a welcome cup of coffee on the quayside on the morning of the first day of February.

He wandered around the Capital and booked into a pleasant enough hotel on the edge of the waterfront. Mr Ravel again used the 'dollar' persuasion to get one of the best rooms available (of which there were quite a number on offer, unlike the 'greenback' he paid over to the delighted receptionist to get it) and he telephoned Arnold Fleischer from there.

The room offered a tremendous view of the harbour, which he slowly surveyed as he waited to be put through to the American. When he was connected, he immediately recognised Fleischer's voice. He apologised to him for his swift departure from Belize but he was comforted when Arnold jokingly stated,

"Yeah, I know all about such expediency myself, so don't worry about it; it's an occupational hazard you might say, eh?"

"Well, yes, that's certainly the case at the moment, unfortunately but hey, I'd like to come over to see you so we can discuss a lot more business, sizeable business, which we might do together. The trouble is I don't have a passport with me to facilitate my travel arrangements at the moment, if you know what I mean?"

"Give me your address and room number there and I'll arrange for one to be sent out to you. As you're, supposedly, a wealthy land agent here in Managua, who's simply lost his passport, it shouldn't be difficult to get a replacement drawn up: pop a passport photo in the post to me and I'll have a quiet word with a couple of people I know here and it'll soon be sorted."

"Right, Arnold, that'll be very helpful if you could; I'm using the alias Ernest Ravel for travelling purposes, don't forget, so I'll get the photo done and in the post to you later today, then. Thank you very much; we'll talk again soon, good bye."

Ernesto rang off and, much encouraged by Arnold Fleischer's offer to help, he went downstairs to the receptionist, requested some writing paper and enquired about having his photograph taken.

He was directed to a general stores along the quayside, which catered for just about everything, including photographic services. He found the establishment without any difficulty and twenty minutes later, he emerged into the sunshine again with a trio of suitable photos of himself.

He'd passed the post office on his way to the all-purpose general stores, so he returned there, purchased an envelope, sat down and penned a short note to Arnold and enclosed the photos of himself and posted the letter.

The next few days were taken up being a pseudo-tourist: he'd never been to Havana before and needed to familiarise himself with the place, in any event. He was also keen to observe the best exit routes out of the City, if he needed to beat a hasty retreat once more. He didn't think that should be necessary really, given Cuba was still regarded as something akin to a pariah state but there was no harm in taking sensible precautions.

Having spent the best part of a fortnight sunning himself in Havana, he was becoming quite comfortable with the place. Although conditions were tough for the locals alright, what with the U.S. embargo still in force and 'make-do' arrangements commonplace, as exemplified by all the cars being models of the fifties or earlier, anyone with a reasonable supply of dollars, didn't lack for much.

'Just like life for the better off generally,' he mused to himself, not appreciating, amazingly, that his own activities had elevated himself into the very position of those he so despised!

He returned to his hotel around midday one sunny Tuesday to have lunch and the receptionist called out to him, as he moved towards the Restaurant.

"Mr Ravel, we have a package for you, sir." He didn't immediately respond to the call, forgetting his new identity momentarily but did so upon the second request from the nice lady behind the large desk.

"Oh, I'm sorry, I was deep in thought about something else; a package, you say?"

"Yes, sir, it was delivered earlier this morning," she said, handing the item over to him.

"Thanks," he replied, as he took it from her and proceeded towards his room instead. Once inside, he opened the package and pulled out a crisp Nicaraguan passport, together with a note from Arnold Fleischer. It read, *'This should do the trick, my friend – call me and we can arrange to meet up.'*

Ernesto carefully scrutinised the passport the American had provided. It was very impressive and certainly looked official, he thought, with his recently taken photo, duly stamped with an impression mark in one corner, looking straight at him. Everything seemed to be in order.

He picked up the telephone, asking the woman on the switchboard to connect him with Arnold's number in Managua and gazed out of his window at the quayside. A few moments later the operator said she was putting him through and he heard Arnold's, rather gruff, voice on the other end of the line.

"Hello, Arnold, it's me, Ernest Ravel. Thanks very much for your letter; it arrived this morning and everything seems fine, very fine, I must say."

"Oh, great, glad everything's okay, your end. When do you anticipate coming down to see me?"

"Whenever it suits you, really; I've no other plans at the moment," Ernesto replied.

"Well, in that case, today's Tuesday, so why don't you arrange to come down here at the weekend and stay over for a few days, eh?"

"Sure, that sounds ideal but how will I know where to find you?"

"You let me know the flight details when you're booked up and I'll send one of my guys over to collect you, that'll be the easiest way, I think. He'll be driving a two-tone, blue, Buick, having a red pennant on the top of the aerial, okay?"

"Okay, then, I'll 'phone you again later on with the flight details, as you say and look out for the car with the red flag flying from its aerial, then."

"Red pennant, though, not red flag, Ernesto - there's no Communism down here, I can assure you!"

"Alright, then, I'll speak to you later -'bye."

Having put the 'phone down, Arnold was still chuckling, as he turned to his number two, Robert Singleton, and declared,

"Well, one thing that guy hasn't got is a sense of humour; I thought my clarification of the car's identity was quite witty, Bob, didn't you?"

"Yeah, I thought so, too, sir," replied his aide, managing a modest laugh in sympathy.

A few days later, Ernesto Alvarez, aka Ernest Ravel, flew into Managua airport, looking quite smartly dressed in a pale yellow shirt, cream coloured suit, bright blue tie and sporting a panama hat.

He carried a sizeable hold-all off the plane, as he joined the queue of disembarking passengers and hoped his new passport would 'do the business' in getting him through customs. He fingered the top of it inside his jacket pocket, as he gradually moved along in the queue of new arrivals towards the immigration desk.

The man behind the desk was engaged in a little banter with a female colleague a few feet away and seemed more interested in impressing her than doing his job properly. Ernest hoped this was a good sign as he approached the officer.

The person in front of him was swiftly nodded through by the man and he turned away from Ernesto to look at his colleague again with another witticism. Upon her reply, he laughed, turned back to look, cursorily, at the Guatemalan, posing as a Nicaraguan land agent, and asked him,

"Are you here long, Mr..eh..Ravel?"

"Only for a few days, this time," Ernesto replied, nervously.

"Okay, sir, thank you," said the official, returning his passport to him and Ernesto moved on through into the arrivals hall. With his hold-all slung over his shoulder, he carried on towards the concourse and then through the exit into the sunshine.

Immediately in front of him was a large, two-tone, blue, Buick, sporting a red pennant atop its radio aerial. Before he could ask the driver any question, a man came up behind him and said,

"Mr Ravel?"

Ernesto half turned to him and replied,

"Yes, that's me."

"Oh, right then, would you like to get in? With Mr Fleischer's compliments, sir," and he held the front passenger door open for him. Ernesto did as he was bid and the man got in behind him, joining another in the rear of the car. It was just gone four o'clock.

The sedan moved smoothly away from the kerbside and joined the main road heading into Managua City. They journeyed through the shabby outskirts of the town and Ernesto noticed numerous slum dwellings where the poor congregated and the smell, on such a hot day, was truly unpleasant.

The car soon left the unfortunate morass behind, as it travelled into the more prosperous, central, part of the city. They journeyed on, through the main thoroughfare and then, northwards and into the foothills overlooking the city.

Some twenty minutes later, the car turned off onto a dusty road, which made the final stages of the journey rather uncomfortable, with the sedan's suspension being put to the test!

The view overlooking the city, however, from their vantage point, was truly breathtaking, Ernesto thought to himself, as he surveyed the panorama.

Then the car suddenly swept past two huge iron gates and along a tarmac driveway, which afforded a much smoother ride to the front of a very impressive, ranch-style, property.

Two guards, standing either side of the portico, moved slowly down the main steps of the building and one of them greeted the rear occupants of the car, as they alighted from the vehicle. Ernesto's door was opened for him and he got out, joining the party beginning to move up the steps into the main house.

A maid, of middle-age and wearing a grey and white uniform, introduced herself to Ernesto, with the salutation,
"Ah, Mr Ravel, I am Salma; Mr Fleischer is waiting for you in the lounge. If you care to follow me, sir, thank you."

She set off along the wide entrance hall, which was lavishly furnished, turned right into a domed atrium and then up a very impressive staircase to the first floor of the imposing residence.

"There is real wealth here," Ernesto said to himself, as he surveyed the opulent surroundings and finally surmounted the stairs. He was shown into a huge room, where several suites of furniture were '*in situ*' amongst numerous antiques on display and many valuable paintings adorned the walls.

A large, well dressed, man rose to his feet and moved towards him. With an outstretched hand, he said,
"Mr Ravel, or should I say Ernesto Alvarez, how nice to meet you at last, Arnold Fleischer, do come and sit down." Ernesto shook hands with him, accordingly.
"Nice to meet you, too and thank you," the Guatemalan replied.

"What would you like to drink?" The jovial American asked his guest, as they moved towards a large settee in the middle of the enormous room.

"Oh, I think a brandy and soda would be very nice, thank you," the Head of the 'Enlightened Way' responded.

"Salma, would you get that please? And I'll have the 'usual,' thank you."

"Yes, sir," replied his maid who turned away towards an anteroom.

Arnold gestured to Ernesto to sit on a settee, next to a large, marble, coffee table and he occupied a corner seat in a similar settee the other side of it.

"You have a very impressive place here, Mr Fleischer, if I may say so," said Ernesto, offering the customary greeting to his, obviously very wealthy, host.

"Well, thank you, Ernesto, I like it and I'll show you around a little later if you like. It's nineteenth century, the main building that is, but most of the additions date from the thirties and I've added a few things on as well, in the last six years since I've been here."

At that point, Salma returned with their drinks on a tray, which she deposited onto the marble coffee table with a resounding 'clunk.' She distributed most of the contents between them and after looking towards her employer, who nodded slightly, she withdrew.

After they attended to their refreshments, Arnold opened the proceedings.

"So, tell me, Ernesto, how come you speak quite good English and what's all this big business about, that you mentioned to me over the 'phone; how can I help you, my friend?"

Ernesto took a sip of his drink and replied,

"Well, I took some books with me when I went into the mountains, a while back and wished to improve my ability in conversing in the World's foremost language. I wanted to make good use of my time there. I also know of you by reputation, of course; my friend at home recommended me to you, if ever I needed any, shall we say, 'special laundering' to be done."

"You mean, Raoul Stiga, yes, he did mention you to me a while back and I know him to be a reliable fellow," Arnold cut in, "but please continue."

"Before I do, Mr Fleischer,"

"Oh, Arnold, please," the American swiftly interjected again, trying to help his guest to relax.

"Thank you, Arnold, then; before I can do anything, I have to know who I'm dealing with, so if you could let me know your background, expertise etc., I will then be able to see more clearly how we might be able to do business together. I know your reputation precedes you and is well - earned, I'm sure but I'd like to hear it from the man, himself; I hope you don't mind and there's no disrespect intended, I can assure you."

Arnold Fleischer straightened up in his corner seat and put his glass, containing his Bourbon and water, down on the marble table with a 'clink.'

Ernesto surveyed his host more closely this time, with Arnold's bow tie hardly visible under his portly chin and his, hitherto well fitting shirt, also showing some strain down the front, if the rather stressed button holes were anything to go by! Now leaning forward to feel more comfortable, he took off his bottle-end glasses, put them down on a magazine on the coffee table, rubbed his eyes and said,

"Fine, fine, now let me see, where do we start? Well, I qualified as an accountant before working for the Teamsters Union in the early seventies. The job was okay, for a time but I soon got the urge to be a management accountant, you know advising companies how better to do things, to improve the 'bottom line' and all that. Their procedures were so bureaucratic and out of date, though, that I threatened to leave." He paused for a moment to sip his drink and then continued,

"The guy I worked for was the head of Internal Accounting and he told me that, whereas there was no way to change the systems the Union employed, there was a way to boost the 'bottom line' by some deft figure work, resulting in bigger bonuses for those 'in the know.' I soon learned the art of 'creative accounting' to advantage but since the Union was subject to a triennial audit and it was coming up soon, I left in good time. The skulduggery was discovered shortly afterwards and my boss took the hit and was fired."

Arnold paused again and refreshed his glass from the bottles on the tray and invited Ernesto to do the same, with a hand gesture to him. He continued,

"After that, I joined a securities firm on Wall Street and got involved in their gold marketing operations. The opportunities there to make a lot of money were self - evident, especially if you worked on the options side of the contracts. You could backdate these, with a little imagination, without any difficulty and when there was a 'fast market' running, it was all too easy. I mean, nobody had time to check anything properly. They were all at it and I made a huge amount of money from it, huge, I can tell you!"

Another pause, as Arnold took a sip of his drink.

"And the rest, as they say, is history. The Feds made a dawn raid on our office in '97 and I, along with a few others in the options department, was indicted on several fraud charges. I knew I wouldn't beat that rap, so I hightailed it out of there and took up permanent residence here.

I'd bought the house a few years earlier with part of my funds at the time and it was just as well I did! I'm still in touch, albeit indirectly, with a lot of guys there and elsewhere around the world, so if you need worthwhile contacts, especially of a gold - orientated / money 'laundering' nature, I'd say I was your man – assuming the price is right, of course!" Arnold concluded, with a chuckle.

Ernesto sat up and said,

"Thank you Arnold, for that potted history; it seems we might well be able to work together. Although my cause is not so much for myself but for others, from which I also benefit, I have to say, I do need the services of someone who really knows how to work the system for me. Let me now tell you, in similar detail, where I stand today and what I'd like to achieve, from a major 'one off' event I am planning."

Arnold, though, cut in and said,

"Shall we do that over dinner my friend? I think they're ready for us now."

"Of course, do please lead on," Ernesto replied and they both got up and left their seats for the dining room.

Chapter Three

So vulnerable, the Goose that lays the Golden Eggs

Situated only ten miles or so off the coast of the Cherbourg Peninsular of Brittany, North Western France, lies the island of Jersey, the largest of the Channel Islands group in the English Channel. The self-governing territory, save for Defence and a few other National requirements, which it looks to the United Kingdom to provide, makes for a 21st Century aberration of the first order.

The States of Jersey, the island's Government, considers the territory to be self-sufficient, largely due to a well - run, yet lightly - regulated, Finance Industry, supporting one of the most attractive 'tax efficient' areas in the developed world. It abhors being described as a 'tax haven,' since such a label conjures up the 'wrong image' to the outside world. In finance, as in most businesses, 'image' is everything.

The wealth residing on the island and held by the deposit taking institutions registered there, is truly breathtaking for a small rock in the Channel; an area covering barely forty five square miles. At the turn of the 21st Century, the aggregate funds held on deposit in Jersey were well over £100 billion.

With so many multi-millionaires comprising the 'local' population of some fifty thousand souls, approximately half the total living there, the per capita wealth figure must be staggering. Easily exceeding the riches of Croesus, the innocuous little island must rank as one of the wealthiest enclaves on earth!

The Channel Islands trace their allegiance to England back to the eleventh century: to 1066, quite literally! They were added to the Dukedom of Normandy in 933 AD and when William the Conqueror, the Duke of Normandy, became William 1 of England upon defeating King Harold at Hastings in 1066, England was added to the Channel Islands and became part of his Kingdom.

The present Duke of Normandy (H.M. the Queen) is still feted by Jersey's senior Seigneur when she pays them a visit: the individual walks into the sea to greet Her Majesty, proffering, on behalf of her loyal subjects, a fattened goose on a large silver salver! A really quaint tradition, that, which says much about the charm of the place.

Such an illustrious history and a tenacious grip on tradition, partly explains Jersey's privileged status in the world today. The principal reason, though, has been the shrewd, post - war, financial positioning of the island as a sympathetic place to do most forms of 'offshore' business.

Whilst husbanding the vast sums on deposit in St. Helier, nowadays, as just part of the huge finance industry operating under its jurisdiction for 'tax purposes,' the island remains independent of the U.K. and the E.U. It neatly straddles both and, thereby, manages to enjoy most of the 'fruits' of this advantageous position. That the Government of the island has managed to keep it out of the clutches of others for so long is quite remarkable.

In recent years, Jersey has adopted some parts of the plethora of European Union legislation being foisted upon so many member states, to placate the critics, as much as anything else. In this way, it hopes not to draw too much attention to itself, in being almost uniquely positioned to benefit so much from the wealth of others.

Such expedience can, and often is, construed as selfishness in the eyes of others; invariably the eyes of the less fortunate, the eyes of envy.

The very well - heeled, having enjoyed a privileged lifestyle there for so long, would inevitably become inured to the feelings of others, nay the resentment of those on the outside, living and sometimes barely surviving, in a very different world. Such self - preoccupation often spawns complacency about the vulnerability to attack; especially where covetous thoughts are augmented by the power of the gun or the bomb.

Despite the colossal wealth of some of its residents and reputation as a 'safe and proper' place to do business, Jersey would be incapable of fending off a serious attack upon it. It fields only a nominal defence force, with little weaponry available to withstand any sort of incursion.

The strength of the Police force is not much greater, with a peculiar contingent of 'honorary' officers, probably weakening the effectiveness of maintaining order, if anything, should the island suffer a terrorist outrage – a real risk in today's world, unfortunately. A few officers, having probably attended some training courses in England, wouldn't be an effective safeguard against a well - organised attack on the wealthy enclave.

Reliance upon the Crown to 'repel borders,' if necessary, is all very well where there is time to spare. In today's climate, though, governments have to respond swiftly and effectively, themselves, to an attack upon their homeland. Time is very much of the essence in such situations.

Could this be Jersey's 'Achilles heel'? Can all that vast wealth really be so unguarded, so vulnerable, so easy to exploit?

Such were the thoughts and musings of Stephen Carvell, a mercenary, who'd been tasked by Omah Djesturi, the operational head of the 'Enlightened Way,' one of the latest radical groups to emerge from South America, to find a real 'trophy' target for him. Omah, Alvarez's right hand man, was determined to see the 'Way' make a name for itself, in as spectacular a manner as possible, to get the other, more established, terrorist groups off the world stage, for a change!

The 'Enlightened Way' was not a terrorist organisation in the strict meaning of the phrase. It was an extremist organisation, certainly, in promoting the rights of the underprivileged to better themselves at the expense of the wealthy, especially the very wealthy, often by force.

The eliciting of 'donations' from the rich to the poor was regarded by them as a 'virtuous act of expiating the soul' deemed good for everyone who'd amassed excessive wealth for themselves – a way to help the lesser brethren of the world for once. Everyone benefited in consequence and made the world a better place for all concerned, although those who'd refused to comply with the doctrine and lost their lives in the process wouldn't have agreed, for sure!

The Founder of the cult, Ernesto Alvarez, was born in Guatemala, in 1950, whose parents were of Mayan descent: despite the lapse of some five hundred years since the Spanish Conquistadores decimated the indigenous Indians, recovery of their wealth at some future date, lives on in their folklore.

Being unwilling to scratch a meagre living in his shanty town, on the outskirts of Guatemala City, Ernesto Alvarez took to the foothills of the Maya Mountains to escape the common hardship. Having foraged there quite successfully for a few years, he returned to his village in 1985, telling his family and anyone else who'd listen, that the many contemplative days he'd spent with Mother Nature, had 'opened his eyes' about resolving the problems of the poor.

Encouraging those who have something to share, even a little, with those who had nothing, was the 'enlightened' way forward, he now proclaimed. Encouragement could be either a gentle plea, an element of coercion or execution of the reluctant benefactor, if need be. Sharing was the main thing, since it benefited both parties, didn't it? Such a philosophy encapsulated much of the spirit of the movement.

The following decade saw Ernesto form his group of 'ne'er-do-wells' into the followers of the 'Enlightened Way': with nothing to lose and much, possibly, to gain, many could see the advantages of joining the cult. Ernesto soon found he had over one hundred adherents to his revolutionary approach to solving the impoverishment of his people and numerous 'Robin Hood' raids on the local 'haves,' followed.

The advent of the Twenty First Century held special significance for Alvarez. He regarded the Year 2000 as the ideal harbinger of an international movement to convince others of his 'Way' of doing things to solve the problem of the World's poor.

The cynic might suggest that going overseas was also an expedient move for him. He had been on the 'Most wanted list' in Guatemala for quite a while and had a considerable bounty on his head, in several South American Countries, too. He didn't feel he was yet ready, though, to give his life for the cause. Enriching some poor people with the reward money from his capture, was not that an 'enlightened' move in his opinion!

He'd moved from Morocco (some said fled) to England in the spring of 2000 and eventually wound up in London, renting a large flat in the Bayswater Road. His landlord was an affable character, Stephen Carvell, who worked for his deputy, as a mercenary, a sort of freelance terrorist, prepared to do anything for money.

Stephen had been tipped off by Omah Djesturi a few weeks before, that the tenant he'd got for him was quite an important character. One who'd be worth getting to know, over time, he'd been told.

Stephen was a ready listener, having much time on his hands, following redundancy six months before Ernesto arrived on the scene.

He was ex-military, having spent sometime in the Middle East 'offering his services' in Oman. When the Security company he worked for lost the contract for supplying professional bodyguards to local 'worthies' he lost his lucrative employment, too. He had some money left from his redundancy pay-off when he first met Ernesto but welcomed the prospect of a new tenant turning up on his doorstep, in the spring of that year, to help defray the outgoings.

Some three weeks later, Ernesto was regularly conversing with his landlord and had soon convinced Stephen of the morality of his cause. Moreover, the prospect of boosting his income considerably also helped the Englishman to make his mind up in joining the 'Way.' Ernesto was not averse to deducting a fee from 'donations' to keep everything going, apparently, which really appealed to the 'ex-minder.'

Stephen Carvell had done quite a bit of research on Jersey, the largest of the Channel Islands, for his boss, Omah, after he'd received instructions from him to closely investigate this place, from a security standpoint, a few weeks earlier.

He'd needed to make sure, though, that this small piece of real estate in the English Channel was really as defenceless as it had seemed, at first sight. He'd visited the Island several times in recent days and 'reconnoitred' it quite a bit, without any difficulty.

He'd also spoken to a few of his chums who'd worked over there, getting their views on their experiences etc., on the pretext of writing a book on the subject. All were keen to help him with their observations of the place and the consensus was that certainly a very relaxed atmosphere prevailed on the Island, reminiscent of the lifestyle of the fifties, one or two suggested.

Further investigations on the Internet from his flat in the Bayswater Road, finally convinced him that the Island was genuinely a very 'soft' target, if that was what was planned. He would convey his opinion to Omah the following day, to facilitate the planning stage, should it be required.

If it was, then a meeting to discuss the 'modus operandi' and assuming general agreement amongst those in attendance, Omah would present the prospective operation to Ernesto and if he sanctioned it, then a more detailed plan would be drawn up for final consideration.

Although Stephen lived in the same property as the 'Way' supremo, he was not allowed to discuss operational procedures or details of the plan with Ernesto privately. He had to go through Omah, the operational head of the organisation, at all times.

"It's the procedure that matters, Steve, everyone knows where they are if they follow the procedures – alright!"

Steve sensed his boss's anger at having to remind him of the protocol once again; he thought Omah, though, was simply jealous of the Founder living in his house, as he, himself, lived half a mile away in a flat in Porchester Terrace. It was Omah, though, who'd found his boss's flat for him, having inspected Carvell's place and recommended Alvarez rent it, since it was fairly close to his place, too.

Chapter Four

The Audacious plan is disclosed

Ernesto Alvarez, the notorious outlaw from Guatemala and Arnold Fleischer, the equally disreputable American financier, living in exile in Nicaragua, moved into the luxurious dining room of the latter's mansion, overlooking Managua harbour, for dinner. The fare placed upon the twenty feet long dining table, which confronted them, was lavish in the extreme. Only the two of them sat down to eat that evening; in attendance were waiters and other members of his staff.

Part way through the six course meal, their conversation was confined to small talk but then Arnold encouraged his visitor to resume their earlier discussion, by waving away the staff, so they wouldn't be overheard.

Ernesto finished his last morsel of the delicious lobster thermidor he'd been served, took another sip of the '85 Chablis which accompanied it and pushed the plate away from him. He discarded his napkin and his host did the same.

"I had a fairly rough life in Guatemala, which I was reluctant to leave but with the authorities, there and elsewhere, keen to be rid of me, I decided to move abroad, one might say, as you know." Arnold nodded and listened intently to the man, studying him closely, too.

Alvarez was a well - built individual, obviously strong and resourceful and looked younger than his fifty years of age. His brown eyes sparkled noticeably under his mop of dark hair but his shirt collar was too big; his lean body, due to years of hardship, no doubt, seemed ill - fitted to suited attire, reflected the overweight American.

Ernesto continued his reprise,

"I've long believed that the wealthy, especially the very rich, could and should, do a lot more to help the poor: Yes, I know they'll always be with us, the downtrodden, the impoverished, those who cannot help themselves, not easily anyway but I think the lot of the 'have nots' could certainly be improved, if the 'haves' cared a bit more. I have, let us say, 'encouraged' quite a few of my wealthy countrymen to do more for their unfortunate brothers and sisters in my time but one or two who refused to do so met an untimely end, I regret to say."

At this last remark, Arnold shifted uneasily in his chair. *'Maybe this guy will consider me 'fair game,' too, if I'm not careful, since I have quite a bit around me here, as he can see, all too well. Better keep a close eye on him, keep him 'on side,' as it were, just in case,'* the American thought to himself.

"I'm sorry, Ernesto, I got distracted there for a moment; you were saying?" Ernesto repeated what he'd just said,

"I was saying that I now wish to pull off one major job and then, if it succeeds, I'd be able to 'retire,' so to speak, since being on the run most of the time now, is not pleasant at all, as I'm sure you'll appreciate." He paused for another sip of his wine and his host chipped in,

"Yeah, of course, I can quite see that....so what sort of a finale do you have in mind, then?"

"Well, I've thought that one major swoop could well make up for fifty or more minor events. I have about one hundred and thirty followers to feed now, so it needs to be big, really big. Ideally, it'll help a lot of people this time, properly reward my 'troops' and also enable me to comfortably move back into normal life."

The leader of the 'Enlightened Way' paused again to finish his glass of wine and Arnold moved to re-fill it, saying,

"My, it does sound big I must say. Have you decided what to have a go at, may I ask?" Ernesto covered his glass in preferring not to drink any more and replied,

"Thank you no, no more for me, Arnold." His host withdrew the bottle, filled his own glass instead and placed it in the wine bucket next to him, as Ernesto followed up with,

"I have in mind laying siege to a small but very wealthy enclave: not in the conventional sense of surrounding the place and starving the inhabitants into submission, since that's impossible nowadays. No, I have in mind utilising the untapped energies of the dispossessed, those you see all too often on the T.V. news, desperately trying to change their wretched circumstances. They'd do anything to get out of their near pointless existence, wouldn't they?"

The Guatemalan looked the American straight in the eye this time, which made Arnold feel distinctly uncomfortable and self conscious at the same time; something he'd not felt like for ages. Ernesto Alvarez answered his own rhetorical question,

"You bet they would; anything resembling a ray of hope and those guys would grab the chance with both hands; wouldn't you in their position? So, I intend to give them that chance, the chance to get some money, at last and try to break free from the raw deal life's dumped on them." Arnold interjected,

"That's fine, truly laudable and we all echo such sentiments, for sure but have you thought about how best to go about it?"

"Yes, I have and I think I know how to pull it off: do you want to hear more?"

"Yeah, yeah, you bet but first let's get some coffees and brandies or whatever in here. Salma!" he shouted and his maid appeared almost at once.

"Yes, sir?" She replied, awaiting instructions.

"Oh, there you are, eh, would you bring in coffee and brandy for us; is that alright for you, my friend?" looking up at his guest for corroboration, which he received via a nod from him,

"And along with the usual additions, of course, thank you." Salma had half turned away towards the door when her boss added,

"Tell me, Salma, have you heard of the 'Enlightened Way' by any chance?" Her immediate response surprised him.

"Oh, yes sir, they're very active up north, aren't they?"

"And what do you think of them, then?"

"Well, sir, for those without a job or anything, they're very popular, I think: they rob the rich to give to the poor, don't they?"

"Okay, thanks, Salma." Arnold turned back to Ernesto, as his maid continued towards the door.

"Well, you seem to be popular down here, too; that's pretty impressive, I have to say. Do please continue while we wait for the coffees etc.,

Ernesto sat up straight and resumed his discourse.

"There are several extremely wealthy areas, small areas, around the globe where the citizens don't care a jot about the plight of the world's poor, as far as I can tell." The American interrupted him, again,

"Yeah, okay but you don't know that for sure though, do you? I mean you cannot possibly know how many people in these places do good works for others, how many donate to charities or what some of their wealth generates by way of employment for others etc., now can you?"

Ernesto seemed a little shaken by Arnold's stout defence of the 'haves'; probably because he was one of them, as was the Guatemalan, too, if only he'd admit to it!

"Yes, I know, that is a fair point but in relation to their extreme wealth, such giving has to be derisory, in all reality, surely?" Arnold sort of conceded the point, through a slight nod of the head and his facial expression.

At this point, Salma arrived with the coffee pot, et al, on a tray and placed it down on the table. Having asked Ernesto how he liked his coffee, she duly attended him and then her boss and withdrew to leave them to their discussion.

Having taken a sip of his coffee, Ernesto continued with his plan, as Arnold took an increasingly keen interest in what was to follow,

"As I said a moment ago, you cannot today lay siege to a place like the old days but you could flood it with refugees all of a sudden and with today's media being able to report on everything, as it happens, the resident government would have to tread very carefully in handling it. No shooting the 'invaders' or 'strong arm' tactics against them could be mounted, without the whole world seeing it. And in today's climate of so much emphasis on human rights and all that, you'd be pilloried by the U.N. and the E.U and all the civil rights groups before you knew it!"

"A good point that," Arnold thought to himself, as his guest continued,

"If you could marshal a good number of them onto a small foreign shore and stage a sort of sit down on the beaches, and then get them to move into the towns, if their demands were not met, there's very little a government could realistically do, in my view. I suspect most, if not all, of them would be very willing to pay a price, a good price, to someone who could arrange for the whole problem to go away. I intend to be that someone, Arnold!"

The American was now sitting upright and was enthralled by the simplicity of such an audacious plan.

"Yeah, I'm with you, I do so agree they would be truly stymied, wouldn't they? I mean what could they reasonably do in such circumstances? So, what about the logistics of it all, though?"

The American re-filled both their coffee cups, as Ernesto expanded on his grand plan:

"There are three areas that need to be dealt with, as far as I can see. Firstly, communication with the unfortunates, shall we call them? Secondly, adequate financing of the enterprise and, lastly, command and control of the operation once it was underway."

Arnold piped up again,

"Well, finance is my game, so I can certainly assist with that, if you want me in. What about the most suitable target? Have you decided on that yet? And what sort of price would you exact from a state to get rid of their problem for them? And what would we get out of it? We mustn't forget that in all this, either, must we, my friend?"

Ernesto held up his hand and said to his enthusiastic host sitting opposite him,

"Let's deal with the problems in order, as I see it, at least:

Communications. Now, I have some friends in 'The Way' who maintain reasonable contact with the Polisario guerrilla movement in Morocco and since Africa has more than its fair share of impoverished peoples, I think that's where I will concentrate upon. I need to make contact with their leaders myself, to see if I can get their co-operation to gather together a large mass of their people for temporary transit to the targeted territory.

Then, there's financing: If it is to be done effectively at the first attempt, I've calculated we'll need three large ships to convey the human cargo to the prescribed destination. All the 'passengers' will need access to smaller craft to ferry them from their ship to the shore of the chosen territory. They must all be unarmed, no weapons with them at all, since we don't want to give the Government of the place we alight upon, any excuse to repel us by force of arms. I cannot stress that enough!

The ships would cost about $3 million to hire for six weeks or so, which I would estimate as the duration of the operation. Then there are other ancillary payments to allow for, along with general costs associated with providing the manpower; in all, I reckon $5 million should cover everything, give or take a bit.

And finally, there is command and control. Now, here it will be up to me to impress upon the Polisario leadership that the only person in charge of the entire project and their people, is me. I, alone, will negotiate with the beleaguered authorities in securing a resolution of the problem we've foisted upon them and the people dumped upon their shores will only take orders from the leader of 'The Enlightened Way.' "

Arnold sat back in his chair and let out a heavy sigh,
"Phew, you've really given this a lot of thought, my friend, I must say; but come on, what will be the price for removing the problem for them?"

Ernesto asked his host for some more coffee at this point and Arnold responded with another shout of,
"Salma! If you please?" and a few moments later, she was back by his side, clearing away the coffee things and being asked for a repeat serving for the two of them.
"Yes, sir, of course; it won't take a minute." and she withdrew, accordingly. The American thought for a moment or two and then repeated his question,
"And the price for all this co-operation on your part, then?"

Ernesto was about to reply when Salma walked back in again, so he waited for her to distribute the fresh coffees to them, along with a re-supply of 'petits fours' and then she left.

32

"That depends on how wealthy the target is perceived to be, how long it takes for them to acquiesce to my demands and their treatment of the unfortunates in their midst, while we wait. The longer it takes, the higher the price, of course."

"Of course," Arnold nodded in agreement. He started to drink his coffee but nearly choked when Ernesto added,

"It'll be in gold, the price payable, I mean; that's your area of expertise, isn't it, Arnold?" His host quickly put his coffee cup down on the table with a 'clang' and said,

"Well, yeah, sure it is but the stuff's very heavy and difficult to transport, quite apart from the need to protect it at all times, of course."

Ernesto, totally unfazed by Arnold's practical misgivings, pressed on,

"Gold will be payable by the 'host' territory to all the journeymen who sail with us, but none of the physical metal will be handled by us; we will profit from the gold market itself and, in particular, gold futures and options. No carrying costs involved nor protection required in our case, you see? That's your specialist field isn't it?" said 'The Way' supremo, looking directly at his host.

Arnold retorted, flatly,

"That's alright, in principle, Ernesto but you'd need a lot of buying power to move the price of bullion, I can assure you."

"That is certainly true, as far as I know, too but if the amount of physical gold to pay over to the refugees was considerable and other countries feared they might well be next, just imagine the speculative demand that might engender. Moreover, when it gets out that only payment in bullion is acceptable to resolve the refugee problem, I'd be very surprised if the price didn't rise quite a bit on such considerations. And we'd be in the long - dated options, long before the news broke about the bullion requirement, eh?"

At this, it began to dawn on Arnold how much money could be made by early buying of 'out of the money' or long - dated gold options, where the 'leverage' or multiplier effect on the price of such holdings would be very substantial, upon even a modest rise in the gold price itself.

He got up from the table and found a pencil and paper and sat down again. He looked across at his guest again and asked him,

"So how much gold will you demand from the unfortunate territory, do you think?" Ernesto thought for a moment and then said,

"Depending on the perceived resources of the location, I'd say, perhaps, $65 - $70 million, which equates to 200,000 ounces or 500 gold bars at the current price of $325 an ounce. I'd prefer one kilo bars to be given to the journeymen, though, given the practicalities of distribution, so that would be around 6,250 one kilo bars. I'd like all those who ventured forth on the sea to freedom to receive, say, $10,000 each. Most of them couldn't earn that in a lifetime!"

The American could see from the set expression on Ernesto's face that he meant what he said. Arnold stated calmly to him,
"Yeah, I agree your general figures," as he looked at the notes he'd made on his pad, adding,
"If you'd like to see everyone who came along for the ride get, say, $10,000, you might wish to consider dishing out a few gold coins, like Krugerrands or Canadian Maple leafs, to them; they're one ounce gold coins, of course."
"We'll see nearer the time, eh?" replied Ernesto, who was getting a little tired, as he tried to stifle a yawn.

It was well past ten o'clock and Arnold invited him to retire early, if he wished to. As he stood up, he asked Ernesto whether he'd had any thoughts at all about the likely target, he might be considering.

"Well, since I'm inclined to launch the 'Freedom ships' from Morocco, the obvious area to study would be Europe. There are a number of very wealthy enclaves there, such as Monaco, the Channel Islands, Andorra and Luxembourg, although the last two would be difficult to get to, being land-locked countries, of course.

I would think one of the Channel Islands would best suit our purposes, since a small island would be much easier to overwhelm than a larger enclave attached to mainland Europe, like Monaco. Yes, one of those would suit us, I would think, wouldn't you, Arnold? That assumes you're keen to be involved, of course; are you?"

Put so directly like that, Arnold suddenly felt pressured to respond in the affirmative and so he did.

"Yeah, sure, count me in, Ernesto; it sounds very exciting, I must say and could well reap substantial rewards for all concerned. Eh, let me get Salma for you and she'll show you to your room. Salma! Are you there?"

The little lady swept back into the dining room and her employer said to her,

"Mr Ravel is going to turn in now, so could you show him the facilities and his room, please?"

"Yes, of course, sir; Mr Ravel, would you care to follow me, please?"

"Sleep well and we'll chat some more in the morning, alright?"

A wave of the arm from his guest signified acceptance of the prospect and the American turned away towards the dinner table once more. Studying his notepad again, he double checked the figures he'd written down and after a few minutes, he slowly shook his head, saying to himself,

"*Some guy, some plan, I must say; it's so outrageous, we might just get away with it!*"

Chapter Five

Target : *Jersey*

Ernesto Alvarez slept well in the luxurious guest room of Arnold Fleischer's mansion and woke at 7 am on the dot, much refreshed. He got out of bed, drew back the heavy drapes and took in the marvellous view of the range of hills in the distance.

The grounds of the property were very well kept, he thought, with a couple of paddocks visible from his window where he noticed a horse and rider jumping some modest fences. Beyond them were a few fields, again well attended, as far as he could tell and they seemed to lead up to the foothills on the horizon. It was a property of considerable acreage to be sure.

He moved away from the window, slipped out of his dressing gown and got into the shower. After a few moments, the water temperature was at a comfortable level and he found the cascade quite exhilarating. Fifteen minutes later, he'd finished his ablutions and got dressed.

There was a gentle knock on the door, which drew him away from the mirror he was using to comb his, usually unruly, mop of hair.

"Are you up, Ernesto?" Arnold called out to him in a subdued voice.

"Yes, I'm just about ready; I'll be out directly," he replied. Putting on a dark blazer, he opened the door and greeted his host,

"Hi, Arnold, I hope you slept as well as I did; the room was very comfortable, thank you,"

"Oh, good, glad to hear it; I sleep very well in this place, it must be the clean air up here, or something. Come on, let's have some breakfast."

The two of them strode along the corridor and back into the dining room. Another impressive array of food was already laid out for them, with Salma in attendance, once again. She curtsied, as he walked up to the table and she asked him what he would like for breakfast. He thought for a moment and then said,

"Oh, just a white coffee, no sugar and some toast, please Salma, that'll go nicely with these," he replied, selecting an apple and a pear from the fruit basket to the side of him and putting them onto a plate.

"Very good, sir and your usual scrambled eggs and bacon this morning, sir?" She looked at her boss for his response and he nodded his approval.

"Yes, I think so, Salma, thank you."

"Breakfast will be along shortly, then, gentlemen, thank you," and with that courteous reply, she walked to the anteroom, closing the door behind her.

"Do sit down, Ernesto and make a start," said Arnold, putting two slices of toast on a plate next to him and reaching for some butter and marmalade. Ernesto crunched on his apple and said,

"I've been thinking about the probable target we should be considering. I don't think Monaco is as good a prospect as one of the Channel Islands, since it sits at the bottom of France and it could easily be reinforced, of course. Not so for the Channel Islands, being surrounded by water; they'd be easier prey for us, for sure but which one?" Arnold swallowed a slice of toast and said, flatly,

"We'll go to my office shortly and look them up on the internet; one of the new search engines should give us all the 'low down' on them we need."

A few minutes passed as they continued eating and then Salma re-appeared with their orders on a large, copper tray and set it down beside them. She distributed the fare to each of them in turn and then retired discreetly, as before.

Half an hour later, with appetites sated, they left the table and walked along to Arnold's office. He started up his P.C. and was soon logged on to the Yahoo search engine. Much information on the Channel Islands was afforded, as they both examined the territories. Ernesto was the first to speak,

"Jersey looks to be wealthier than Guernsey, in terms of residents living there and their finance industry is a good deal larger, too – look at the money on deposit that Jersey has, compared to Guernsey; they have half as much again, apparently. Let's look at the topography of the two of them."

"That's this page here, then, it seems," the American replied, as he 'clicked' on it and their respective maps appeared on the screen. After a few moments, Ernesto piped up again,

"Jersey is a good deal flatter than Guernsey it seems and has several large, sandy beaches, which would be ideal for getting the journeymen ashore. There's one here at St. Helier," he said, pointing with his finger,

" Another a bit further along to the west, called St. Brelade's Bay and look, one on the west coast, named St. Ouen's Bay : we could land the people on all three, simultaneously, that's perfect, Arnold, just perfect. Jersey's the one, I reckon!"

Arnold looked away from the screen at him and said,

"It does seem to have all the right characteristics, I must say, especially those three, wide beaches; there shouldn't be any problems arriving on those. I agree that Jersey seems to be the ideal location."

"I'd better ring Omah in London; he's still on the lookout for a worthwhile territory for us and now I can say we've found it for him!"

"Use my mobile 'phone over there; it's more secure than the landline, probably."

"Oh, right, thanks, I will."

Ernesto punched in Omah's number and a few seconds later he was in contact with him. The call lasted about five minutes, during which time Ernesto also explained to his Operations Chief that he intended to visit the Polisario people in Morocco, in a day or two. He needed to get the boats arranged, the people organised and everything else established to ensure a smooth implementation of his grand plan, when the time came to put it into practice. He was confident he could persuade the leadership of the Polisario rebels to participate on the promise of a worthwhile payment to them.

After hearing from his leader, Omah was keen to alert his number two, Stephen Carvell, who was in charge of planning, to concentrate on the Island of Jersey from now on, as this seemed the ideal place for their purposes. Their leader had said so, he relayed to Stephen, so everything else to date should be discarded and every effort made to get all the relevant information about Jersey in place to facilitate a final presentation of an action plan. Stephen, having acknowledged the instruction, now turned his full attention to the little, unsuspecting island in the English Channel.

Meanwhile, back in Managua, Ernesto spent the last few days of February enjoying the facilities at Arnold's luxurious residence. His host accompanied him on most occasions, although not on the couple of mounted treks into the hills overlooking his property, since Ernesto's horsemanship was far superior to his and he didn't want to be a drag on his guest's exploratory enjoyment.

Over dinner, on the third night of his stay there, Ernesto informed Arnold that he must go over to Morocco to 'make arrangements' with the Polisario leadership about his grand plan.

"At the weekend, I'll fly to Marrakech and meet one of our contacts there, who has connections with Polisario. He should be able to get me a meeting with one of their leaders and, hopefully, I can persuade them to get involved." Arnold interjected,

"And what if you can't, if they don't like the idea, what then?"

"The price for their co-operation, then, would have to rise until they couldn't afford to turn it down, eh? You have to remember that a few thousand dollars for the wealthy, is an inconvenience but for them, it is a King's ransom!"

"Yeah, I do appreciate that, really, it's all relative to one's environment, I suppose," chipped in the American, rather wistfully.

An hour later, Arnold suggested his number two might book the flight to Marrakech for him and he also offered to lend him one of his mobile 'phones to help him keep in touch. Arnold had several, so Ernesto was happy to accept. When he gave it to the Guatemalan, along with its charger, he said,

"Don't forget to charge it up, on this, when the batteries are low; you might need to get an adaptor over there, possibly, depending on the local voltage but that shouldn't be too difficult, if you need to. Oh, one other thing, before I forget. How about a photo of us together? On the threshold of this great endeavour, as it were, eh?"

Ernesto was reluctant, initially but after Arnold said he had several such photos as reminders of enjoyable times past with other visitors (he hadn't) the Guatemalan agreed.

Robert Singleton, Fleischer's number two, duly obliged, taking two photographs of them together and Arnold promised Ernesto, the picture would be placed in a prominent position in his library.

Later on, when Ernesto was out of earshot, Singleton asked his boss about the photo taking,

"Why the picture of you two together, Boss? You've never done that before." To which Arnold replied, rather chillingly,

"You never know when we might need it; a guy like that might turn on us, one day! Regard it as a form of insurance, eh?" His boss turned away and went back into the house. Singleton hadn't thought of that but had to admit it seemed a sensible idea, under the circumstances.

Two days later, Ernesto thanked his American host profusely for his exceptional hospitality. Both hoped their forthcoming 'enterprise' would prove very rewarding for all concerned and especially so for them.

"Do keep in touch now," Arnold Fleischer said, as he waved his guest goodbye and Ernesto said he would. The Buick set off for the airport and the portly financier turned back into the house.

The leader of the 'Enlightened Way,' Ernesto Alvarez, embarked upon the next leg of his grand plan, when he set foot on Moroccan soil on March 2nd 2000. One of his aides had made contact with the Polisario leadership prior to his arrival at Casablanca airport and he was met there by a 'representative' of the guerrilla group.

Having exchanged greetings of a brotherly nature, he was ushered into the back of an old, white, Mercedes 280 saloon, which had clearly seen better days. However, the veteran motor lived up to its reputation for reliability and covered the one hundred and twenty mile journey to Marrakech without difficulty.

Finally, the car stopped outside the entrance to a rather ramshackle, three storey, house on the outskirts of the town. It looked late nineteenth century, as did most of the buildings in the dusty street they'd just travelled along. Either side of the double-door entrance, were brightly coloured awnings, suggesting the property was more imposing than the others in the vicinity.

Ernesto's passenger door was opened by an individual standing at the bottom of the three steps leading up to the front door. Fortunately, he spoke Spanish, too and the Guatemalan was invited to follow the man upstairs into the house.

It was quite dark inside and it took Ernesto a few moments to adjust to the gloom. As the door closed behind him, he looked around and saw two armed men, dressed in black robes of some sort, looking dispassionately at him. A voice, in English this time, greeted him from a corner of the room. He turned towards it, seeing a man extending his right arm to him, saying,

"Welcome to my home, Mr Alvarez: I am Jousef Manakurh. We've spoken about each other, or rather our deputies have but we've never met, until now."

"Hello, at last, Ernesto is my first name; I am very pleased to meet you after all this time."

Jousef Manakurh snapped his fingers and another man appeared from behind a beaded curtain. A swift instruction, in Arabic, was acknowledged by the acolyte and he disappeared behind the curtain, once more.

"I've called for some tea, I hope that is acceptable; we muslims are not permitted alcohol, as you may know but other refreshments are available, if you do not care for tea."

"No, no, tea will be very nice, thank you," replied Ernesto.

"Come, please sit down here and we can talk while the tea is being made," gestured the older, bearded, man, to a chair next to him. He swirled his black robes over the back of his own chair in one swift movement and Ernesto did as he was bid.

"Now, tell me, Mr Alvarez, of your proposition for us. We know of your efforts to help the poor in South America and would like to assist such a just cause, especially if it concerns our people here or those in Africa, as a whole."

Ernesto was about to relate his grand plan to the emir, when tea arrived. They sat in silence, as the small cups were distributed to them, along with a very tall teapot. Jousef poured out the tea into Ernesto's cup and handed it to him. He waited for his host to complete his own pouring and then they each took a sip of the refreshment.

It took about half an hour for Ernesto to 'flesh out' his plan to the Polisario leader who sat impassively for most of the time. Only at the end of the discourse, did the emir ask a few questions, principally about the timing of the endeavour, its likely duration and 'modus operandi' as far as he and his men were concerned.

Seemingly satisfied, he finally asked the $64,000 question:

"How much will Polisario be paid for our help in all this?" Ernesto hesitated for a moment, since any response would be pure guesswork at this stage. He opened the bidding with,

"Fifty thousand dollars, U.S. dollars, of course."

"Not enough, my friend. I will need to call upon several hundred of my men, if not a thousand, to gather all the people together, get the small boats brought to Agadir on time, attend to security all the while and so on and then there's......."

Somewhat exasperated, Ernesto cut across him,

"Oh, alright then, one hundred thousand, how about that?"

"Still not enough, my friend; we'd like to help, of course but there's everyone to feed, arms to supply.." Ernesto cut him short,

"No, no weapons are to be taken on board the freedom ships, absolutely none. If we're armed, they'll have every excuse to open fire and probably sink us; that would be the best solution for them and would discourage others to follow."

"Yes, on reflection, I can see that; the democracies of the West would be loathe to take such drastic action, what with their Human Rights laws and everything, unless they were provoked into doing it. We mustn't give them that opportunity – Five hundred thousand dollars!"

The emir's riposte, at the end of what seemed to be a sympathetic response to his 'no arms' stipulation, caught Ernesto by surprise. He thought for a moment, *'This man isn't going to come cheap, despite his professed empathy with the plan to help the poor amongst us.'*

He was offered some more of the tea and he held up his cup for the refill, with a nod, before replying,

"How about if we met in the middle? Three hundred thousand dollars, would you agree to that?"

The emir looked into his tea cup and then relented,

"Very well, as it's such a just cause, we'll agree on Three hundred thousand dollars. I would like one third before we start and the rest of the money at the end: that would be when the last freedom ship has set off for this Island of Jersey in the English Channel, yes?"

"Yes, that would be the conclusion of your involvement and I'm happy to pay a third of the money upon commencement and the balance at the end, as you prefer. That's agreed, then?"

"We have a deal, Mr Alvarez," the emir confirmed and offered his hand to Ernesto, who readily shook it and replied,

"Thank you, sir, thank you very much."

"And now we have finished our business, you will have a meal with us, Ernesto, yes?" The emir enquired.

"Well, yes, thank you, I would like that," said Ernesto. Another snap of the fingers and the acolyte was by the bearded leader once more and a torrent of Arabic followed. Several nods by him ensued and then the 'flunky' went back behind the curtain again.

Josef Manakurh rose to his feet, drawing his black robes off the back of his chair and said to Ernesto,

"It is better we eat away from here, since the town is often subject to Government soldiers, in some numbers, making house to house searches for us, after dark. We'll travel to my base in the mountains, an hour's drive from here, where we will be much safer and we can relax, my friend, alright?"

"Yes, of course, if you think it is wiser to do so; you know the local situation all too well, I'm sure but I need to find somewhere to stay for a few days while I'm here and…" The Polisario leader held up his hand and replied,

"Now we have agreed to help each other, you are my friend, Ernesto and so you are very welcome to stay with me at my home in the mountains above Taroudannt. It is quite near Agadir, where the boats will gather to sail away on their epic voyage to a new life, we hope."

At that moment, a few vehicles roared up to the front of the house, braking sharply and sending a cloud of dust across the threshold.

"Come…our transport has arrived," said the bearded leader, as he strolled out of the room and Alvarez took that as his cue to pick up his hold-all and join him outside.

The sunlight was still quite strong and Ernesto squinted as he adjusted to it. The heat remained insufferable, too, as he surveyed the convoy of vehicles at the foot of the steps.

There were five of them; two Toyota pick-up trucks in front of a black Mercedes and two more behind it. The all-terrain, rugged, Japanese trucks (seemingly the favourite conveyance of gunmen) were all armed with a heavy machine gun in the rear with several 'soldiers' in attendance around the weapon. Most of them carried the iconic AK 47 assault rifle or, the equally formidable, RPG rocket launcher.

Ernesto walked down the steps and followed the Polisario leader into the Mercedes 450 saloon. As soon as his door was closed by a guard and he'd jumped into the back of the Toyota pick-up in front of them, they were off and at some pace, as the convoy raced out of town.

However, some three miles out of Marrakech, it came to a screeching stop, generating a huge dust cloud!

"Wait a moment for the dust to die down and we'll change vehicles," stated the emir, reassuringly; Ernesto thought for a moment they'd encountered a Government patrol or some other danger, so he was much relieved to hear the voluntary 'all change' explanation for it!

He followed the leader once more out of the limousine as two armed guards vacated the cabin of the pick-up in front of them. The four of them exchanged places, without a word passing between them; Alvarez simply following Jousef Manakurh into the Toyota. There was sufficient room for the three upfront, rather surprisingly, he thought.

The convoy set off again with all due haste; the ride being much less comfortable now, though, as they charged along the, barely made up, road to Taroudannt!

"You're wondering why we changed places, yes?" The emir asked his new friend, looking straight ahead.

"Well, yes….security, I suppose, eh?" The Guatemalan replied, looking at the profile of the emir. He held his gaze, trying to study the man, as he gave his reply,

"Yes, for security reasons, we do it, of course," said the Arab, still looking at the road ahead of them. He continued,

"It is quite possible our swift exit from Marrakech was reported by a spy to one of the numerous army patrols around here and they could easily ambush us before we get to our destination. My car would be the obvious target, since I got into it, as we departed. Some of them are quite accomplished with an RPG and a hit is almost always a sure 'kill'," he affirmed.

"What about the men who swapped places with us, don't they mind?"

"No, they'd die for me and the cause and they know they're expendable anyway and I'm not!" was the matter of fact reply.

Ernesto finished studying the man at this point. He looked about seventy years of age, the turbaned figure sitting next to him, Ernesto thought, with his weathered face and grey beard attesting as much. However, when he asked the Arab leader how long he'd been engaged in his struggle and he'd replied,

"Since 1956, when Morocco gained its independence from France; I joined the guerrillas at the age of ten, running errands for them, things like that and joined Polisario when it was formed, in 1973," he realised Jousef Manakurh was no more than fifty five!

The Toyota led convoy sped along around 100 kmph, generating a sizeable dust trail, despite hitting the odd pothole or pebbles strewn across their path, every so often. The journey was quite uncomfortable for the passengers in these pick-ups, as they bounced along, with Ernesto holding on tightly to the steadying handle over his door.

Just as he was beginning to get sort of used to it, there was a tremendous bang in front of them; the leading Toyota was hit by an RPG or mortar bomb, as it veered off the road in a wall of flame and smoke and overturned.

Their pick-up swerved violently to avoid it and any crater if it was a mortar attack upon them and they rushed through the heavy smoke of the impact. Ernesto and the Polisario leader both looked behind them to see what was happening to the others. How those in the rear of their vehicle held on, Ernesto couldn't fathom at all but they did and 'opened up' on the opposition, immediately to their left.

The Toyota juddered violently as the heavy calibre machine gun stammered out a volley of rounds towards some nearby hillocks. It was peppering the tops of them, as Ernesto saw the two rear vehicles responding in like manner.

The Mercedes, though, had gone off the road and was receiving a torrent of 'incoming' fire and it suddenly burst into flames! Whether the petrol tank had ignited or another mortar bomb or rocket propelled grenade had found their mark, was impossible to know. Anyone inside the saloon, though, had probably had it, Ernesto thought to himself, as they charged on and the sound of gunfire subsided.

Their speed was now up to 125 kmph with the bumping around no longer such an intolerable problem to bear. With only twenty miles or so to go before the end of their journey, he was told, it seemed they would get to their destination, after all.

Ten minutes later, the Toyota slowed down to around its previous speed and Yousef reached for the 'walkie-talkie' radio in the glove box. He rattled off something in Arabic into it and a few seconds later a voice responded to him. The Arab leader muttered back a reply and put it down on his lap. He said nothing and just stared ahead, until Ernesto couldn't bear the suspense any longer, so he asked him,

"Well, what's the situation, then?" The 'old' man looked at him for the first time during their trip and said,

"It was quite a large government patrol of some fifty men, it seems. Our first vehicle was hit by an RPG and they're all probably dead, as are, almost certainly, the others in the Mercedes. Two others in the trucks behind us were injured, too, apparently but we got some of them, as well, according to the driver of the last pick-up."

"Well, that could so easily have been us in the Mercedes, couldn't it?" Ernesto gasped, to which his poker-faced friend next to him, Jousef Manakurh, simply replied, with great aplomb,

"I thought the change of vehicle an hour ago was a sensible move, despite the bumpy ride for most of the way, before dinner!"

Chapter Six

Polisario's lofty sanctuary

It was just past six o'clock when their Toyota pick-up truck turned off the 'main' road, after their hair-raising ride and dice with death and stopped.

"We'll wait for the others to catch up," stated the bearded and turbaned one, as he stepped out of the vehicle, looking back towards the way they'd come. Ernesto joined him.

"They'll be along in a few minutes; they have orders to slow up any possible pursuit to give us time enough to get away and then they will accelerate away to rejoin us. The jeeps and trucks the Army use are no match for these Toyotas," Jousef confidently exclaimed, as he slapped their model, proudly, on the front wing!

Some twenty minutes passed and then, in the distance, both could see a growing dust trail heading their way. A few minutes after that, the two remaining, white pick-ups roared towards them and braked sharply alongside their vehicle. The first driver jumped out and spoke rapidly to his leader, as the dust cloud they'd generated moved beyond them. After a rapid discourse between them, Jousef Manakurh held up his hand and the man returned to his truck.

"They're about fifteen minutes away, so if we turn off here, they won't follow us into the mountains; it's too dangerous for them. Come, we go!"

The trio of Toyotas moved off along a dusty track, heading for the foothills in the middle-distance and, beyond them, the safety of the mountains beckoned.

It was still quite hot and sticky as the sun started to set behind the largest peak ahead of them. Ernesto glanced at his watch, showing it was nearly 6.30pm and longed for the very bumpy ride to end.

By 7 o'clock, they were tackling a noticeable gradient and although this had reduced their speed to only 20 kmph or so, the bumping up and down was now constant. A few moments later and they stopped behind some sizeable boulders and were surrounded by about fifty, heavily armed, men. *'Jousef's men, of course,'* Ernesto thought to himself, as he jumped out of their vehicle, after the Polisario leader had done so.

"The last mile or so will be on horseback; that's alright for you, Ernesto, isn't it?" asked the turbaned one.

"Sure, no problem; it will be a nice change being able to roll with the undulations for a change!" the Guatemalan replied.

One of the guards surrounding their party produced a couple of horses for them; Ernesto was given a strong - looking, black stallion and both he and the Arab rebel leader then mounted up.

By 7.25pm, having picked their way around various obstacles on the rocky incline they were trekking along, they came to a large clearing of flat terrain, at the far end of which were several huts and a couple of utility buildings, which Ernesto took to be bunkhouses. Obviously, this was Jousef's camp.

At various points around this area were sighted some heavy machine gun posts and, on either side of the entrance to the 'plateau,' were two, double-barrelled, anti-aircraft guns, probably fifty calibre weapons, Ernesto thought to himself, as he dismounted from his steed, mimicking his host's actions.

"We like to be able to defend ourselves, if we have to, my friend, as you can see!" said Jousef, with a laugh, as he proudly displayed his well - armed hideaway with a wave of his arm.

"Very impressive, I must say," replied Alvarez, taking it all in.

"We have around three hundred men here and many more in the countryside, of course," Manakurh boasted, concluding with,

"Come, dinner awaits us, my friend," as he strolled off in the direction of one of the bunkhouses and Ernesto followed suit.

As they approached the larger of the two of them, Ernesto suddenly realised they were, in fact, sited well under an over-hanging cliff, so there wasn't any chance of these buildings being bombed from the air -*'good strategic thinking that,'* Ernesto thought to himself, as he followed the leader inside. He was amazed how spacious the interior was and also surprised by the wholesome array of food laid out on a large table before them.

"Come, let's eat, drink and relax, while we consider, in more detail, the complexities of your plan to improve the lot of some of our brothers and us, too, of course!" Jousef said, as he gestured to Ernesto to sit down alongside him at the table. There were just the two of them.

"Well, yes, of course, I will and thank you," he replied, sitting down.

Ernesto waited for the bearded leader to help himself to a selection from the various dishes on the table and then he did likewise. After a few minutes, Jousef asked his guest,

"So, tell me, Ernesto, how many people are you planning to send over to this little island you have in mind?" The Arab leant forward and selected two further slices of lamb from the meat dish in front of him, as he awaited his reply.

"Well, ideally up to ten thousand, to make for as dramatic an impact as possible, I would have thought but fewer would serve the purpose adequately. No less than half that number, otherwise the effect would be seriously lessened. Between six thousand and ten thousand refugees, hopefully nearer the higher figure, I'd guess."

The Polisario leader didn't immediately reply, so Ernesto took the opportunity to replenish his plate, too. As he poured himself some more of the, passable, wine that was provided, his host responded,

"Yes, I agree it would be essential for the 'landing party,' shall we say, to be as large as possible; I can provide ten thousand men without too much difficulty but what about the ships for them? Where do we get those from?"

The Guatemalan terrorist finished eating and took another sip of the red wine in his glass,

"I have given this part of the plan considerable thought. With the need to provide for up to ten thousand 'journeymen' for a five to six day voyage, I've calculated, I think three passenger / car ferries would do the job for us. The larger ones can accommodate some eighteen hundred passengers and hold over two hundred cars in their car bays; if the vehicle space was given over to the 'human cargo,' as well, I think each of them could carry an additional twelve hundred people, with ample room for palliasses, bedding etc., quite easily!"

Jousef looked very surprised when Ernesto added,

"I have a friend, a sympathiser, who lives in Greece and owns a shipping line. He has four of these large car ferries in his fleet and reckons I could lease three of them for two months, fully crewed, at a very good price. I have a twelve months option on them already.

Now we have our agreement, I can give my man in London the 'go ahead' at any time and they'll soon be on their way to us. The car ferries operate out of Piraeus, the main port of Greece and Stelios, that's my friend over there, states that he needs only a week's notice to have them ready and available for us. It would take about a week for them to get here but if the weather's fine, the two thousand five hundred mile journey could be completed in five or six days. They could berth, offshore, for a few days and then move closer to Agadir to take on their 'special cargo,' when the time comes."

Ernesto Alvarez paused for a moment to eat some more food and take another sip of his wine. His host piped up,

"I am very impressed with your plans, thus far and how advanced they seem, my friend." Ernesto finished eating and continued,

"You say you can gather up to ten thousand 'journeymen,' without too much difficulty, Jousef but what about boats? They'll need many boats to get them out to the ferries to get on board for the journey; do you think that will be a problem for us?"

The 'old' man sat back in his chair and took a large sip, or gulp more like, of his cordial and caressed his bearded chin, before responding to Ernesto. A few moments passed and then he said,

"If we have a few weeks beforehand, sufficient craft can be found, I'm sure. Most families on the coast have a fishing boat, or even two, if they're successful at making a living from it. Say each boat carries twenty people or so, that would require...eh...five hundred boats, would it not?"

Ernesto nodded but thought it better not to speak at this point, for fear of interrupting his train of thought. Jousef Manakurh spoke again,

"How close to the shore can these ferries of yours get?" He asked, looking at Ernesto.

"Well, I don't really know at this stage, Jousef but I can find out: how deep is the water, say, a quarter of a mile offshore, do you think?" Another pause by the Polisario leader,

"I would think a good twenty metres; I will let you know tomorrow. The fishermen will know, of course and I'll get one of my men to find out."

"Yes, do. If the water is that deep, then the ferries, having quite a shallow draught of only five or six metres could get in quite close, I'm sure but I...." Jousef interrupted him and said,

"If they can get within a few hundred metres or so of the beach, then we might not need anything like that number of boats; I mean, we could do four or five trips with only one hundred boats over that short distance, eh?"

Ernesto didn't like the idea of the collection exercise taking too long, for that would draw unnecessary attention to the conveyance procedure; he much preferred a 'one-off' event, to complete this early stage, as quickly as possible. He expressed his concern to his host but felt re-assured when Jousef stated,

"We won't know for a week or so, how many boats we can call upon, nor how many people would want to make the trip; my men will make discreet enquiries and I'll let you know the approximate number, in each case, shortly." And then, with a wry smile, he added,

"If it turns out that we need to make two or three runs out to the ships, in getting them all aboard, we could always make out it was a relay race, of some sort; you know, 'to keep the 'locals' happy in having something else to do' eh? That should keep the Authorities relaxed about all the activity and any inquisitive naval interest at bay, too, don't you think?" He added, laughing out loud,

"Oh, that would be really funny, wouldn't it?" Ernesto was already laughing with him as their mirth gathered pace, reaching a crescendo a few moments later.

When their laughter subsided, the Arab leader looked at his watch and said,

"Well, my friend, do you think it is time to sleep? It is approaching 11pm and we rise early here." Ernesto took the hint and they both got up from the table. Jousef stretched and said to his guest,

"Come, we sleep in the other bunkhouse. I'll show you your quarters." With that, he strode for the door, with Ernesto following a few feet behind.

There were two doors to go through to exit the building. The inner one triggered the 'off' switch to the electric light bulbs strung loosely from the ceiling of the dining room. These were powered by a generator outside the far wall of the bunkhouse and, after a while, the 'hum' it made became less intrusive.

The inner door being opened, ensured the exit to the outside was completed in darkness, to avoid giving away the location of the camp to the enemy, obviously.

'A good security feature, that, I must say' the Guatemalan said to himself, quite impressed, as he stumbled in the dark after his host towards the second bunkhouse. He noticed, in the moonlight, that there were quite a few guards posted around the camp, even though it was very quiet.

Jousef stopped at the foot of the steps to the second bunkhouse and whispered something to the sentry positioned there while waiting for Ernesto to catch up with him. As soon as he did so, the Arab leader walked up the half a dozen steps to the door, opened it and they both went inside.

Once again, the double - door arrangement made for an entry to the inner room difficult, until the outer door had closed but once it had, the electric light bulbs came on to illuminate a much larger interior than seemed possible from the outside. The inside was huge, in fact, measuring some two hundred metres long, by approximately thirty metres, wide.

Ernesto looked up at the timbered ceiling and saw the woodwork finish some twenty metres into the room, beyond which was a deep cave, housing most of the dormitory accommodation. *'There must be two hundred or more beds in here,'* he thought to himself, as he surveyed the surroundings. Most were occupied, as far as he could tell.

At the cave entrance, the beds were arranged in four rows into it; one either side of the natural hollow in the rock, augmented by two bed rows in the middle, with ample room in between them, extending to the back of it.

Jousef Manakurh was the first to speak. With a sweep of his arm, he said,

"You see, my friend, we are well catered for here. Whenever the Government planes fly over to attack us, those in here simply rush down there, amongst the beds, until the threat has passed; nature provides our protection, as well as our food. Hopefully, those outside will be successful in bringing down the intruders, too, eh?"

"Well, you certainly seem to have the capability of doing that, Jousef, I must say," rejoined the Guatemalan, smiling back at his host.

"Come, your room is over here, my friend," said the Arab, pointing to a small office type room to their right. Jousef opened the door and walked inside, followed by Ernesto Alvarez.

It also was more spacious within than seemed likely from the outside. There was a small desk opposite a single bed along the wall; a modest chest of drawers between them, with a mirror on top of it, at the end of the room. It measured about fifteen feet by ten feet, Ernesto guessed.

"You can stay with us here for as long as you wish, my friend; this will be your office and accommodation for as long as you require it," declared the bearded leader, with an engaging smile.

"That's very kind of you, Jousef, thank you, thanks very much," replied Ernesto, adding,

"I would like to visit Agadir tomorrow with your men; to see the beach and port areas and to survey the possible embarkation point for our 'journeymen,' you understand?"

"Of course, I'll come along with you, too, so we'll both see the departure point of the historic journey, then, eh? In the meantime, my friend, have a good sleep and we'll speak again tomorrow, okay?" With that, the Polisario leader withdrew and closed the door.

Ernesto put his hold-all down, unpacked a few things and, finding a full jug of water next to a large bowl, cleaned his teeth and then got into bed.

He awoke the next morning to quite a commotion outside his window. He lifted the blind away from it to see two rebels fighting, when another came between them and, after some difficulty, managed to separate them.

Ernesto looked at his wristwatch and saw it was 6.45am; *'Time to get up, I think,'* he said to himself and attended to his ablutions. He got dressed and opened the door of his 'office' and found the huge dormitory empty.

He spied an open door to what appeared to be a toilet and went inside. Having completed that necessity, he ventured outside into the sunshine. It was already quite warm, for even that time of the early morning, in stark contrast to the coolness of the dormitory.

He spotted Jousef at the top of the steps of the dining room bunkhouse and walked over to him.

"Ah, Ernesto, did you sleep well, my friend?" The Arab leader asked him.

"Yes, I did, Jousef, thank you; and you?"

"Oh, yes, I always sleep peacefully here, amongst my men; come, let us have some breakfast," motioning the Guatemalan to follow him into the dining room bunkhouse once more. He did so.

After another fulsome meal, they discussed the trip to Agadir.

"We will take the horses down to the road again and collect the pick up trucks, once more. If we leave in half an hour, we'll be there in two hours or so, around ten o'clock," said the Arab, looking at his watch.

On the way over to the stables, Ernesto asked Jousef what the two men outside his window were fighting about earlier.

"Oh, them, yes, one had accused the other of falling asleep at his post, on sentry duty and since failure to stay awake, while guarding the camp and one's friends, usually leads to the guilty being executed, he was desperate to plead his innocence. However, an accuser needs two witnesses, at least, to corroborate such a charge and since nobody else came forward, he was released. He was probably seeking revenge on the person who accused him of such waywardness."

"Oh, I see," said his guest.

"We have to be strict about such things, otherwise a surprise attack, while we're all asleep, could be the end of us all here, eh?"

They arrived at the stable door and walked in.

"Are you happy to ride the same horse as yesterday?" The emir asked Ernesto, as he pulled his own steed out into the yard.

"Yes, and a fine animal he is, too," he replied, spotting the black stallion a few bays beyond him. He walked up to the fine looking creature and it looked round at him, as he patted the animal and spoke softly to it,

"Come on, boy; do you fancy another trek down the mountainside this morning, then?" He led the animal outside and saddled up the stallion, mounting it a few minutes later.

The emir and Ernesto, along with a dozen or so other riders, trotted out of the encampment and began their descent down the quite steep hillside.

By 8.45am, they'd reached the foothills where four of the white Toyota pick up trucks were awaiting them. No heavy machine guns in the back this time, though, Ernesto noticed.

Once dismounted, they got aboard the vehicles, with the turbaned leader and the founder of 'The Enlightened Way,' getting into the second of the quartet. Once the rebels were installed in the rear of each of them, they set off for Agadir.

The bumpy ride was no easier for them and all yearned for the outskirts of the destination to emerge beyond the next hillock, as the surrounding scrubland flashed by.

Chapter Seven

The stage is set for a 'Go' from Agadir

The convoy of Toyotas slowed down as they reached the outskirts of the Arab quarter of the town. They cruised calmly through it, observing the speed limit signs as they did so, in order to avoid drawing undue attention to themselves.

Ernesto was able to enjoy the colourful scenery for a change and in some comfort, too. The streets were mostly cobbled in this, the oldest part of town but the passing years and regular traffic over them, made for an unusually smooth ride.

The old buildings lining the streets, either side of the convoy, were adorned with bright awnings and hanging tapestries once again, expressing a tranquil atmosphere, while hiding from view some dilapidated stonework, to be sure. With the Sun not yet overhead, part of the streets were in shadow, with the other side bathed in sunshine.

The vehicles trundled along and soon arrived at a huge square, in the middle of which was a large roundabout, adorned with palm trees and numerous flowers, making for a blaze of colour. The construction was clearly well - tended.

Beyond the circular junction, in stark contrast, was the modern part of Agadir, with tall office buildings and smart rows of shops lining the pavement. These were built in the mid-sixties, after this area of the town was destroyed by an earthquake in 1960.

Their convoy of Toyotas nosed its way into the circulation of traffic around the roundabout and exited the junction directly opposite the street they'd travelled along and continued towards the docks. They duly arrived at the Moroccan port at just after ten o'clock in the morning, without any interruptions from Government patrols, fortunately, unlike the previous time Ernesto travelled in this iconic vehicle.

It was boiling hot with the sun shining fiercely in a cloudless sky. The temperature was already 35 degrees centigrade and climbing.

The pick-ups moved slowly along the waterfront and parked alongside what appeared to be the wall of a large warehouse. The driver and his chum in the front of the first vehicle got out and walked back towards the second Toyota occupied by the Arab leader and Ernesto. Their automatic weapons were hidden under their flowing white robes but in this heat, Ernesto thought, their dress made them look rather conspicuous.

The driver leant on the door of the second vehicle and received instructions from Jousef Manakurh, in rapid Arabic. A few moments later he nodded his understanding to his leader and beckoned several of the others to follow him back along the waterfront. Jousef turned to Ernesto and said.

"I've told them to make enquiries of the locals about the water depth out to one hundred metres from the shore and also, discreetly, how many people might like to make a journey with them for a few days and earn quite a bit of money doing so. They will return here in a couple of hours and then we'll all go and have some lunch with a café owner friend of mine. Meanwhile, we'll go and look at the shoreline to see which area offers the best pick up point for all the travellers, yes?"

With that, the emir alighted from the vehicle and Ernesto did the same. With the remaining members of his 'entourage' numbering about ten men behind him, the party set off. They walked along the promenade for a few hundred yards and then down some steps leading to the beach.

Jousef and Ernesto both stopped near the waters edge and surveyed the shoreline in both directions. The bay they were scrutinising was huge; it must have been over five miles long, Ernesto thought to himself, with the white sandy beach stretching back from the sea some two hundred metres, at least.

It was incredibly hot now and the Guatemalan was encouraged when the Arab leader turned to him and said,

"What do you think of this, my friend? Is it wide enough for our purposes, do you think?" He moved his arm in a slow, sweeping motion of a semi-circle to emphasise the grandeur of the vista before them.

"I would definitely think so, Jousef and look where the seaweed is up to on the beach; it's only ten metres or so higher up from here, so there's plenty of room to gather people at high tide. If the water's deep enough fairly close in, then I'd say this bay would be ideal."

Ernesto, shading his eyes from the sun with his hand, squinted at his host awaiting his reply. The emir continued looking in both directions and finally said,

"Yes, I agree we wouldn't find a much better spot than this; see, the tidemark of the seaweed is quite uniform all along the sand for as far as we can see. If you're happy with it, then I am, too," he declared.

"If this is to be the place of the 'grand departure,' then let's go and celebrate finding it so easily, in my friend's café. It is over there," he said, pointing towards a blue and white striped awning on a building further along the promenade.

"Yes, I agree that's a splendid idea; this heat is quite something and I, certainly, would like to get into the shade with a drink in my hand, too."

The emir laughed at him, saying,

"You're not accustomed to all this sunshine, my friend, that's all; we're used to it here and this is quite normal. Come, this way," the bearded leader said, moving back towards the promenade, with his 'minders' dutifully falling in behind him.

Ten minutes later, they arrived outside the café and Jousef beckoned one of his men to him A short instruction in Arabic followed and the white robed individual walked inside, keeping his AK 47 well concealed under his apparel. The acolyte soon returned with a rather fat man coming out of the establishment behind him.

"Here is my friend, Anwar, who owns the place," said Jousef, just before he was enthusiastically 'bear-hugged' by the big man. The emir reciprocated, as best he could in the circumstances, Ernesto thought to himself, and then the tight embrace gave way to some conversation between them. After a few moments of this, Anwar stood aside for his venerable friend to step forward into his 'humble parlour' and gestured to Ernesto to come in, too.

Anwar shook the Guatemalan's hand as he walked passed him, bowing slightly and with a genuine smile, which Ernesto returned.

He hadn't got more than a few feet into the interior, though, when a couple of gun shots were heard in the distance. These were followed by a few short bursts of automatic fire and Jousef rushed passed the Guatemalan into the street. After a short pause, as he looked towards the far end of the beach, he turned to Ernesto and beckoned him outside, too, saying in an urgent voice,

"Come, we go now," tugging his guest's arm and Ernesto followed, as the emir waved goodbye to his friend, Anwar, with his 'minders' in his wake.

They all walked quickly along the promenade but stopped a few hundred metres from their parked pick-ups. The bearded leader issued some instructions to his, white-robed, followers and half a dozen of them set off for the far end of the beach. The rest stayed with Jousef and Ernesto and then their reduced party set off again, with renewed urgency in their step, towards the safety of their vehicles.

They arrived at the parked Toyotas, just as further gunshots were heard. They all looked towards the far end of the beach and saw some of Jousef's men running towards the second group he'd just despatched towards the fracas. Their flight away from the beach persuaded the others to turn back and all were now running hard towards their vehicles.

A jeep appeared, armed with a machine gun on the roof of the cab, with several soldiers in the back of it. A staccato of shots were fired at the fleeing Polisario rebels, giving rise to a line of sand spurts in front of them.

At this, two of the rebels turned and let off a fusillade of automatic fire from their AK 47's at the pursuing vehicle. The rounds peppered the lightly armoured jeep, shattering the windscreen and it then veered off into the surf. The machine gunner was silenced, too, being seen to slump over the weapon, as smoke began to pour from the driver's position. It stopped with its bonnet underwater.

Shouts of glee were heard from the two members of the rearguard, who turned to catch up with the main bunch in front of them. They all arrived safely, although out of breath after their involuntary four hundred metre dash across the sand. As soon as they'd clambered aboard the pick-ups, the vehicles reversed back into the main road and sped off, one by one, back into the centre of town.

"That was a close encounter, my friend," said Jousef Manakurh, in a much understated sort of way, as they raced into the main thoroughfare, around the roundabout, with everyone desperately hanging on to whatever they could, as the convoy sped off up a side street.

The Arab leader continued his appraisal of the situation,
"There will be more of them on the outskirts of town, I would think; you never come across a single jeep and they might have radioed ahead to warn them about us. We will see," he stated calmly.

They were taking a different road out of Agadir this time, Ernesto thought to himself, as they sped along, with screeching tyres, as they swerved around another bend or avoided another vehicle. The driver of the pick-up in front of them, though, clearly knew his way around this town, as did the others, seemingly, for they were rarely more than a dozen metres apart!

Eventually, the lead Toyota slowed down somewhat, as they approached the outskirts of the town. It was stifling inside the pick-up without the air - conditioning working properly, if at all, with the glare of the sun adding to their discomfiture.

Suddenly, the Toyota in front of them slowed up quite a bit, flashing its stop lights repeatedly to signal danger ahead. It had just reached the crest of the hill they were climbing. The emir muttered,
"Get ready now; it seems we might have run into them again!"

He reached into the glove box in front of him, took out his 'walkie-talkie' radio and fired off some orders into it. Two acknowledgements came back to him. He looked over to Ernesto, just as the sight of two jeeps, nose to nose across the road, came into view, some two hundred metres ahead.

"Hold on, my friend, the ride gets a lot bumpier from now on." The convoy had slowed to about 30 kmph and closed ranks, as it approached the road block. Ernesto shrank back into his seat, as he spied both machine-gunners on the two jeeps train their weapons on them.

They continued their fairly sedate approach towards the army vehicles and nothing more was said. When the lead pick-up got to within ten metres of the soldier in the middle of the road flagging them down, it suddenly roared into life, and he leapt out of the way just in time. It rammed the front of the jeep on the left of them, whilst Jousef's Toyota did the same to the other one on the right!

Both trucks bounced off the military vehicles, forcing the jeeps off the road and scattering half a dozen soldiers in several directions. Both machine - gunners lost their bead on them and had to traverse the weapons to regain their targets. Not quickly enough, though!

The four pick-ups were through the road block in just a few seconds and then the rebels in the rear of each, opened up on the disorientated jeep crews, with withering automatic fire. They concentrated on the two machine gun positions, initially, to eliminate the greatest challenge to their well - being.

The hail of bullets, from a dozen or more Kalashnikovs, tore into the jeeps, taking out both machine gunners, as they struggled to return fire. A few isolated shots ricocheted off the back of the last Toyota, wounding one of the rebels in the back of it but that was the extent of the reply.

They bounded along the main road at over 120 kmph and Ernesto, recognising a couple of landmarks he'd spotted the day before, realised they were fast approaching the junction where they'd turn off to head for their mountain sanctuary.

The pick-ups barely slowed down to negotiate the crossroads and they all took the turn very widely, veering off the road onto the scrub bordering it but fifty metres further on, proper traction had been regained.

Once the drivers were convinced there wasn't any pursuit to worry about, the convoys speed reduced to 70 kmph or so, giving the occupants some respite from the succession of bumps they endured along the track up to the foothills but not much!

Alvarez was the first to speak,
"Well, that was quite something, Jousef, I must say…pretty frightening." The bearded man looked at him and smiled, saying,
"We don't come across such dangers very often but those soldiers would have mowed us down on any excuse; I don't know whether they knew some of their friends were killed by us earlier but four Toyotas, all with men in the back, would have been intimidating for them. So, it was better to strike first in protecting ourselves, yes?"
"Yes, to ensure our safety, sure; nobody could argue with that," Ernesto replied, pensively.

Jousef Manakurh picked up his 'walkie-talkie' again and loosed off another message into it. He waited for a couple of minutes and got his reply, which he seemed to acknowledge, as he immediately switched it off afterwards.
"I've radioed ahead to request the horses are ready for us when we arrive at the change - over point. It's not for another hour or so yet but at least the animals would have been fed and watered in good time. Pinah will be looking forward to seeing you again, I'm sure," he said, with a smile, as they bumped along the track.
"Pinah?" enquired his guest.
"Yes, that's his name, Pinah, the black stallion you've ridden a couple of times now. A horse likes a competent rider and stallions have to respect their masters, more so than mares, eh? You ride very well, so I'm sure he'll be pleased to see you soon!"

Ernesto felt quite flattered by the compliment and visualised the proud, black, stallion neighing towards him when they next met. He replied,
"Well, thank you, Jousef, for those kind remarks and pleasant thoughts. Let's hope you're right!"

It was still baking hot that afternoon as the convoy trundled along the rutted track, their speed now down to 50 kmph or thereabouts. They were some ten miles from the foothills and it was just past 3pm, when a lookout in the back of the truck in front, shouted out something, pointing skywards.

Jousef instinctively turned round and saw the men in the back of their truck getting very agitated.

"There's a plane up there….no, two of them, it looks like," Jousef shouted, as he got out the 'walkie-talkie' again and rattled off rapid Arabic into it.

The Toyotas broke file and fanned out, beginning to zigzag, as they picked up speed in their dash for the hills ahead.

"They've seen us, I think!" Ernesto shouted, leaning out of his side window and looking up behind them.

"They'll know what to do, my men, you'd better hang on tight; it's as well the sun is still overhead, otherwise they'd dive at us with it behind them and we'd never see them open fire on us, then," Jousef shouted back at him. Their speed picked up rapidly, as did the bumping and bouncing, with one hundred metres or more between the trucks now.

He rattled off another message into the pocket radio, which Ernesto took to be further instructions to his men. He clicked off and shouted to Ernesto again,

"I've told them up ahead that we're under attack from the air and to delay sending the horses down to the change-over point; we wouldn't want Pinah and the others to get frightened unnecessarily, eh?"

Ernesto was about to reply, when their Toyota driver suddenly slammed on the brakes and the vehicle juddered to a stop. Two rockets zoomed past them and hit the ground some one hundred metres in front of them, creating a big dust cloud. Before Ernesto could gasp, their truck charged off again, continuing to zigzag, like the others were doing.

Another vehicle stopped suddenly and again, two missiles thumped into the ground ahead of it but rather closer this time, Ernesto thought.

The two jets screamed overhead, after their unsuccessful first pass at the group of them and all eyes in the trucks were focussed upon the aerial assailants, wondering whether they'd turn and have another go at them.

"They're coming back again!" Ernesto screamed to anybody listening to him above all the commotion and bouncing around, as the pick-ups continued their charge for the relative safety of the foothills, now only a couple of miles away.

As soon as flickering from the leading edge of the wing of the first jet lining up for another run at them was seen, their vehicle veered violently to the left and then to the right to avoid the stream of cannon fire aimed at them. The scrub to the right of them was peppered with a line of rounds from the strafing jet and then another, shorter, burst just missed them, as the fighter zoomed over them.

The second jet came at them from the side, at nine o'clock, this time and again, the vehicle juddered to a stop, as soon as the wing edges 'glittered' at them. It also loosed off another two rockets at Ernesto and Jousef's Toyota but again their driver was up to the challenge, fortunately for them.

The cannon fire slammed into the ground ahead of them, once more; the violent braking occurring just as the fighter pilot pressed the trigger button on his fifty calibre machine guns. Once the driver of their vehicle had spotted the two remaining objects slung under the wings of their attacking aircraft begin to drop, followed by a 'tell-tale' puff of smoke behind each of them, he knew two missiles were on their way, as well.

He turned the Toyota sharply to the left and accelerated as fast as he could, hoping to get under the trajectory of them, just as the plane screamed overhead. He just managed it in time, with the two rockets whizzing over his roof, too and thudding into the ground, with a tremendous bang, some one hundred metres behind the pick-up.

Fortunately, no 'hits' by the jets had been sustained and the pair of them were then seen peeling away to the west and were soon out of sight.

No return fire had been possible, with everybody clinging on to the vehicles for dear life but after the aerial danger had passed, a few 'victory' volleys were loosed off into the air.

The convoy was still intact, fortunately, albeit spread over quite a wide area. The trucks slowly drifted back together, over the remaining mile to the safety of the foothills and a few moments later, were safely back under cover of the rocks. Their occupants were so relieved to be alive and to be able to simply sit upon them.

Ten minutes later, the horses were down alongside them and Ernesto did think, when he spotted Pinah amongst them, that he'd given him a 'relieved' look in his eye, when the stallion cast a sideways glance at him. He could have equally imagined it, though!

Jousef had strolled over to his Guatemalan guest a few moments before the equine transport arrived, saying,

"You see if Pinah is not pleased to see you, then?" Both looked for the animal when the group were down with them; the emir nudged Ernesto in the ribs when he came into view,

"I told you so; you can see he's looking for you already, no?"

"Well, I'm not really sure; he seems more interested in that clump of grass he's now nibbling, don't you think?"

"No, no, he's just a little shy, that's all. Give him a whistle and see if he doesn't come over to you, eh?"

Ernesto did so but no apparent response from the proud, black stallion. He whistled again and then his previous mount looked up from the grass tuft he'd been munching on and wandered over to him.

"You see, I said he'd be pleased to see you," chortled the Polisario leader, with a big grin on his face.

Ernesto got up and patted the horse on his neck and it snorted an acknowledgement at him.

"Maybe, you're right, Jousef, he does seem to know me, just a little, anyway."

He looked up at the sky to see the sun moving nearer the horizon now. It was still very humid and he mopped his brow with his forearm and turning to his host, asked him,

"Do you think they'll be back? The enemy, I mean."

"Probably, in a day or two; they prefer to send over a few planes in the morning, drop a few bombs and then retire, allowing some ground troops to get in position below here and then follow up with an assault on my camp. They don't know the trails up there, though," he said, waving his arm upwards towards the mountain behind them,

"Unlike us and we'll be ready for them, as usual. After a few have been killed, they normally give up and go back down again," he concluded, rather dismissively.

"Come, we go!" the emir declared, as he moved towards his own horse, mounted it and turned towards the trail leading up the mountain, with his men and Ernesto doing likewise.

There was an hour's daylight left, Ernesto estimated, as they trekked back into the rebel encampment, dismounted in front of the stable block and gathered outside the main bunkhouse.

Alvarez told his host he'd like to shower and change before they sat down for dinner and also draw up a plan of the forthcoming endeavour to discuss between them over their meal.

"Please go ahead, my friend, that's a good idea; I'll look forward to seeing your list of ideas for us. The meal should be ready by seven o'clock, so I'll see you then."

"Okay, I'll see you later."

Ernesto Alvarez wandered off towards the other bunkhouse which comprised the main sleeping area for the rebels and his temporary 'office.' He had about an hour and a half to complete his ablutions and draw up a summary of his plans for the 'Great Adventure' which lay ahead. If Manakurh agreed with the schedule, then the onslaught would start from here.

Chapter Eight

The countdown begins....

Just after six o'clock that evening, Ernesto Alvarez emerged from his shower, duly refreshed and towelled down. He changed into some clean clothes he'd retrieved from his hold-all he had with him, combed his unruly mop of hair and sat down at the desk previously assigned to him by the rebel leader.

After a few moments thought, he wrote down the following list of requirements and instructions comprising the *'modus operandi'* of the audacious plan he envisaged. He decided to name it 'The Croesus Tithe' and duly headed his sheet of A4 with that title. He wrote down the following stipulations:-

1. *Polisario will supply between 6,000 and 10,000 men who are willing to spend a few days at sea and up to a month away from their families.*

2. *None must bear arms - any journeyman found with a weapon will be severely dealt with!*

3. *The 'Enlightened Way' will provide three Car Ferries as transport.*

4. *The ultimate destination will be known only to the leaders of the two movements and the Captains of the Ferries after they're underway.*

5. *Polisario will appoint 'leaders' of each squad of 500 men beforehand.*

6. *They will be personally responsible for their 500 strong detachments and solely answerable to the leader of the expedition, Ernesto Alvarez.*

7. *Upon arrival at the destination, they will organise their group to get ashore and 'phone Ernesto Alvarez's mobile when this has been done.*

8. *He will demand from the Authorities that every journeyman be paid approximately $10,000 in gold, in the form of a one kilogram bar, for each of them. Such bars contain 32.15 ounces of pure gold. With gold worth $310 per ounce, this equates to some $10,000 per kilogram bar.*

9. *Upon joining his vessel, every journeyman must be told of his anticipated 'prize' and after that, give his unswerving allegiance to Ernesto Alvarez, carrying out his instructions, without question, until the voyage is declared over by Ernesto Alvarez. If the man is unwilling to give such commitment, he will not be allowed on board.*

10. *Polisario will be paid one third of the agreed sum for its assistance to the 'Freedom Way' upon confirmation the Ferries have set forth, with the previously agreed complement of journeymen on board. The balance of the agreed sum to be paid upon, either, the Ferries returning to Agadir to discharge their 'cargo,' or confirmation of the end of the operation by the leader of 'The Enlightened Way,' Ernesto Alvarez.*

11. *Ernesto Alvarez will have sole charge of the operation throughout and any major disputes will be <u>exclusively</u> settled by him.*

12. *It is understood that strict secrecy must be observed, by both sides, until the event is announced in the media. Thereafter, discretion will apply in addressing any unforeseen circumstances.*

Signed.....................................
Ernesto Alvarez
Signed.....................................
Jousef Manakurh

Having read his document twice and made a copy of it, the Guatemalan placed the papers in a folder he found in the centre drawer of the desk he sat at and walked with it outside.

It was still very hot, although a cooling breeze had got up, which freshened the air somewhat. He looked at his watch, showing 6.50pm and then strolled over to the main bunkhouse, with the folder under his arm, saying to himself,

"Well, I hope the emir likes what I've drawn up, since I don't think there's anything too controversial in it and as long as he gets his money...."

As he approached the dining room, he found the very man waiting for him at the foot of the steps.

"Ah, my friend, I hope you're feeling much refreshed and I see you have with you your list of, shall we say, 'requirements.' I hope they're acceptable, eh?"

"Yes, I have and I hope you'll be happy with everything I consider essential for the plan to succeed," Ernesto replied.

"I hope so, too; shall we go inside?" the Polisario leader suggested, motioning his guest to mount the steps in front of him.

Once again, a lavish spread of cold meats, stews, vegetables, salads and fruit were set out on the large dining table awaiting them, along with the customary assortment of juices and some wine.

Ernesto waited for his host to sit down, out of courtesy as before, and then he did the same. As previously, the meal was to be shared by just the two of them; the emir preferring to learn the details of what was planned before his followers, as befits a revered leader.

Jousef Manakurh tucked into the fare, filling his plate but not excessively so, poured himself a glass of orange juice, took a sip of it and then began to read the schedule Ernesto had placed beside him. While he busied himself with that, his guest made his selection of food and filled his glass with some red wine, took a sip and waited for the emir to respond.

A few moments elapsed without comment from him, so Ernesto started to eat his meal. He'd swallowed several mouthfuls and still no word from his host, who continued to, quite studiously, read his schedule. He felt a little embarrassed at the silence and looked up at the two servants in attendance. Neither noticed him, or his anxiety, since they continued to stand to attention and, impassively, stare across the table at each other.

Then the Polisario leader finally put the paper down and spoke,
"Well, my friend, I'm sorry for taking so long; I hope you didn't think I was being rude but I read it twice, very carefully, to make sure I understood everything."

"Uh oh, he doesn't like it; I wonder which clause he objects to?" Ernesto thought to himself, fearing the worst. He was quite wrong, though, for Jousef smiled broadly and continued,

"You have done a thorough job here, I think, Ernesto; the stipulations are lucid and sensible and most important of all, you have reiterated the terms of our financial agreement, precisely. I will happily sign the schedule for you now," looking up towards one of the attendees to provide him with a pen to do so.
"Well, I'm pleased you're happy with everything, Jousef; I tried to convey the minimum requirements to avoid any misunderstandings...."

The taller steward, having moved away from the table to accede to his leader's request, swiftly returned with a ballpoint pen, which distracted the Guatemalan in mid-sentence. As he was about to sign the document, Jousef looked up at the Author of it and asked,
"How do you or the 'Enlightened Way' get paid for all this, eh? There's no mention of it in here, I've looked carefully for it." The signature was pending, Ernesto noticed, as he responded,
"The movement and I will not receive any payment like the kilogram bars due to the men, nor will any fee for cessation be demanded from the Island Authorities."

The signing hand still hovered over the requisite place on the schedule, as Jousef continued to stare at him, awaiting his answer.

"No, I have made arrangements with a friend of mine in Nicaragua to invest in the gold market, with him, before the news of payment in gold leaks out. Hopefully, we'll benefit from a rise in the price of the metal, afterwards. In this way, nobody can accuse us of making money ourselves out of our desire to provide for the poor.....such altruism reinforces the integrity of purpose, wouldn't you say?"

Jousef laughed loudly at that, saying,

"Not directly benefiting, of course!" as the signing hand hit the document and a quick scrawl ensued. Jousef Manakurh handed him the paper and said,

"That's very shrewd, my friend, really quite clever, I must say. Would it be in order for Polisario to buy some gold, too, in good time, I mean?" The wily old leader enquired, adding,

"We have some money for our purposes in a bank or two, you understand and it would be sensible to boost our reserves, wisely, if we could."

"I don't see why not, if you were discreet about it; I cannot guarantee the price of bullion will rise on the news, of course but you would need to wait until the right moment, I would have thought; perhaps just as the ferries arrive and disgorge their cargo onto the Island of Jersey."

"Yes, we'll give that some thought and about that time would seem the moment to do it, I agree, my friend, thank you."

"You keep your copy of the agreement safe in the meanwhile, Jousef and I'll do the same," Ernesto replied, putting his copy of it in his pocket.

Jousef tucked his away inside his robes and they continued dining. During the meal, Jousef asked him,

"Oh, yes, I almost forgot to ask; why call the operation 'The Croesus Tithe'? I mean, who or what, is Croesus? " Ernesto swallowed the wine he was sipping and replied,

"Croesus was an extremely wealthy King, I mean, ostentatiously so, who lived about two thousand five hundred years ago. His wealth was mainly in gold and legend has it, that it was so vast, that it couldn't be counted; only estimated. That seems an appropriate description of this little island of Jersey to me; the wealth they superintend there is truly enormous, apparently - that's why I've called it that."

"So what will the tithe cost them, then, do you think?" the emir enquired of him.

"That depends on the number of men you can muster, Jousef; if it's the minimum number of 6,000, then at $10,000 per man, that would amount to $60 million but if you get up to the maximum of 10,000 impoverished souls, then it would be $100 million, wouldn't it?"

After another sip of wine and a short pause, Ernesto continued,

"While that does sound a lot to you and me, you need to realise there is over £100 billion on deposit there alone, or $150 billion and that's quite apart from the, very considerable, individual wealth, residing on the Island. It would only be a nominal tithe, really."

"Well, that explains it, my friend, thank you. I see the Croesus connection, now. I'm sure they won't mind donating just a tiny part of it to our 'unfortunates' when they see them!"

When they'd finished, he asked Ernesto when he was thinking of returning home,

"Presumably, you'll be going over to London, shortly, to get everything organised your end, yes?"

"That's right; I would like to get over there as soon as possible, as there's a lot of work to do and I want to be in a position to move quickly, after you confirm how many people you've managed to enlist for the journey. I wouldn't mind going to Casablanca airport tomorrow morning, if that isn't too inconvenient for you, Jousef?"

"No, not at all; I can arrange for the Mercedes to be available to pick you up at the crossroads after breakfast and then you'd be well on your way."

The emir motioned to the principal steward to come over to him, which he did. He spoke rapidly in Arabic to the man and a few moments later, the acolyte withdrew. Jousef turned to Ernesto and said,

"The car will be waiting for you there from 9.30am, so you'll have a couple of hours to journey down to the trucks and get there. I'll send a couple of my men with you to Casablanca, in case you get stopped on the way to the airport; you know, just in case," he concluded, as he rose from the table.

"Right, that's fine, thank you very much, Jousef; I'd better get a good night's sleep and I'll see you here for breakfast, then," and he did the same.

"Sleep well, my friend," replied the bearded one, as he went outside.

Ernesto awoke bright and early the next morning and arrived at the main bunkhouse, with his hold-all ready for departure, at 6.30am. The Polisario leader was already inside and got up from the table to greet him.

"Good morning, my friend; I hope you slept well and do come and sit down here," the emir said, pulling out a chair for him.

"Yes, I did sleep well, thank you," he replied, sitting down next to his host.

During their meal, Ernesto asked Jousef to ensure all the 'squad leaders' of the 500 man groups were issued with mobile phones, with his telephone number recorded in the data bases of them.

"You know, in case they forget my number in all the excitement surrounding them at that time; recording the number in each of the memory packs will ensure that doesn't happen. I need to be in ready contact with any and all of the men, at any time, of course. Before you issue them with their 'phones, you need to list their numbers and let me have them, before the ships sail, eh?"

"Yes, of course, I'll ensure that is done and let you have the list in good time."

Forty five minutes later, they'd finished breakfast and were outside, firmly embracing reach other. Jousef had given him the list he'd asked for, as well as three different mobile numbers Ernesto could reach him on. Jousef was bragging that he had over a dozen mobile 'phones with him at the base, just in case one or two got broken, during 'defensive operations!'

The horses were brought up to them a few moments later and Jousef remarked,

"Pinah will miss you for sure, my friend," patting the animal on the nose and it gave a short snort in response, which made them both smile, as Ernesto mounted up.

"I think you might be right, Jousef. Is he smiling as well; only I can't see from here?" They both grinned at each other, as the Guatemalan led his horse into the centre of the group trekking down to the Toyotas awaiting them down below.

"Have a good journey, my friend and we'll be in touch soon, yes?" the emir called out after him and Ernesto waved back in acknowledgement, as they set off for the downward journey to the transports.

The sun was beating down on them, as usual, with the heat becoming intense, as the party joined up with the Toyota people down below. Three of the riders dismounted, including Ernesto and they quickly boarded the second pick-up. The Guatemalan waved goodbye to his stallion, as it was wheeled around for the return journey up the hill but the animal didn't respond.

The trio of Toyotas set off on their bumpy journey for the last time, as far as Ernesto was concerned and he wouldn't be missing this part of his experiences in Morocco, for sure!

An hour or so later, the three vehicles had stopped alongside the white, Mercedes 280 and two of the guards joined Ernesto in getting in the car. He got into the front passenger seat and they got into the back.

One of them spoke English fairly well, fortunately, Ernesto thought, as the vehicle drove off behind only one of the pick-ups this time. The English speaker in the rear, proffered the explanation,
"The leader thought it better to minimise your presence on the journey to Casablanca; a convoy of vehicles is more…how you say?…conspicuous, I think is the word, eh? Only one Toyota out front could be anybody travelling along and they wouldn't know this car had an escort, therefore and no machine gun in the back of it, either, you see?"
"Yes, I do; that all sounds sensible, I think," Ernesto replied, rather nervously.
"We will drop you off on the outskirts of the City and you can change into a taxi for the last leg of the journey to the airport; the leader has already 'phoned ahead for one of his people to drive you there, okay?"
"Yes, thank you, that's very thoughtful of him; I appreciate it," he replied, still a little anxious.

They sped along around 100kmph out in the countryside, with a less bumpy ride and air-conditioning aiding the comfort level in no small way. Several villages flashed by as the car hurried along and by noon, they had stopped for lunch in Marrakech.

Suitably refreshed and relieved they'd not encountered any difficulties, thus far, they resumed their journey to Morocco's Capital. With the condition of the roads improving, as they got nearer their objective, they were able to maintain a higher cruising speed of some 130 kmph. They covered the 280 mile journey in just over four hours, arriving at the agreed place for the taxi exchange at 4.15pm.

This occurred uneventfully and Ernesto waved his escort goodbye. The Peugeot he was now settled into, drove away for the short run to the airport. He arrived there some fifteen minutes later and said his farewell to the taxi driver and went into the concourse of the building.

He looked around to get his bearings and saw there was a London - bound flight scheduled for a six o'clock departure and joined the small queue at the Air Morocco check-in desk. There were several seats available, he was informed, so he bought a ticket for the flight, without difficulty.

He sauntered over to a nearby coffee shop in the airport, sat down and telephoned his Number two in his organisation, Omah Djesturi and told him of his flight details. Omah informed him that he'd got his boss a flat in the Bayswater Road, not far from Omah's place; the Landlord seemed a nice chap, an ex-military, called Stephen Carvell.

Ernesto, now travelling under his passport name of Ernest Ravel, was pleased with his lieutenant's efforts on his behalf and told him so. Much encouraged by his boss's contentment, Omah offered to pick him up from Heathrow when he got in and he did.

His plane took off on time and the leader of 'The Enlightened Way' thought through much of what lay ahead of him during the three hour flight to London. The time soon passed and he arrived at Heathrow Airport at just gone 7pm GMT on the 4th March, 2000; his first trip to the United Kingdom. He was looking forward to his stay in England.

Having got off the Air Morocco 757 Jetliner with the other passengers, he collected his hold-all from the luggage carousel and wandered towards the immigration desk handling 'Foreign Nationals,' trying to look as casual as possible.

Once again, he fingered the top of his passport in the inside pocket of his navy jacket he was wearing and said to himself,
"Well, Arnold Fleischer's handiwork has proved convincing so far; I hope my luck still holds, otherwise......best not think negatively at this stage......I don't want to convey the wrong impression......"

His musings were interrupted by an official, who called out to him,

"This way, sir, if you please…" pointing to another immigration desk which had just opened up.

"Oh, right, thank you," he replied, moving as confidently as he could up to the official, manning the newly opened position.

He got out his passport and placed it on the top of the desk. The officer looked at it closely and then looked up at him and then down again at the 'Fleischer special' and said,

"It's Mr Ravel, is it? Mr Ernest Ravel from Managua?"

"Yes, that's right, officer."

"Are you here on business or on holiday?" The immigration officer asked, looking directly at him, this time.

"A bit of each, actually; I'm staying with a friend of mine who lives in Bayswater, for a few days and then I intend doing some business, while I'm over here," he replied, with a smile.

"Oh, what sort of business might that be, Mr Ravel? I see here you're listed as a land agent, is that right, sir?"

"Yes, I'm involved in property development in and around Managua, mainly and advise several local and International companies specialising in this field, including some of your largest concerns here, who wish to invest in my country."

"That sounds very interesting, sir," said the customs official, sensing he was getting a little out of his depth on this line of enquiry. He changed the subject, accordingly,

"Do you have anything to declare at all, Mr…eh…Ravel?"

"No, nothing at all; would you like to look in my hold-all, officer?"

"No, thank you, sir; just make sure you go through the 'green' channel on your way out then and have an enjoyable stay here," handing him back his passport.

"Thanks, I will." The official nodded to him and called out,

"Next, please," looking over Mr Ravel's shoulder to the person behind him.

The, much relieved, Guatemalan strolled towards the exit doors to the main concourse, remembering to go through the 'green' channel beforehand. He did so, unchallenged by the two staff members manning this section, who only glanced at him and he emerged into the public arena.

Having fleetingly scrutinised the sea of faces in front of him, he walked slowly through the throng, hoping 'his man' would soon spot him. A few moments later he did. A smiling Omah Djesturi suddenly stood in front of him.

"Hello, Ernesto, it is great to see you, sir." The leader of 'The Enlightened Way' scowled at him, though, saying in a hushed tone,

"It's Ernest, Ernest Ravel, not Ernesto....not until I'm clear of this place, anyway; remember that when I'm travelling, Omah, Eh?"

He looked around him to ensure he hadn't been overheard. In all the noise of the concourse, there was little chance of that but he wanted to impress the point on his Number two. Omah was suitably chastised.

"Sorry, sir, I got too excited at spotting you in the crowd. It won't happen again, I can assure you."

"Alright, no harm done this time; are you going to show me your flat, then?"

"Yes, yes, of course, this way," he replied, heading for one of the exit doors from the building. Mr Ravel duly followed.

During their car journey to Omah's place, Ernesto Alvarez gave his deputy a short résumé of events thus far, including some of his more dramatic experiences in Morocco.

He also told him how well his meeting with the Polisario leader, Jousef Manakurh, had gone and that he would stay with Omah for a fortnight or so, pending an update on the Agadir situation, from him. Once he'd been in touch, he would see to putting the other arrangements in place.

It took just over an hour and a half for them to arrive at Omah's flat, No. 22 Porchester Terrace, in Bayswater. Ernesto commented on the traffic to him,

"I have never seen so many vehicles, Omah, how do you manage to get about around here?" His deputy smiled at the road ahead,

"With difficulty; you should see it in the daytime! You just get used to it, you have to!" They both laughed.

At 8.35pm, they drew up outside the three bedroomed townhouse, which was situated mid-terrace, amongst a block of eight, late 60's built properties, each having a garage opposite them, in the cul-de-sac. The quiet location was just a few yards from Porchester Street, one of London's quite fashionable areas.

Having parked his car on the tarmac standing in front of his garage, Omah locked it and led Ernesto to his front door. Inside the property was an unusually spacious entrance hall, leading to a modest dining area. On the next elevation was a comfortable lounge, well decorated with bright curtains and soft furnishings. A few traditional landscape paintings adorned the walls, several being individually illuminated by overhanging lights.

The room had been temporarily converted, though, into a sizeable office by the look of it; two draughtsman's drawing boards occupied much of the central area of the room and a desk, with much paperwork on it, was located behind the door. Most of the furniture had been pushed up against two walls to accommodate the 'working' environment.

"You have a very nice place here, Omah; life must be treating you well, eh?" the Guatemalan stated, with a wry smile.

"Yes, I must agree this is a very nice spot, very peaceful, with light and airy rooms making for an enjoyable working place," his Operational Head replied, rather nervously.

"Come, you see I'm already drawing up plans for the enterprise you envisage," inviting Ernesto to look at his workings on the drawing boards.

The leader of 'The Enlightened Way' took a few steps forward to see a large aerial view of Jersey on one of them and detailed maps of each of the three likely landing areas, Ernesto had already expressed an interest in, on the other.

The aerial photograph was marked with three red crosses, one on the west coast and the others at two points on the south coast of the island. These were shown as St. Ouen's Bay on the west coast and St. Brelade's Bay and St. Aubin's Bay. The capital, St. Helier, was situated near the south - east corner of St. Aubin's Bay.

Omah pointed to the aerial photo and said,

"You were right about these areas for a landing. See the island is quite rocky in the north and for much of the east side, too but here, in the west and the south, it is quite low lying and the beaches are wide, flat and sandy; ideal locations for our purposes."

He moved over to the other drawing board having the detailed maps of the three bay areas on it. He continued,

"We could arrive here, here and here, without difficulty," he stated confidently, pointing with his forefinger at St. Ouen's Bay, St. Brelade's Bay and St. Aubin's Bay,

"And the arrivals could be undertaken simultaneously, to maximise the element of surprise. Moreover, if you stayed at one of the hotels overlooking the front in St. Helier," pointing with his finger again at St. Helier, he continued, excitedly,

"You could witness the onset of your journeymen onto the beach in St. Aubin's Bay from a good vantage point and know the other bays to the west of you, were experiencing the same thing!"

Ernesto Alvarez studied the three maps closely and then said,

"Omah, I like it. You've done well; now how about some dinner, eh?"

"Yes, sir, of course. Would you like to go out or shall I get something sent round? I usually 'phone a 'take away' place I know around the corner when I'm working but we can always…."

"No, a 'take away' sounds fine and we can then continue our discussion about all this," he said, looking away towards the drawing boards again.

"Would a 'Chinese' be alright, then?" Omah tentatively enquired.

"Fine, fine, for me, thank you," Ernesto replied, deep in thought, as he looked at the three maps once more.

While Omah Djesturi telephoned in their 'take away' order, Ernesto muttered to himself,

"Yes, I like it.….I really do like it, I must say.….I have a good feeling about it already!"

Chapter Nine

Everything's set ....as an island slumbers

Ernesto Alvarez stayed just over a fortnight at his Deputy's house in Porchester Terrace and much of the time was taken up with laying the foundations of his Grand Plan.

Jousef Manakurh, the Polisario leader, had telephoned him the day after his arrival there with the good news about the water depth off the beach at Agadir, they'd both considered. It was quite shallow a few feet from the shore, apparently but beyond that, some twenty metres out, the sea floor dropped steeply, giving a water depth of over thirty metres!

"That's more than enough for our ferries, Jousef, they only have a draught of six or seven metres, un-laden and even full, they'd need only ten metres or so. That's very good news; now what about the journeymen?"

The emir was quite upbeat about that, too; his men were taking reports from all over the port of willing participants and at the latest count, he'd secured over four thousand 'confirms' and was confident he'd be able to double that number by the following week.

"The word has spread like wildfire, my friend, so you'll soon have the ideal number you're after, I'm sure; the prospect of gaining $10,000 in gold, for just a few weeks away from their families, is irresistible to them, as you can imagine!"

"Don't let them get over excited, though, for we don't want the authorities to get wind of what we intend to do now, do we?" cautioned Ernesto. Jousef's response was fairly reassuring, though,

"I've instructed my men to tell all those who've applied, that if they, or their families, talk too much, they won't go and if the authorities make enquiries about all the rumours, then we'll simply deny it and who'd ever believe such a crazy story, anyway, eh?"

Ernesto counselled the emir, nevertheless, that it would be unwise to let the 'offer of riches' get out of hand, however, since the element of surprise at the outset was just as crucial as the landings at the end of the voyage.

Equally though, he didn't want to discourage his ally, since there was no denying he was doing splendidly for him; he just wanted to ensure a worthwhile gathering of several thousand souls was available, when the time came.

The next few days were taken up with more detailed planning, augmented by a couple of visits by Stephen Carvell, their planning operative, who lived in the Bayswater Road, where Ernesto would take up residence.

Apart from being finally introduced to his prospective tenant, the leader of 'The Enlightened Way,' he brought his military training to bear upon the project, which much increased its credibility. He'd already carried out several 'recce's' of the landing sites, as well as the island as a whole and was able to confirm the place was genuinely, a very 'soft' target.

"The place is wide open, gentlemen, as far as I can see; such an incursion would be very 'do-able,' as things stand," he'd assured the pair of them.

Carvell was a big man but still a very fit forty two year old, ex-marine. Despite a successful and quite varied career in the Royal Navy, he'd subsequently felt that the World had passed him by, during his enlistment. Having had little success in 'Civvy Street' afterwards, either at home or abroad, he was determined to make up for lost time, whatever it took to do so.

"Well, thank you Stephen for all your preparation work; we'll consider all you've said and let you know what's decided in a few days, then," Omah had told him.

"Right you are, Gentlemen, thank you," he'd replied but as he got to the door to leave, Ernesto said,

"I'll be over to stay in your flat, in a few days, Stephen; I gather Omah, here, has attended to all the arrangements with you…."

"Oh, yes sir; everything's been attended to and it's all ready for you."

"Good, good….I'll be in touch soon, then," the Guatemalan replied, as the burly mercenary opened the door, nodded in acknowledgement and quietly closed it behind him.

Three days later, on the 10ᵗʰ March, Alvarez got another call from the leader of the Polisario, Jousef Manakurh, who confirmed he'd now got up to seven thousand men lined up for the trip and hoped that would be sufficient for him.

"Any more would be increasingly difficult to control, I think, given the communication problems, security risks and so on…," he'd stated.

"That's fine, Jousef, just fine; that's about twenty four hundred journeymen per ferry, which would be virtually a full complement for each of them.

Let's call this part of the plan complete, then; you don't need to get any more now, alright? Well done, Jousef. I'll speak to my friend in Greece and let you know soon when he can get his ferries to Agadir, to give you time to prepare for loading them all, okay?"

"Okay, my friend, I'll wait for you to call - goodbye."

"Did you hear that, Omah? Jousef's already got seven thousand men and he's keen to go, as soon as possible. I'd better ring Stelios, you know, my man in Greece, to get the ferries ready for us," he called out to his deputy, who was making coffee for them, in the kitchen.

"Things seem to be falling into place, quite nicely, eh, Boss?" Omah called back to him.

"Oh, hello, could I speak to Mr Makarios, please? Mr Stelios Makarios, yes, that's right," Ernesto confirmed to the telephonist at Makarios Marine, the Mediterranean shipping line, when he got through.

"Hello, Mr Makarios here, who's calling?" Ernesto heard the shipping magnate ask, a moment later.

"Stelios, it's me, Ernesto Alvarez; how are you, my friend?"

"Oh, Ernesto; it's good to hear from you. How's it going, your quest to right the wrongs of the World, eh?"

"Fine, things are coming along fine. I just wanted to let you know that we are now ready our end, for the boats you've set aside for us…."

"Boats, what boats? Ships you mean, my friend, ships; I don't deal with boats, they're too small. I only deal with big things; you know that, of course!"

The multi-millionaire roared at his own joke down the 'phone and Ernesto had to hold the handset away from his ear and feign his jovial response to the overweight tycoon,

"Yes, of course, Stelios, how silly of me, I meant to say, ships; how are mine coming along, you know, the ones I've leased from you?"

"After your last call, I've had the three ferries crewed up, with extra fuel on board and have sent them onto Algiers; they should arrive there tomorrow. They can stay in port there for quite a while, if you like, without any questions being asked; the Algerians need the business, these days, you know," the boss of Makarios Marine, chuckled.

"That's very helpful, Stelios, thank you; how long would it take them to get to Agadir from Algiers, would you guess?"

"Hold on, my friend, let me find out for you." Ernesto heard the tycoon barking some enquiries down another 'phone in his office and then he got back onto the line,

"It's only a thousand miles or so to Agadir from there, apparently, so they could travel that distance in two or three days, depending on the weather, of course."

"Well, that's tremendous news, Stelios; do I request them to move to Agadir through you or should I speak to the Captains directly?"

"No, you instruct the senior Captain on the "Makmar Empress", the main ship from now on. Have you got a pen and paper there?" Stelios enquired.

"Yes, I have, go ahead," Ernesto replied,

"Right then, I call all my ships "Makmar" this or "Makmar" that… I like to put my name on my floating assets, you know," chortled the shipping magnate and, again, Ernesto responded to the jocular remark, without really appreciating the mirth,

"Well, I would too, if I owned your empire, Stelios," humouring the fat man on the other end of the line.

"Now, where was I? Oh, yes, the "Makmar Empress" is captained by Robert Stegman, known as 'Steggles' in the trade, if you know what I mean, my friend. The "Empress" is the biggest of the three, some four hundred feet long, carries two thousand passengers and two hundred and forty cars, which you won't be needing, of course, eh?" Another laugh down the line, which Ernesto chose to ignore, this time.

"The other two are French built, both in 1973 but that doesn't concern you, of course; they're three hundred and fifty footers, carry about eighteen hundred passengers, with room for two hundred and twenty cars, again more space for people, instead.

The "Makmar Queen" is captained by Peter Wilkinson and he's the Second in Command throughout the voyage and the other one is the "Makmar Princess", under the command of Captain Michael Rollings, or 'Rollo' to his friends, apparently.

They're all 'Ro-Ro' ferries, do you know what I mean by that, Ernesto?" The Guatemalan thought for a moment and then said,

"Well, I'm not too sure; you'd best explain, Stelios, just so I do understand, if you would."

The Greek replied,

"Ro-Ro is an abbreviation for 'Roll on - Roll off,' my friend, enabling the vehicles to roll on board and roll off afterwards; it means the ships are fitted with bow doors and a ramp, rather like a landing craft used by the military. It should suit your purposes, ideally, I would have thought, no?"

Ernesto hadn't really thought of that. What a bonus to be able to load and unload in shallow water from the front of the vessel.

"What sort of draught are we talking about, Stelios?"

"The "Empress" is about five and a half metres un-laden and seven metres when fully laden. The others are about the same but a little less, why do you ask?"

"Well, it would be a major advantage if our people could simply swim a short way out to them to get on board and then exit from the bow to the shore; I mean, twenty feet of water, what is that, really?"

The Greek shipping magnate cautioned him, though,

"Only in calm water, my friend; if the sea's rough, you couldn't open the bow doors and lower the ramp, otherwise, the water would come in and you might well sink the ship and that wouldn't do at all, would it? Not good for you, nor me, eh?" Another belly laugh down the line to the Guatemalan ensued.

"No, of course, not. The Captain would know whether it was safe enough to open the bow doors, obviously but if the weather's fine and the sea is becalmed, then that facility would be a tremendous boon, for sure, that's all," Ernesto replied, rather indignantly.

"You'll notice all the Captains are British on my ships; I regard them as the best there is on the high seas and with all their training, which is more exacting than most, they're second to none. Not the cheapest but the best!"

"That's good to know, Stelios; how do I contact Captain Stegman, then? When I'm ready for the boats...oops...ships, I mean, to move?"

"Nowadays, you can simply use your mobile 'phone; write his number down and I'll speak to him after this call to tell him to expect to hear from you."

Stelios gave him the number and Ernesto wrote it down and then called it back to him. It was correct. The Greek magnate continued,

"I've told him, this six week odd voyage is a private affair that I've arranged for you. You are an extremely wealthy, eccentric but philanthropic, friend of mine, who wishes to benefit several thousand of Africa's poor people. It's an opportunity of a lifetime for them. That's certainly true, isn't it?"

"What did Captain Stegman say when you told him that, Stelios?"

"He thought the idea was extremely novel and commendable; the very wealthy can afford to do things like that, if they wish to, he said. I've told him to accede to all your requests, regarding the voyage and he said he would do so, of course, provided they were reasonable requests, not imperilling the ship, or anything like that!"

Ernesto thought for a moment and then said,

"Does he know where we're heading for?"

"No, not exactly; I've told him we intend picking up the people from Agadir, some twenty metres from the shore, rather than use the port, as it's a type of team race out to the ships for the men. He's confirmed the water's deep enough at that distance to use the bow doors, weather permitting and all that. He knows that he'll be making for The English Channel with the three ships afterwards but nothing more than that, at this stage. That's alright, isn't it, my friend?"

"Yes, that's fine. If he's agreed to take the passengers on board through the loading ramp, I just hope he'll agree to let them off the same way and not via a port, either. How do you think he'd react to such a request, Stelios?"

There was quite a long pause and Ernesto thought they might have been cut off,

"Hello, are you still there, Stelios?" he asked.

"Yes, yes, I'm still thinking about that one." Another pause and Ernesto waited patiently this time. Then the Greek spoke up,

"I don't know the man, personally but I imagine he'd be reluctant to do it, very reluctant. It would not be viewed as a reasonable request, even to accommodate an eccentric philanthropist, known to his owner. Even if it was safe to do so, in becalmed waters, he wouldn't do it.

He would be censured by the Jersey Authorities, for sure, since he wouldn't have requested docking facilities, still less, permission to dump thousands of people on unsuspecting beaches. No, he'd lose his licence definitely and they would sue the pants off him for doing such a thing."

Ernesto was becoming rather downcast, at this point. Then the Greek piped up again,

"I think, upon reflection, that there are only three viable ways to get the Captain to do your bidding, Ernesto. They would be bribery, mutiny or endangering the ship and its passengers."

"Well, I..." Stelios interrupted him,

"Let me continue, my friend," he requested,

"Sorry, please do," Ernesto replied, somewhat chastened.

"Of the three, I think bribery is the weakest option and remember, there are three of them, so even one honourable man could easily thwart such a proposal and I don't know any of them, personally, anyway, as I've said, so that's out, I'd say.

Endangering each ship is better, since saving the vessel and, more importantly, the passengers and crew, is of paramount importance to a sea Captain...always was...and will always be so. However, in shallow water like you envisage, one or more of them might not think the risk to the ship and the people on board, would be that great in refusing to comply."

Another pause, while Ernesto exercised patience once more and then he spoke again,

"No, you'd have to arrange for the passengers, or some of them anyway, to take over the ship as it neared the Island. That would ensure you were in control of the situation and after all, the Captain's blushes would be spared in commanding a ship which disgorged its passengers onto the beach, if he wasn't able to prevent it!"

"That's the answer, Stelios, I agree entirely. I can arrange with my man in Agadir to implement the mutinies at the right time and the Captains will emerge blameless, which is both sensible for us and only fair to them."

"Don't tell anyone I suggested it, though, eh?" Another belly laugh down the line from the Greek tycoon but this time, the Guatemalan felt genuinely able to join in with him.

"Okay, Ernesto, it's been nice talking to you; let me know, if you need any more help and the best of luck with your endeavour, eh?"

"Thank you, Stelios, for all your assistance; when you see it all unfold on the TV soon, you'll have to remember to look surprised at seeing your boats…eh, sorry, ships, I mean, having been hijacked by pirates, terrorists, or whatever. Just don't start rooting for us, okay?"

"Yeah, right; hear from you soon, then, one way or the other - 'bye!"

Having put the 'phone down, Ernesto turned to his deputy and said,

"One thing I hadn't thought of, Omah, was how to persuade the ship Captains to unload the journeymen onto the beaches, bearing in mind the illegality of it."

"What did Stelios say about that?"

"He said we had three choices open to us; bribery, which he didn't really think would work; mutiny, which he reckoned was the best bet and then there was threatening to endanger the ship and its passengers."

"What?! Putting a bomb on board each of them and threatening to blow them up, if they didn't comply? That doesn't seem plausible for a man intent on improving the lot of the underprivileged, does it?"

Ernesto sighed heavily and had to agree with him,

"No, not really, especially as we've stipulated no weapons are to be taken on board, too!" Omah had a further thought, though,

"As the explanation for getting the people on board through the bow doors was due to the start of a relay race, supposedly, why not try to finish the journey that way, as well?"

Ernesto suddenly thought he might have something there,

"You mean, persuade the Captains that they all need to dash off to the beaches, through the bow doors and then return the same way to complete the race? Otherwise, the race would be void.

Yes, that does sound a crazy idea, too, doesn't it? Something an eccentric benefactor might well request, don't you think, eh?

And then they'd actually carry on into the interior of the Island? You know, that might just work, Omah, especially if the ships arrived early in the morning, too, with no people on the beach at that time. Only one or two, possibly, anyway."

Ernesto looked across to Omah for encouragement but was greeted by him putting something of a damper on the notion,

"What if they refused, though? Then you'd have to take over the vessels to get the men ashore, wouldn't you?" He contended.

"As a last resort, yes, I suppose you would have to, unfortunately but, at least, the Captains couldn't be accused of collusion and their reputations would remain intact."

Omah got up to make another pot of coffee for them, while his boss pondered some more.

As he returned to the table with the fresh pot of coffee, Ernesto said to him,

"I think I'll call Jousef; the race was his idea and he will have to select which individuals will overpower the Captains and their crews, if it has to come to that."

"Yes, that's a good idea and you'll also need to remind him about letting us have the names of the squad leaders, you know, those in charge of five hundred men or so, who'll be answerable to you, upon landing on Jersey."

"I've thought about how best to deal with that, logistical, problem; I think I'll get Jousef to make up ten squads of, now seven hundred odd, men and have all the leaders of them wear different coloured hats. That'll avoid me using the wrong names, or forgetting who is leading which section and so on."

Omah liked that idea, adding,

"It would make for visible recognition, too, if you have to address the men around you and there's some confusion at the time."

"Exactly," stated Ernesto, as he picked up his mobile and rang the Polisario leader in Morocco.

Half an hour later, he concluded his conversation with the emir and, smiling broadly, turned to his Number two and said,

"Jousef basically agreed that the 'eccentric' request for the relay race to be completed the same way as it started was well worth trying.

He also mentioned that the Captains would always feel a certain obligation to their employer to accede to requests but if they didn't, then he would deputise a group of men to take over the ships, without any difficulty.

He went on to say that, with $10,000 in gold available to everyone on board, much more than that could be arranged, if it was necessary!"

"What about the colour codes for the section leaders?" Omah asked.

"Oh, yes, he's already arranged for a couple of dozen of his own men to travel on each ship, 'just in case,' as he put it and they'll ensure the right men will be selected to lead each squad. He liked the idea of the coloured hats and will arrange for them to be acquired, accordingly. He will let me know the assortment he comes up with, shortly!"

"That's good, then; all we await now is confirmation from him that he's ready, with Stelios's ships waiting for the signal to move to Agadir and after that, the little flotilla can get underway towards that Golden Isle!" Omah chortled.

"Yes, that's about it for now on the positioning front," Ernesto replied, adding,

"I'll need to ring Arnold Fleischer in Managua, to bring him up to date and also give him a likely departure date of the 'flotilla,' as you put it. He needs to time our entry into the gold market, as finely as possible, to maximise our reward for all this investment and effort of ours, eh?

Come on; let's go out for lunch for a change. I'll call the American later on; he'll be fast asleep now, anyway."

"Okay, Boss; I know a nice Bistro just around the corner we can go to and, oh, bring your passport with you, since I've arranged drawing facilities for you at the Bank along the road but they need to see you and your passport to finalise everything."

"That's good, thank you, Omah; I'll go upstairs and get it, then."

"Right Boss, I'll just go and lock up, before we go," said a smiling deputy, enjoying the gratitude of the 'Enlightened Way' leader.

It was a nice sunny day, as the two of them stepped outside. Omah locked the front door and led the way out of the close and they rounded the corner, heading for the 'Al Fresco' Bistro. When they got there, though, there was more dining inside the establishment than outside, Ernesto observed. They got a table, without any difficulty, however, and sat down to study the menu.

They quietly discussed their plans and, in particular, the *'modus operandi'* they should follow once the ships were on their way.

"We'll need to be over there, in Jersey, I mean, to oversee everything and undertake the negotiations with the Island's Authorities."

"Would that be safe for you, Ernesto?" asked Omah, rather anxiously.

"Well, I won't be alone, of course; you and Stephen Carvell will accompany me and, anyway, if we're arrested, then nothing gets done about solving their problem, does it?"

The waiter arrived at their table with their orders and the conversation was suspended for a few minutes. After he departed, Omah resumed their, low-key, chat.

"I'm not sure we should take Stephen with us; I mean, I haven't known him that long and you've only briefly met him!"

"You said he was completely mercenary, didn't you?"

"Well, yes, but…"

"Money, or the prospect of a lot of it, is their sole motivation and, anyway, as he has a good idea of what we're up to, it is much better to have him along with us, where we can keep an eye on him, don't you think?"

"Well, put like that, I suppose…" Ernesto cut across him again,

"You've heard of the saying, 'Keep your friends close but your enemies closer, eh?"

"Yes, I have, of course," stuttered Omah,

"Well, then, it is better to have him in view all the time and don't forget, he knows the place very well and has a good number of friends over there; we might yet be glad of both, you never know! I'll go round to commence my tenancy at his flat tomorrow and I'm sure I can 'get him onside,' as it were, if he's not already. Don't worry; we have far more important things to discuss from now on."

"Okay, you're the Boss," Omah said, meekly.

"Yes, that's right...I am," Ernesto responded, flatly.

An hour later, they'd left the Bistro and strolled along to the bank. When their turn came at the cashier's window, Ernesto introduced himself as Mr Ravel and pushed his passport under the grill between them. He explained that his colleague next to him had already made arrangements with the bank for him to have drawing facilities there and the cashier studied the passport.

"Would you please follow me, gentlemen," the smartly dressed young lady said to them as she left her position and walked into a waiting room at the far end of the building and held open the door for them.

"Somebody will be along to see you, shortly, sir; do please take a seat," she concluded, with a smile and left them there, closing the door behind her.

No sooner had they sat down, than a man knocked on the door and walked in.

"Mr Ravel, nice to meet you, at last, sir," extending an outstretched arm to Ernesto, whilst smiling at Omah, too. The Guatemalan shook the hand offered to him and replied,

"Yes, me, too."

"Now then," the banking man started the interview in his usual manner, while sorting out some papers he'd brought into the room with him.

"I just need to ask a few questions of you, Mr Ravel, to complete the formalities, you understand," commencing his routine.

Near the end of the 'necessities,' he asked Ernesto whether he had any other documents, like a utility bill or some such, to corroborate his identity for him,

"Money laundering regulations, you understand; life's a lot more demanding these days, unfortunately," looking up at him, with a smile.

Ernesto was conscious of blushing, somewhat, at the mention of the phrase but Omah came to his rescue, fortunately.

"Mr Ravel has no utility bill to show you, because he's only just arrived here on a business trip; he's my boss, so I can vouch for him, if that'll do. He's 'very well to do' in Nicaragua, you know."

"Well, thank you for that, Mr Djesturi, I'm sure...." The interviewer looked over to Omah, smiling appreciatively at his enthusiastic support for his boss, saying,

"I'm sure Mr Ravel's reputation is beyond reproach; it's just that we are duty bound to ask such questions, under the regulations, you understand. However, everything does seem to be in order, so I'll arrange for a cheque book and credit card etc., to be sent off to you at...eh.. Mr Djesturi's address, then, shortly," he concluded, looking up at Ernesto.

The man got up from his chair and, with the extended arm offered again, and the customary salutation,

"Gentlemen," Ernesto shook his hand and said,

"Thank you, Mr...eh.."

"Anderson, sir, Tim Anderson," replied the bank man, again with a smile.

"Right, thank you, Mr Anderson, thank you very much," replied a relieved Ernesto Alvarez, as he walked through the door, held open for him by the obliging Mr Anderson and waited for Omah to walk alongside him and out into the street.

As they walked towards Porchester Terrace, Ernesto said,

"I'll telephone Stephen when we get back to your place and arrange to go around to the flat tomorrow. The sooner I get to meet him properly, the better, I think." Omah nodded his understanding and added,

"Don't forget to ring Arnold Fleischer, too, you said, earlier."

"Yes, that's right, thanks for reminding me; it's still a bit early for him right now, so I'll call him later on."

He duly called the American around 6 o'clock. Arnold was very pleased to hear from him and invited him over to stay a few days again with him and added,

"We can then go through all the details to fine tune our purchases; timing, in the investment game, is everything after all, don't forget!"

Ernesto had agreed to do so, at the end of the month, despite being a little concerned about the possibility of bumping into the notorious Ronaldo Martin, or one of his men, there. Also, he'd been unable to make contact with his 'retributionist,' Manuel Cortez, back home in Guatemala, which concerned him more; he hadn't heard from him since he left the Country and that was a while ago now! *'That's not like him, not like him at all,'* he thought to himself. *'Maybe he's got a new woman, or something?'* he further mused.

The following day was overcast and rain threatened. Ernesto gathered up his modest belongings and Omah drove him round to Stephen's flat in the Bayswater road.

Upon their arrival, Omah rang the bell and the burly, ex-marine, opened the front door to meet his new tenant.

"Mr Alvarez, nice to meet you again and to see you, Omah; do come in, won't you?" The trio walked upstairs into a spacious lounge; it was reasonably well decorated, although looking rather 'tired' Ernesto thought, as he surveyed the new surroundings.

"Put your things down here, won't you? And we can go up to your flat, Mr Alvarez and you can look around; I hope you like it, sir,"

"Oh, Ernesto, please, Stephen," the Guatemalan said, inviting cordiality between them.

"Ernesto, it is, then; right this way, gentlemen, if you please," with Stephen Carvell leading the way up another flight of stairs. At the top of the house, the atmosphere noticeably changed; under three skylights, the landing was bright and airy and the smell of recent decoration hung in the air.

"I've just done it up for you, sir,..eh, Ernesto; I do hope you like it and it's to your taste," the big man said, rather nervously, hoping the new occupant's response wouldn't be in the negative, as he opened the door into the lounge.

This room was huge, newly decorated obviously and well furnished, to a high standard. The owner of the property was pleased with his tenant's reaction,

"It is extremely pleasant and well appointed, Stephen; I will like it here, for sure," Ernesto enthused, as he took in the plush environment. The two bedrooms, kitchen and combined bath/shower room were all of the same high standard and Ernesto's positive impression continued, as he looked around the place,

"Very nice, yes," he said, each time he came out of one room and into another. Stephen was clearly well chuffed by it all. An hour or so later, Omah bid them farewell and left them to it.

In the evening, Stephen cooked up dinner for the two of them and Ernesto took the opportunity to get better acquainted with his Planning operative.

"So, tell me Stephen, how did you find Jersey, then? Is it as vulnerable, as I'm led to believe?" Ernesto enquired, holding the man's gaze, as he gave his reply,

"Oh, very much so: I've been over there several times of late to confirm my initial reading of the situation and I have to say, it is extraordinarily vulnerable, as things stand."

"That's good, very good, for what we have planned. Has Omah informed you of what we hope to achieve over there?"

"Not really, although I've naturally got my suspicions that something is about to 'go down' shall we say?"

"Yes, it is about to 'go down' as you put it but let me tell you what we envisage and why, then."

Ernesto Alvarez, the founder of 'The Enlightened Way,' then proceeded to enunciate the *'raison d'etre'* of his organisation, at some length, hoping to persuade the ex - marine of the legitimacy, as he saw it, of the hijacking of this small Island, called Jersey.

Their discussion, not all in agreement, initially, went on into the wee small hours of the next morning but, eventually, there seemed to be a growing accord between them.

It took several further discussions, over the next fortnight, in fact, to finally convince the tough ex - marine, that Ernesto's cause was just and fully warranted, in the circumstances.

The cynic might suggest that Ernesto's closing remarks, about the 'sizeable rewards' which should accrue to all, from a successful exercise, clinched it for the man! He'd promised him 10% of the profit on their gold dealing activities, which might equate to $1million, if all went well.

He agreed to accompany Omah and Ernesto over to Jersey when the time came, mainly to act as the latter's bodyguard, at Ernesto's request but also to ensure they didn't run off with his share of the sizeable loot he'd been promised.

On the 1ˢᵗ April, Alvarez caught the BA Jumbo to Managua. On the way over, he got talking to an Englishman, who was also in property, apparently but his fellow passenger just couldn't stop talking, which irritated him. He did manage to get some sleep, eventually but couldn't understand the man's closing remark about it being *'April Fool's Day'* today.

It must be some kind of English joke, or something, he thought to himself: *'I hope I'm not being an 'April Fool' in going over to see the American. I could have discussed everything with him over the' phone, I suppose…..."* were his final thoughts, as he nodded off to sleep.

A gentle shaking of his shoulder, accompanied by a soft, female, voice saying to him,
"Mr Ravel, sir, we'll be landing in a few minutes, so if you could please sit up and fasten your seatbelt again, I'd be grateful, thank you."
Coming round swiftly, he replied,
"Yes, yes, of course,…I…eh…must have dozed off, thank you, miss."

The big airliner landed smoothly ten minutes later and fifteen minutes after that, he breezed through 'arrivals,' passing the man at the desk, thankfully unchallenged and out into bright sunshine.

As before, he was greeted by a 'suit' and ushered towards the 'red pennanted,' two-tone, blue Buick, parked a few yards along the kerb, outside the terminal building. The party soon pulled away from the 'drop zone' and headed upcountry, towards Arnold Fleischer's palatial home.

While they were on their way, the American remembered Ernesto's photo hadn't yet been framed and put on display in the library, which he'd promised the Guatemalan it would be, as he departed, last time.

He rang his right-hand man, Robert Singleton, on the internal 'phone, saying,
"Bob, that guy from Guatemala we had over here a few weeks back, is on his way to us again and I've just remembered his photo's not on display

in the library, yet. Can you find it, frame it and put it on show, before he gets here? You remember, you queried why I got you to take his picture; 'just in case' I said and all that."

"Oh, yes, now I recall him. I know where it is and I'll have it on show, directly, sir," Robert Singleton intoned to his boss.

By midday, local time, they'd pulled up outside Arnold's place and Ernesto was being greeted once more by his maid, Salma; the two guards either side of the front door, having stood aside for him to approach the threshold.

"Nice to see you again, sir," said Salma, in a cheery voice, adding,

"Mr Fleischer is waiting for you in the lounge, sir."

"Right, thank you, Salma," replied Ernesto, following her along the corridor and passing Robert Singleton coming out of the library, as he did so. He nodded in his direction and the man reciprocated.

"Ah, Ernesto, my good friend, good to see you again," the overweight, American fraudster, greeted him, as he rose from his armchair, with some, initial, difficulty. Ernesto shook his hand and sat down next to him.

"Good to see you, too, Arnold. I've been quite busy since I saw you last."

"I'm sure you have, my friend, bearing in mind the massive 'coup' you intend to pull off shortly. Ah, Salma, there you are; what would you like to drink, then?"

"Well, since it's only noon, I think just a cup of coffee would be very welcome, thank you," he replied to his host but looking towards his maid.

"The usual for me, Salma, thank you; you know I'm not too fussed about the time of day and all that...eh, no offence, of course," he said to his guest.

"None taken, Arnold, none at all," Ernesto replied, graciously.

They made small talk for a while, waiting for their lunch to be announced. Arnold had said he preferred to await all the details of Ernesto's exploits until then; taking their time over a meal, aided concentration, he contended - his at least!

Bang on 1 o'clock, Salma came back into the lounge and proudly announced that,

"Lunch is now served, Gentlemen." They both got up and walked leisurely towards the dining room, accordingly.

Chapter Ten

The upcoming clash of the Titans

Half an hour later, the two of them were well into their delicious meal and confined their conversation to small talk. Ernesto was leaving it up to Arnold to dispense with his staff prior to getting on to the main topic, as he'd done previously.

When their dishes were finally cleared away and brandy and coffees were ordered, Arnold gestured to his staff to depart. Salma arrived a couple of minutes later with a coffee set on a porcelain tray and after bringing in a large bottle of 'Napoleon,' accompanied by a couple of balloon glasses on a silver salver, she left them to it.

"So you're all ready, then?" said Arnold, as he poured out their coffees, adding,

"Do help yourself to the 'Napoleon,' won't you, Ernesto?" The American passed his guest his cup of coffee, as the Guatemalan poured a generous measure of the brandy into his glass.

"Thank you, Arnold…yes, I think everything is now ready and I hope to give the order to 'go' shortly.

Arnold Fleischer settled back into his chair, after pouring himself a 'double' from the black bottle and cradled his glass in his hand, gently swirling around the contents.

"Do you have an actual departure date and, more importantly for our investment programme, an ETA, you know, when you expect to be landing your guys on Jersey? An actual date for that would be critical for determining which gold options we should buy, of course."

Alvarez assumed the same relaxed posture as his host before replying. He then took a mouthful of Napoleon and slowly swallowed the 'nectar,' enjoying the warm afterglow from doing so.

"Well, today is the first of the month and, first of all, I want to go to my village to make contact with one of my senior operatives there. I've not heard from him for quite a while, which concerns me, I have to say. After that, I'll return to London to finalise everything and double check all the arrangements. This will probably take a week or so. Then, I and two colleagues, will go over to Jersey a few days before the 'landings' to set up our 'HQ' as it were, in a suitable room of one of their hotels, overlooking the bay in St. Helier; St. Aubin's Bay, I think it's called."

"Okay, okay but when will that be, Ernesto?"

"I would think some three weeks from now, I'd guess."

Arnold sat up in his chair to address matters.

"Look, Ernesto, I know it's your show and all that and you 'call the shots' as to when it goes down but I need a specific date for when your people will land on that foreign shore. It'll be all over the media a few hours later but we need to be in the gold market before the event, not running after it. You do see that, don't you?"

"Yes, of course…you need to be in there for us before the announcement of it…I do realise that, Arnold."

The American was not wholly convinced the Guatemalan appreciated the significance of the precise date, though, so he persisted,

"We're not going to buy gold bullion, gold coins or gold shares, Ernesto. No, to maximise the benefit of our 'inside information' that you exclusively have, we'll buy gold options; short dated, 'out of the money,' gold options. Those which are close to expiring worthless and then, all of a sudden, 'Bingo'! They rise dramatically in value because of a jump in the gold price, just before their expiry date. That's where you get the real 'leverage' my friend; ten or maybe twenty times the price we paid a few days before!"

Ernesto sat up at this. He didn't know much about investing in gold, still less, the vagaries of gold option trading and with such a possibility of multiplying one's investment so fast, he wanted to know more!

"Do elaborate on these options for me, Arnold; I'm not as conversant with them as you, of course." Arnold Fleischer obliged his guest.

"Sure. Let me see, now. With the market price of gold standing at $300 per ounce at the moment, all gold options are based on that valuation, as we speak. The options have different, fixed, gold price levels attached to them and expire, worthless, at different times, too. When they're near to their expiry date, they fall in value on the market, in anticipation of that happening. This is especially true of 'out of the money' options, as traders call them. These carry a fixed gold buying price on them of more than the current market price of bullion; in other words, who wants to buy a gold option with a $325 buying price attached to it, when you can buy gold itself in the market today for $300? Answer: nobody! Especially, as it might have only a few days left to 'live' on the market before it expires worthless."

Arnold stopped, momentarily, to have a large sip, nay gulp, of his brandy, before continuing,

"Now, if the gold price in the market suddenly jumped by, say, 10% to $330, that, hitherto uneconomic, $325 gold option to buy at its fixed price, which is about to expire, suddenly acquires a value of $5, doesn't it?" Moreover, if you'd bought that option to buy gold at $325 a day or two before the gold price jumped by 10%, you would have paid only pennies for it. Maybe, say, fifty cents, or even a quarter; since it had a negative value then, with gold at only $300 in the market, eh?"

Another gulp of his brandy ensued, as he licked his lips over the upcoming payoff,

"Say we paid fifty cents for that $325 gold buying contract yesterday when it was effectively worthless, with gold at only $300 in the market. Today's price would be at least $5 for that $325 buying contract, with gold now trading at $330. Well, you can do the maths yourself, Ernesto, fifty cents becoming five dollars, equates to ten times your investment and if you got it for only a quarter, then a twenty times multiplier applies and overnight, virtually, too! That's what I call making money, my friend!"

Ernesto was fascinated by the prospect of making ten or more times his money almost overnight and to think he was the unique 'insider' of all this, too!

Before he could respond to Arnold's enthusiastic explanation of such an exercise, the American piped up again,

"You see how crucial that day is now? Yesterday, misery but today, jubilation! That's why it is critical for me to know when your guys land on the Island; the media run the story etc., to ensure we're in there the day before. That's the way we make it big, yes sir, really big!"

Alvarez sat upright, had another swig of his brandy and asked the American the obvious question of an anxious novice,

"What can go wrong, though, even if our 'event' is precisely on time and you're in there for us, the day before the media revelations, etc.,?"

"That's a fair question, Ernesto, since there's no such thing as a guarantee in all this, even for a 'copper - bottomed' scheme like this one.

Firstly, because the gold market is specialist and International, it takes a fair bit to move it; the US economic outlook affects sentiment towards it, as does the Federal Reserve in its fight against inflation and all that.

Even bullion sales by the big banks occur from time to time and such news can adversely affect sentiment towards the yellow metal.

Conversely, a falling dollar or rising inflation, economic disasters of one form or another, usually drives the price higher, as does any threat to stability, or undermining of the *'status quo.'* People don't like threats to the system they're used to, so unexpected negative developments, etc., usually see them rushing into gold as a defensive move.

That is what I hope to see in reaction to your 'landings' my friend; the realisation of Jersey having to buy a lot of gold to solve the problem of all those squatters and then......'who might be next'?

If the news of the 'landings' breaks on a quiet day in the gold market and the media give the story a really good airing, with numerous negative connotations doing the rounds, then I reckon we'll do very well. But I do need to know the exact date the story will break to get us positioned a day or so before, in the cheapest of the 'out of the money' gold options."

Arnold looked Ernesto straight in the eye to ram home the profundity of the timing element. It clearly did the trick, for then Ernesto stood up and declared, somewhat imperiously,

"The date we land on Jersey will be the first of May, precisely one month from today. I'll need a few days to go upcountry to my village and see my friend, as I say and then I'll fly back to London. Another few days to get everybody involved aware of the departure date and the ETA on Jersey some three or four days later. That'll take us to the middle of this month, another few days for us getting over to Jersey, setting things up there and allowing for any bad weather en-route for the ships to contend with etc., I reckon a landing on that day is perfectly feasible and we will make it so."

"May Day, then; how apt that would be, eh?" the American rejoined, with a smile, as he stared into his, now empty, brandy glass.

After a few moments, Arnold Fleischer piped up again,

"Okay, then, we know the date; how much do you want to invest in these gold options, if they appeal to you, my friend?"

"Oh, they certainly appeal to me, with that sort of return possible from them; how about $5 million? Would that be alright?"

"Sure.....and I'll do the same; that'll be $10 million between us, then. If you arrange for your bank to send the money over to my bank in a few days, I'll make the investments for us, at the most judicious moment, provided the ETA date doesn't change, of course. If it does, you must let me know immediately, otherwise, we'll lose our shirts, almost for sure."

"It won't, I can assure you; only if a calamity happens, will it not go ahead on that date, now I've decided upon it and I'd let you know instantly if it did, since we'll have so much riding on it, too!"

"Precisely," the American replied.

The following morning, Ernesto made the necessary arrangements for transferring $5 million to Arnold's Bank account and later, reminded him of his wish to pay a visit to his village, San Luis, north east of Guatemala City.

"How far away is that from here?" the American asked him.

"About four hundred miles or so; it would be nice to drive there for a change, take a few days holiday getting there and back, you know."

"Why don't you take one of my cars, rather than go into town to hire one? I've got several you can choose from, out back?"

"That's very kind of you, Arnold; that would save me a lot of trouble for sure, if you don't mind. I'll bring it back in a few days."

"Not at all. I'd be glad to oblige you, now we're partners and all, eh?"

Ernesto chose a maroon Oldsmobile sedan, from the selection in Arnold's garage around the back of his substantial property. He noticed it, too, had a red pennant attached to the radio aerial, just like the blue Buick, Arnold's men used to transport him to and from the airport.

As he drove the saloon from the garage to the front of the house and stopped to load his few things for the journey, Fleischer came out to wish him a good trip.

"I see this car carries a red pennant, as well as the other one, Arnold," Ernesto said to his host, with a grin, adding,

"Have you got a 'thing' about red pennants, then?"

Arnold laughed,

"No, no, we usually travel around in two cars at a time, you know, in case we have a breakdown; the roadside assistance services aren't very good in Nicaragua and if we get stuck in traffic, you can usually see the other car without any difficulty, which is quite handy. And people know us and the vehicles around here, too, which helps!"

"Ah, that's a good idea, come to think of it…oh well, I'll see you in a few days, then -'bye!"

"Cheerio, my friend," the American replied, as the Oldsmobile pulled away and he waved him goodbye.

Ernesto Alvarez enjoyed the long drive home and was relatively familiar with the route, having journeyed to the border with Honduras and traversed that Country a month or two earlier with his 'retributionist,' Manuel Cortez.

Sticking to the Inter-American highway, he was able to cover the four hundred and fifty odd miles in just over seven hours and he arrived at his native village, San Luis, at just gone 4 o'clock in the afternoon.

It was very hot, although he didn't appreciate how hot it was, until he exited the air-conditioned sedan, having parked it in a side street, a few hundred yards from his Mother's wooden house. He decided to stroll the remaining distance to stretch his legs and also avoid attracting too much attention to his presence there - just in case.

The village seemed strangely quiet to him; there were a few people going to and fro and a number of kids were playing around an old car wreck, which was quite normal but there seemed to be....what was it?...a sort of vacant air to the place, he thought. He stopped on a corner, some fifty yards from the house where he spent most of his childhood.

He looked around, having withdrawn into a doorway to mask his presence there a little more....he felt that might be wise but he didn't know why? He studied the scene for a few moments and didn't think anyone had noticed him.

He looked up the road to his Mother's house....nothing stirred....all was quiet...too quiet. And then the commotion of the kids playing around the wrecked car, stopped. He looked back towards the abandoned vehicle and the children were nowhere to be seen. *"Now, that is odd!"* he muttered to himself. No curtains moved, nor other signs of life were evident; San Luis seemed to have become a ghost town, all of a sudden.

'It must be me....it's all in my imagination...it's still siesta time, that's what it is,' he told himself, as he moved away from the doorway and strode, warily, towards his Mother's house.

A breeze got up and some tumbleweed rolled down the dusty street towards him, as he approached his old home. Sitting on a window sill of the shack which adjoined his Mother's house, was a mangy, ginger cat, basking in the hot sun, watching him approach its position. As he got to within three feet of the animal, it suddenly spat at him, baring its teeth, with ears flattened back onto its head, which startled him and then it shot off the ledge and ran down the street.

'Something is amiss here...it's not my imagination...there's definitely a tension in the air, for some reason...' he told himself, as he knocked on his Mother's door. No answer. He knocked again, trying the door, this time. It was locked.

He decided to try the back of the house and as he moved towards the alleyway alongside the wooden shack, he noticed a curtain move, ever so slightly, from the shack across the road. He looked directly towards the opposite property and was sure he saw a figure move out of his sightline.

He got to the side gate of his childhood home, opened it and found his mother at the far end of the vegetable patch, hanging out some washing. He walked up to her, as she turned around and upon immediately recognising her son, she flew into his arms.

"Oh, Ernesto, my son, you're alright, thank goodness; they said they'd kill you, too, if they ever found you!"

"Who said that, Mother?" Ernesto asked, as he hugged the frail lady who'd given birth to him, some fifty years before. He held her away from him, fleetingly, to look into her eyes. The frightened look was unmistakeable. He repeated the question,

"Who said that to you, Mother; tell me who it was, who was it?"

"Come, my boy, into the house, not here," she replied, ushering him towards the back door of their home.

Once inside, she turned to him and said,

"A few weeks ago, some men drove into the village and started to ask questions about you. Where could they find you? What did anybody know about you? Where was your house? Who were your relatives and where might they be found? Things like that."

"So what happened next?"

His Mother began to sob and he put his arms around her again. He waited for her to regain her composure and after a few minutes, she replied,

"These men went from door to door asking such questions but nobody told them anything. You know how we view strangers around here."

"Yes, yes, but what then happened?" Ernesto asked more urgently, this time.

"They then offered anyone $1,000 for any information about you, your family, or your friends. At first, there remained silence; still nobody said anything to them. But, after they threatened to shoot two people, on the hour, every hour, as well, someone whistled to them from the corner of the street and one of them went over there. I don't know who whistled to them, nobody seems to know that."

She paused for a moment, pouring herself a glass of water from a bottle on her draining board. Ernesto helped himself to a glass, too and then she resumed her recollection of those events,

"Whoever had whistled to them and it was a horrible, shrill, sound, I remember, obviously gave into them and told them what they wanted to know. Whether it was to stop any of the threatened murders or to get hold of all that money; that's a fortune around here, of course, or both, I don't know."

She paused again for another sip of water and her son did the same.

"The men immediately went over to Manuel Cortez's house and barged in his front door. He was a friend of yours, wasn't he, Ernesto?"

"Yes, you know he was, Mother, he was one of my best friends and very loyal, too. So what happened then?"

"He was obviously ready for them, since he shot the first one as he burst into his shack but was wounded by the other one, who'd gone around the back of his place. He shot Manuel in the back and then tortured him, before he died but he didn't give you away. The second man ran off down the street, shouting he'd be back with his friends to find out where you were. They haven't returned yet but we're still waiting....waiting to hide from them, when they do."

Ernesto finished his drink and said to his Mother,

"I know who was responsible for all this and I will avenge Manuel's death, to be sure. They will come back, almost certainly, so you should leave here Mother; go into the hills, where I used to live for a time, you know; they'll never be able to find you up there."

"I don't think I can bother with all that at my age, son; I have your father's gun in the kitchen drawer over there and if they do come back and come to see me, then I'll...." Ernesto replied,

"Well, if you really want to stay, do so but make sure you have enough ammunition to defend yourself. Here's some money to ensure you have enough and also some extra to get by on until I've dealt with the man I have in mind; permanently dealt with him," Ernesto said to her, putting $500 in notes on the kitchen table.

She smiled at him, as he did so and then said, with a determined look on her face,

"You'd better go; whoever betrayed us might well know you've returned and they could be informing on you, right now, so go carefully, my son."

He gave her another hug and agreed it might be sensible to go, without delay, in case he had been spotted. He added, with a smile,

"They must have thought I was one of them returning to the village, when I arrived half an hour ago, since everything went very quiet, all of a sudden."

"Yes, I'm sure they did. You be careful now and look after yourself; come back to see me, as soon as you can, won't you, dear?" She returned his hug, kissed him and with a tear in her eye, said goodbye to him.

Her son left the ramshackle house and walked purposefully back towards his parked car. A couple of curtains moved slightly on his return to the vehicle, he noticed but he was relieved, upon turning the corner into the side street where he'd left it, to find it was still there.

He turned the Oldsmobile around and sped off the way he'd come, passing two villagers walking up to the main street, who both looked behind them, at his departure. He had been spotted and by the 'whistleblower,' too!

On his return journey, Alvarez wondered who the informant had been and, more importantly, how and when to deal the fatal blow to that monster, Ronaldo Martin.

He was angered by the man's audacity to terrorise his village in trying to get to him, and his mind raced with numerous ideas about how to finish him off.

An hour or so after he crossed the border back into Nicaragua, he stopped at a garage to fill up with petrol. While he was paying the attendant for the fuel, another car pulled up behind his vehicle. Neither of the two occupants got out, though; one was seen to be using a mobile 'phone, while the other kept a close watch on the customer who'd filled up the Oldsmobile in front of them and was now paying the bill.

Were they plain-clothed policemen, possibly? The mystery vehicle had followed the maroon sedan all the way from the border to this filling station, without the driver noticing, seemingly. Or were they in the employ of someone else....Ronaldo Martin, maybe?

The driver of the Oldsmobile had noticed his 'tail' though. Moreover, he reasoned they were Martin's men, who'd probably been tipped off a while ago; after he left San Luis, given those moving curtains, staring bystanders as he drove away, and so on. How to resume his journey, though, without being shot at? That was the question of the moment, for him.

Ever resourceful, however, Ernesto had an idea how to get away from them. He was unarmed, so he was at a major disadvantage in any prospective 'stand off' with them. However, they couldn't know whether he'd spotted them or not and they wouldn't risk a shoot out in a garage forecourt with all that petrol about, surely?…. *'Yes, that petrol would be a problem for them, wouldn't it?'* He thought to himself.

"I'll have a couple of bars of that chocolate over there, I think and also, a can of coke, too, thank you," he said to the attendant behind the counter.

"Eh, in a carrier bag, a large one, if I may," he added to the young man, eager to complete the order. He returned to the counter and Ernesto asked him if he could use the toilet, as well,

"Sure, thing, sir, that's out back and that'll be….forty two dollars, fifty, thank you very much."

Ernesto gave him a $50 bill and said,

"Keep the change and I tell you what, I'll give you another one hundred dollars for your baseball cap and bomber jacket."

The kid behind the counter looked at him, in disbelief.

"I beg your pardon, sir?"

"Alright, two hundred, then. Look, those men in the car behind mine are after me and I need to get away. No! Don't look over my shoulder at them; here's the two hundred bucks; it's all yours. I'll go into the toilet and you follow a few moments later, give me your cap and jacket and stay in the back room and I'll deal with them, alright?"

Not wishing to pass up the opportunity of making two hundred bucks so easily, the young man replied,

"Okay, then, you go through and I'll follow directly," as he picked up the two $100 bills and put them into his back pocket. Neither of the men in the car behind the Oldsmobile had made a move, as Ernesto went out back to the toilet area.

The youth duly followed a few moments later and completed the exchange. Alvarez, having put his own jacket in the carrier bag, donned the kid's garb and walked out of the rear exit from the toilet. He emerged around the far side of the forecourt, put the carrier bag down against the wall and strode up to the car behind his vehicle, keeping himself aligned with their 'blind spot.'

He arrived opposite the open window of the driver's door, pulled away the 'super unleaded' petrol pump hose from its cradle, since that was the nearest dispenser of fuel to the mystery car and said to the driver,

"Right, sir, how much would you like?"

He squeezed the trigger on the pump and the fuel gushed over the two of them. The driver exclaimed,

"What the....what the hell are you doing!?" His passenger tried to shield himself from the petrol gushing over him, as well and it took a few seconds for them to grasp the seriousness of the situation.

The Guatemalan wasn't finished yet, though. As the fuel cascaded over them, he reached into his pocket and pulled out his cigarette lighter, just as the man in the passenger seat put his hand inside his jacket and pulled out a pistol.

"Not advisable in your position, I'd say, gentlemen; one flick on this and you'll be toast, before you know it!" He waggled his hand holding his lighter, with his thumb over the flint wheel, so they could clearly see it and the mortal danger they were in. And still the fuel gushed over them.

"So who do you work for then?" Ernesto asked them, as casually as he could. They were coughing and spluttering now and still the petrol cascaded over them.

The passenger made to get out of the fuel-logged car but Alvarez was quicker,

"I don't think so, you'd never get away from the flame; it would be on you in a flash and your friend here would already be burning to death!"

The driver pulled the passenger back into his seat to share the same fate as him. Still Ernesto kept his finger pressed on the pump trigger and the inrush of fuel continued.

"There must be twenty gallons of fuel in this car by now and you still haven't answered my question, gentlemen."

"Ronaldo Martin...we work for him," the driver exclaimed, his eyes transfixed on Ernesto's hand holding the lighter.

"We got a call from him about two hours ago that you'd been spotted coming away from San Luis in Guatemala and we were to await your arrival at the border, verify it was you and put you away," he concluded with a splutter.

"Look, can we get out of here? We're suffocating with all the fumes!" said the passenger,

"Yeah,…at least release the pump trigger, can't you?! We're all but drowning in here, for pity's sake, man!" the driver pleaded.

Ernesto relented, at last, by releasing the trigger of the petrol pump. The stench of fuel was almost overwhelming, even for him.

"You tell your boss to leave my family and my village alone. If he doesn't, I'll do more than this to him and all his men; if you agree to relay that message to him, I'll not light this, this time!" waggling his lighter hand again.

"Yeah, yeah, of course, man!"

"Give me your weapons, then; slowly, very slowly, if you please," taking their handguns from them.

"Right, you can now get out of the unexploded bomb you're sitting in and wait over there," motioning to the far corner of the forecourt. He put the nozzle back into the cradle of the petrol pump, as the two men exited the flooded vehicle they were sitting in.

The cashier, having emerged from the back of the shop a few moments earlier, had seen the end of the 'saturating' of the two mystery men. He went up to the Guatemalan, obviously very shaken, and said,

"They'll be back for me, after you've gone, you know, for selling you my jacket and cap, won't they?"

"No, they won't, believe me. I suggest you close for the night, leave the doors of their car open to allow the petrol to vapourise and in the morning you can tow the vehicle to a safe spot and set light to it; I know I would… and, oh, here's your cap and jacket back. I don't need them anymore and you can keep the cash, as a 'thank you' from me, eh?"

The terrified youngster took back his gear and moved back into the shop, turned off the overhead lights of the forecourt, leaving just the small showroom lights on. The 'closed' sign was duly illuminated.

Ernesto walked over to the two men at the far end of the, now darkened, forecourt and said to them,

"You'd better get out of those sodden clothes; you're a major fire risk, you know!" They did so, stripping off everything down to their underpants and shoes.

"Well, it's a warm night and in an hour or two, your underwear should have largely dried out and be less of a health hazard for you. You'd better start walking towards the City; it's a couple of hours away, in that direction," pointing to the glow on the horizon.

The men shuffled passed him, one muttering,

'We'll never forget this, never," whereas the other told him to shut up, promising to relay his message to Mr Martin, when they got back to town.

Ernesto Alvarez stayed with the frightened lad in the shop for a further ten minutes or so. He assured him the men wouldn't trouble him any more and that he'd best call the fire brigade to dispose of the petrol sodden car, if he didn't want to haul it away the following morning. He could always ring the boss of the garage and let him decide what to do, of course.

The youth decided it was best to ring his boss but only an hour after Ernesto had driven away, at the Guatemalan's request, to give him time to make his escape.

"If the police ask you which way I went, you will tell them that way, won't you, eh?" pointing towards the border with Honduras, and added,

"After all, you wouldn't want me coming back now, would you?"

"No, sir, definitely not….eh, but you know what I mean! No disrespect intended, sir."

"None taken, young man and thanks for helping me out earlier."

The youth touched his cap and nodded, as Ernesto walked over to his carrier bag, retrieved it and finally got back into the Oldsmobile. He reeked of petrol, too, so he opened all the windows, put the fan on 'max' and drove away into the night.

A few minutes later, and a mile or so from the garage, he came across two, scantily clad, men walking towards town. He slowed down as he caught up with them. They thought a kindly motorist was about to give them a lift, since they couldn't see who the driver was until he was right alongside them but then it was too late.

Four gunshots rang out in the balmy night air. Ernesto had felled both of them with the first two shots from the car. He stopped, got out and finished the job, from point blank range, got back into the car and sped off towards town, muttering to himself,

'They would have been back for the kid, for sure and it was none of his doing…..he shouldn't have witnessed what needed to be done, to protect him from them, either……it's man's work! Hope he didn't hear the shots, but then again, if he did, he might be able to truly believe what I told him,….. that they wouldn't come back to trouble him, not now!'

Ernesto arrived back at Arnold Fleischer's house at just before midnight. The guards on the gates recognised the red pennant on the aerial of the car, which made them more relaxed as they peered at the driver.

He was allowed to pass through and on to the house. He drove up to it and then slowly around to the back of the property, parking outside one of the garages. Having got out of the car, he walked around to the front of the house clutching his large carrier bag and walked up the steps.

He was greeted at the top of them by Salma, as the two guards either side of the portico, stepped aside for him.

"Good evening, sir, Mr Fleischer has recently retired I'm afraid but I can always get you something, if you wish."

"No, no, thank you, Salma. I'm pretty tired, too, so I think I'll turn in, as well." The maid turned aside to let her boss's house guest through into the long hallway and Ernesto strolled along to his bedroom, the route now being quite familiar to him. Salma followed behind and then said,

"Good night, then, sir," as she peeled off into a side corridor.

The next morning was very overcast, with storm clouds gathering in the distance, Ernesto observed from his window, after pulling back the drapes in his room.

He could hear some activity outside in the corridor, so he had a shower and was dressed soon afterwards. Having combed, or tried to, his mop of unruly hair into something suggesting it had been attended to, he went outside and walked along to the dining room.

His host was already tucking into a hearty breakfast. He looked up at his house guest,

"Ah, there you are, Ernesto, did you have an enjoyable trip yesterday? I thought you'd be away a bit longer," the overweight American asked.

Alvarez selected a couple of fruits from the dish in front of him, as he sat down.

"The journey was fine but not the outcome, unfortunately. When I got to the village, I discovered my friend there had been murdered and many inhabitants intimidated, including my Mother," he stated, in a very matter of fact, sort of way, without looking up from what he was doing.

Arnold was stunned at the news. He put down his knife and fork and said,

"So what did you do? Was your Mother alright? I mean, do you know who was responsible for doing such things?"

"Oh, yes, I know who was behind it alright. I killed two of his men on the return journey; it was unfortunate but necessary, I'm afraid," he declared, maintaining his deadpan manner. Arnold coughed in disbelief,

"Are you saying you are a 'target' of someone? You know....what's the expression...eh...on someone's 'hit list' or something?"

The Guatemalan finally looked at his host and with a determined expression on his face, said,

"Yes, I am; I'm on Ronaldo Martin's 'hit list' but I will get him before he gets me, Arnold, believe me!"

"What on earth have you done to him?...I mean, I don't know the man at all, just his reputation, which is pretty fearsome, I have to say," replied Arnold, still stunned by Ernesto's predicament, despite his resolute statement over which of them would triumph over the other.

"Ronaldo Martin is an extremely evil man. You and I make our money out of relieving people of theirs; yes, it's illegal but in my case, justifiable, I would argue, since it largely benefits others, too. Martin relieves people of their lives, the most valuable thing they have and makes millions from doing so. His activities enslave thousands, maybe millions, in visiting drug addiction upon them. My operations are the opposite of what he does. He doesn't deserve to live and I will see to it that he doesn't do so much longer!"

Arnold paused before responding to Ernesto's profound utterance. He sensed his reply would go some way in determining whether the Guatemalan would, ultimately, regard him as an eventual 'fat cat' to be approached for a donation, or not. He finally said,

"Well, I regard my business as pretty harmless, really. I mean, nobody gets hurt or injured, still less addicted to anything, because of me. The big players in the markets are the ones who get 'burnt' financially, when I win but then that's the name of the game. They know the risks as well as I do and when I lose….." He took a sip of his coffee, before continuing,

"It is true, that a good number of naïve folk mostly lose out on my pyramid selling capers but in all cases, they only lose through stupidity! What they lose, though, can always be recovered later on, if they so desire.

I have no truck with drugs, never have had and never will. I think it's a disgusting business and consider those indulging in it, to be the lowest of the low!" Arnold meant what he said; more importantly, though, Ernesto believed him.

After another pause, Arnold piped up again,

"So what now, then? I mean, I hope this Martin fellow and your determination to bring him down, won't interfere with your Jersey plans. You've spent so much time and effort on…."

Alvarez burst out laughing at the American's last remarks, stopping him in his tracks.

"Spoken like a true capitalist, I must say!" Ernesto blurted out, still roaring his head off. Arnold suddenly saw the funny side of it, too and joined in the hilarity, as well.

When the laughter subsided, Arnold repeated his question,

"So,…what then? Any change of plans at all?"

"Absolutely not; he's not worth it, after all the effort put into it, as you rightly say. No, everything goes ahead; we land on Jersey on May 1st."

"Good, good, my friend, that's what I like to hear, true commitment!"

They both laughed out loud once more.

Ernesto Alvarez flew back to London a few days later, arriving at his flat, rented from his planning operative, Stephen Carvell, on the 9th April.

The next week was taken up with final preparations for the launch of his 'freedom ships' ensuring they were in place and readied for the 'off'.

He also had a long discussion with Omah Djesturi about Ronaldo Martin and his determination to get rid of him, as soon as possible. Alvarez wanted something in place soon to ensure the elimination of the man before he could get to him but **not** at the expense of the Jersey operation.

Omah made a particularly cogent point towards the end of one of their discussions on the topic. He remarked to his boss, that their main strength, against a man like Martin, was their superior numbers in the field.

Upon asking Omah to develop his argument, his deputy said,
"We can muster over one hundred armed men, more than twice the number of 'soldiers' Martin has, by all accounts but he's now very much on his guard against you. He'll be taking extra care over everything he does, where he goes, etc., and be very difficult to get at. But if you combine our numerical advantage, with the element of surprise, there's no way we couldn't succeed in finishing him off."
"Do continue, Omah, this sounds very interesting."
"Well, if we take the offensive, while he's distracted, we'll have the element of surprise on our side and overwhelming firepower to finally take him out."
"So how do we distract him, then?" Ernesto asked, with increasing curiosity. Omah sat forward in his chair and continued,
"Ronaldo is eaten up with getting you, especially after you despatched two more of his men a fortnight or so ago. His reputation now depends upon doing so, right?"
"Right, so?"
"If he knew where you were or, more precisely, where you'd be on a particular date, he'd pay strict attention to that, wouldn't he?"
"I still don't follow you, Omah, do get on with it; the suspense is killing me!"
"You'll be on television, almost certainly, on the night of May 1st, you know, on Jersey television; wouldn't he be at home watching his arch

enemy, regardless of anything else he had to do, if he knew you were to be on TV? I'd say he would, so we let him know the date a few days before and when he's at home, with all his 'soldiers,' watching the box, thinking you were thousands of miles away, temporarily out of his reach, we then strike - WHAM! - he'd never know what hit him!"

A knowing smile gradually spread across Ernesto's face. He said, quite slowly,

"And all the while, I'd be grinning at him on his television, as a hundred of my men burst into his place, blasting him and all his people away. Omah, I like that, I really do like that, especially the irony of it!"

A few moments later, Ernesto said,

"You get in touch with our people during the next few days and arrange for them all to be in striking distance of Martin's place in Managua on the first of May. They've got two weeks to get there, so that's ample time for them to prepare and get into position.

His hillside retreat can be discreetly surrounded, without too much difficulty on that evening and when I'm on the T.V, looking into the camera at him, he'll be passing into history!

Yes, Omah, the more I think about your plan, the more I like it. So, do it will you? Do it for all our people and, especially, for me, eh?"

"Yes, sir; leave everything to me. It will be done!" Omah affirmed.

Chapter Eleven

An incoming tide.......of Humanity

A couple of days later, Arnold Fleischer got a telephone call from somebody he didn't wish to hear from......one, Ronaldo Martin!

The feared drug baron wanted to discuss something very important to him and asked if he could come around to have a chat with him. Not wishing to appear intimidated by him and thinking a refusal on his part might be misinterpreted as rudeness he, reluctantly, agreed.

The American was in his study, checking out the most suitable gold options and their prices with one of his brokers, when the ogre knocked on his door.

His housemaid, Salma, answered the door, as usual and invited Mr Martin and the 'aide' with him, to wait in her employer's library for him, which they did.
She said to them,
"Mr Fleischer is expecting you, gentlemen; I'll tell him you're here. I'm sure he won't be a moment," and with that, Salma, sauntered off to find her boss.

While the two of them were sitting down waiting for Arnold, they looked around the lavishly decorated room. Ronaldo sat nearest the, highly polished, grand piano and was admiring this piece of furniture, when he spotted the various photos atop the musical instrument. He nodded to his aide in the direction of it, saying,
"That's an interesting photo, don't you think?" Ronaldo got up to look at it properly, as did his 'minder.' Martin picked it up and said to the man,

"Yes, I thought so; it is him, look," handing the photo frame to his bodyguard to verify.

"Yeah, you're right, boss, that is Alvarez, alright!"

Ronaldo Martin carefully returned the picture to its position on top of the grand piano and remained standing, with his arms behind his back, as he studied some paintings on the wall nearest him.

"There's some nice stuff here, boss, don't you think?"

Ronaldo was about to reply to his man, when Arnold burst into the room, in a bit of a fluster, saying,

"Sorry to keep you waiting, gentlemen, there's a bit of a panic on in the markets at the moment and I couldn't get off the 'phone easily; I hope I haven't kept you waiting too long."

"No, not at all, we were just admiring your pictures, Mr Fleischer; sorry, Ronaldo Martin, thank you for agreeing to see me at such short notice," the drug baron said, extending his hand to him.

Arnold shook his hand and the other man's, too, who just nodded without giving his name. Arnold replied,

"Please, sit down; what would you like to drink, then?" Ronaldo held up his hand, as he replied,

"No, no, thank you, it is too early for us," and looking towards his henchman for corroboration, who nodded in the affirmative.

"Well, coffee or tea, then?" Arnold countered, nervously proffering an alternative.

Ronaldo shook his head in declining that, too.

"What can I do for you, then, Mr Martin? You said on the telephone something was bothering you and I might be able to help."

Ronaldo Martin sat up in his chair, looking quite imperious in his smart suit, well cut shirt and sober tie. Arnold felt rather scruffy, all of a sudden.

"Let me get straight to the point, Mr Fleischer; you're obviously a very busy man and I don't wish to take up too much of your time. I'm looking for someone you might know; someone who recently killed two of my men."

The fat American gulped at hearing the statement, so flatly delivered. He knew he was referring to Ernesto. The drug baron added,

"Yes, this man was seen driving one of your cars as he made his getaway, apparently. I'm hoping you can tell me where I might find him."

"Driving one of my cars, you say? One of my men, no, you must be mistaken, surely; why would one of my people want to tangle with you, Mr Martin? He'd be silly to do that, I mean, you have quite a reputation and all...."

"I didn't say it was one of your men, Mr Fleischer; I said someone was seen making a getaway in one of your cars, a maroon Oldsmobile, I think it was."

"There are lots of those around, there must be. What makes you think it was one of my vehicles?"

"The red pennant on the top of the radio aerial, that's what; there cannot be many of those around, now can there?"

"What's his name, this chap you're looking for; maybe he stole one of my cars, without me knowing...."

"Ernesto Alvarez is his name, Mr Fleischer, do you know him?"

"No, I can't say I know the name; is he local?....I've been here a few years now and....."

"This is the man, Mr Fleischer," said Ronaldo, reaching for the photo frame on the Grand Piano, turning it around to show Arnold and staring at him, with a rather menacing look on his face.

"Ooops, I'm right in it, now!" he thought to himself and, instinctively, he exclaimed,

"That's not whatever you said his name was; that's Ernest Ravel. I said you must be mistaken."

Ronaldo looked confused. He looked towards his 'minder' who also had a puzzled look on his face.

"Well, I'm sure this is the man we know as Ernesto Alvarez; maybe he's changed his name, or uses an alias, or something. Where is he now?"

"He's gone back to Europe; he was only over here with me for a few days holiday. That picture was taken a while ago; are you sure you've got the right man? I've only known him as Ernest Ravel; there must be some mistake."

"No, that's him, alright, I'm sure of it. He must have changed his name. Ernest is very similar to Ernesto, too, don't you think?"

The well dressed, Ronaldo Martin, straightened his tie and added,

"Where in Europe has he gone too, did you say?"

"To London, I think; whether that was a stop-over to somewhere else, I'm not sure. He telephones me, from time to time; would you like me to mention that you'd like to see him, when he's next….?"

Ronaldo interrupted the American,

"No, no, I'd be grateful if you'd let me know when he next comes over, though, or 'phones you; do ask him for his number, or where he's located, that would be much appreciated."

Turning to his henchman, he then concluded the conversation,

"Come, Raoul, we've taken up enough of Mr Fleischer's time. I thank you, sir," Ronaldo holding out his hand to Arnold again, which he duly shook and bade them farewell.

Later that afternoon, Arnold got on the telephone to Ernesto, to tell him of Martin's visit to him. The 'Way' leader wasn't unduly perturbed by the news but as he thought more about it, he suddenly remembered the need to get the drug baron to watch his TV on the 1st May.

"Say, Arnold, why don't you tell him, say, the day before our ETA on the first of May, that he'll see me on TV then, in all probability, eh?"

"What's the point of doing that, Ernesto?"

"Well, he'll know, then, you took his request to keep him informed of my whereabouts seriously and he might glean something of my location, from the news coverage. That's got to be helpful to him and it avoids you actually telling him anything about my whereabouts and what I'm up to."

The American thought for a moment,

"Yeah, it does, too, doesn't it? He will appreciate getting the 'tip off,' at least, I would have thought and it should get him off our backs for a while, as well. I'll call him the day before and tell him to watch the TV news on the night of May 1st, then. Yeah, that's a good idea; I'll do that!"

Ernesto put down the 'phone, with a big smile on his face. Omah was with him and he asked what was so amusing? Still smirking, Ernesto replied,

"Arnold's just had a visit from Ronaldo Martin, asking about my whereabouts. I told him to tell him to watch the TV news on the night of

May 1st. He liked the idea and said he would tell him to do so. Isn't that great news, Omah, eh?" Both fell about laughing.

With ten days to go before the 'off,' Ernesto finalised everything, including having gained agreement from Captain Stegman that he would land his 'human cargo' onto the beach at St Aubin's bay, provided it was in the early morning. His fellow officers were willing to do the same, on the expectation they'd be on their way again by 0700 hours. *"As it's a 'one off' for charity purposes, we'll be happy to oblige you, sir,"* he'd confirmed to Ernesto, when he'd telephoned him.

Omah had booked the three of them into Jersey's Hotel Royale, which was right on the seafront, overlooking St Aubin's Bay. Their two rooms were on the top floor and afforded a grandstand view of the bay. Omah and Ernesto were to share Room 410, with Stephen occupying the room next door, No 412.

The trio arrived there on the twenty fifth of April, for their fortnight's stay on the Island. They posed as tourists during the first couple of days, ostensibly sight-seeing but, in reality, they were reconnoitring the place for the last time.

They hired three mopeds for themselves, from a friendly motorcycle hire shop on the front, to get around the island swiftly, especially if traffic snarl - ups occurred a few days later!

All agreed Jersey was a pretty island and had much to commend it to the holidaymaker. They all knew, though, the place represented much more to them than that; it offered the opportunity of a lifetime.

The wealth was everywhere, from the institutions proudly displaying their plush offices on the front and in the centre itself, to the most expensive cars often seen driven on the roads. A good number of motor showrooms offered most of the top marques, whilst the numerous jewellers retailed top quality pieces, as the 'norm.' The restaurants were notable, too, with many exclusively catering for the 'well to do' on the island, quite obviously.

Jersey was clearly 'comfortable' with itself, as it basked in the late April sunshine of that notable year, the year 2000.

With three days to go, Ernesto got the call from Jousef Manakurh that all the journeymen had been picked up and the 'flotilla' was now on its way. All those participating in the 'race' had been issued with coloured armbands and the 'marshals' were wearing their coloured caps. He gave Ernesto the list of the nine squads, comprising approximately seven hundred men each:-

"Makmar Empress," for St Aubin's Bay - squads - Red, Blue, Green (Capt Stegman)

"Makmar Queen,"　for St Ouen's Bay -　-do-　- Yellow, White, Pink (Capt Wilkinson)

"Makmar Princess," for St Brelade's Bay　-do- - Orange, Purple, Grey (Capt Rollings)

Each 'marshal' was issued with a mobile 'phone having Ernesto's number in its memory and theirs were called over to him.

Having written down the details, Alvarez thanked Jousef for all his hard work in getting everything off on time and would now release the first tranche of the agreed payment to him. The Polisario leader thanked him for remembering this part of their arrangement without any prompt from him and concluded their conversation in upbeat mood,
"It's over to you now - goodbye and good luck!"
Ernesto then 'logged in' all the marshals' numbers into his mobile.

One thing almost slipped Ernesto's mind after doing so: Ring Arnold and remind him to suggest to Ronaldo Martin to watch the TV news on the evening of May 1st.

Arnold Fleischer duly obliged on the day before the big event. He'd just completed their gold option purchases, all $10 million worth and was pleased to see the bullion market rising a bit, subsequently, as he picked up the telephone to speak to the infamous drug dealer.

Martin appreciated the call and told Arnold that he'd certainly look out for the broadcast the following evening. The American apologised to him that there wasn't time to ask his friend, Ernest Ravel, where he was heading for, because he'd been called for his flight and had to dash off. Maybe, he could determine his location from the news bulletin? "You know, just a thought!"

"Yes, maybe I can, thank you, Mr Fleischer," replied Martin, as he put down the 'phone. He then turned to his acolyte and said to him,

"Raoul, get our people together tomorrow night, will you? There's going to be something happening then, on TV, apparently."

On the morning of the first of May, Ernesto, Omah and Stephen all woke early, around 5.30 am. Half an hour later, they were in position in Room 410, with binoculars at the ready. The balcony doors were open.

It was a beautiful morning, as the Sun slowly emerged on the horizon, spreading the first light of dawn across a calm sea and a deserted beach. Little stirred, apart from two early morning joggers and a lone car travelling along the coast road, as far as Ernesto could tell, from his sweep of the bay with his binoculars. The air was still.

'Such tranquillity; it seems a pity to spoil it, really, but it would be for the common good, eventually.' Ernesto thought to himself, as he swept his gaze back across the bay from his vantage point.

Omah suddenly nudged him, excitedly,
"Look, there they are!"
The Guatemalan immediately moved his gaze from the beach to the horizon and saw three ships approaching from the west.

"Oh, yes, I see them, too; they're quite big, aren't they?"
A few moments later, he saw two of them peel off to the right, heading for the other bays. The largest, the "Makmar Empress," maintained its course and was soon only a few hundred yards or so from the beach.

Ernesto noticed one of the others had turned inwards towards St Brelade's Bay, some three miles along the coast from him, while the remaining ferry pressed on around Corbiere Lighthouse, on the southwest headland of the island. St Ouen's Bay was a couple of miles further up the west coast.

He turned his binoculars back to the "Empress," which had now stopped, on the high tide, some two hundred yards offshore. The ship loomed so large in his binoculars, he had to 'zoom out' to get the complete picture ahead of him.

Then with a long creaking sound, the bow of the ship was raised to a near perpendicular position, the doors were opened and a landing ramp lowered onto the minimal swell. Once the small splash had dissipated, there was a tumultuous roar from the car deck, as a wave of humanity ran down the ramp and into the sea.

The noise continued for a few more minutes but when all the 'journeymen' were off the ferry and swimming for the shore, silence descended. All that could be seen was a myriad of black people threshing about, as they made their way towards the safety of the sandy beach which lay ahead.

Ten minutes later, all were ashore and were beginning to line up in their three coloured ranks; the marshals of each, having donned their respective caps, now went about organising their 'teams' in a military fashion. Ernesto was quite impressed with the discipline shown!

He 'phoned the leader of 'Red' group to congratulate him on their organisation and told him to tell the other two 'leaders' the same. He also instructed him to ensure that all the people should stay in their positions, until he gave them further orders.

"Yes, sir, thank you; I'll pass those orders down the line and we'll await your further instructions."

"Very good, Red leader," replied 'Commander' Alvarez, switching off and, smiling to his cohorts, turned his attention back to the Empress.

Nothing was happening, although he could see Capt Stegman on the bridge, spying the assembled throng on the beach. He seemed a little anxious, since he looked at his wristwatch a couple of times, between viewings of the beach scene.

Ernesto's mobile rang and he answered it. On the line was 'Orange' leader from the "Makmar Princess" group.

"We're all ashore here at St Brelade's Bay; no casualties and we're lining up on the beach, as instructed, sir."

"Good, good, well done Mr 'Orange'. I want you to keep order with your other squad leaders and stay where you are until I call you, alright?"

"Very good, sir, thank you."

Alvarez clicked off as two blasts on the horn from the Empress distracted him. He turned his binoculars back to the bridge of the vessel.

Capt Stegman seemed to be getting a bit agitated there, he thought to himself, as his 'phone rang again.

"Hello?" the Guatemalan enquired into it.

"Mr 'Yellow' from the Queen group reporting in, sir; all is well and we're lining up on the beach here at St Ouen's Bay. All got ashore okay, I'm pleased to report and we await your further orders, sir."

"Well done, 'Mr Yellow,' that's good to know. Please pass on my satisfaction to your fellow squad leaders and stand by for my further orders. Keep everybody in their squads on the beach, will you and I'll call you again shortly."

"Very good, sir, thank you," replied 'Mr Yellow' who then clicked off.

The leader of the 'Enlightened Way' turned to his companions and said,

"Well, gentlemen, I'm pleased to say ...." three more blasts from the "Empress" (and longer this time) interrupted him but he ignored them and continued...

"As I was saying, before I was rudely interrupted by all that noise, all our 'troops' have been safely delivered onshore and now we can set about dispersing them to advantage."

Picking up his binoculars again, he spied the bridge of the "Empress" once more, saying,

"But first, I have to reveal to Capt Stegman our change of plan, don't I? He does look extremely agitated now, I must say; I wonder who he's on the radio to?"

He looked at his watch, as Stephen volunteered to order breakfast from 'Room service' for them,

"Yes, good idea, Stephen, thank you; I'm sure we all could do with some sustenance, with all this excitement going on, eh?"

It was just gone 7.15am and Ernesto noticed more traffic was about now and several cars were slowing down to survey the assembled company on St Aubin's beach below him. One or two pedestrians had also walked onto the beach and were speaking with 'Red' cap, or even beginning to remonstrate with him, it looked like.

A series of short blasts from the "Empress" echoed around the bay, this time.

'Time to enlighten the Captain, methinks, before he goes completely ape!' Ernesto thought to himself.

He rang the sea Captain on his mobile, who responded quickly,

"Captain Stegman; who's this?!"

"Ah, Captain, it's Mr Alvarez, here, I…" The naval man cut him short,

"Mr Alvarez, at last! Now, when do you expect your people to return to their ships? I've sounded the horn at them several times and they don't seem to be taking a blind bit of notice; they just seem content to wave at me and…"

"Well, Captain, I'm afraid there's been a change of plan…"

"Change of plan? What change of plan? I've got the coastguard on the radio asking me what the hell I'm doing here and…." Ernesto interrupted him again,

"Now that everybody has been disgorged onto the various beaches, we intend to stay a while, I'm afraid…." The Captain now did the same,

"Stay a while! What on earth do you mean by that, may I ask?

"Exactly that, Captain. We intend to stay on this island, while we request some help from the good and wealthy people here; hopefully, the Jersey Authorities will see the justice of our cause and financially assist those now confronting them."

"Are you mad, Alvarez?!" The Captain screamed at him, with Ernesto noting the omission of 'Mr' this time, as he continued,

"You can't just abandon them like that; I mean I have to answer to the authorities…" Ernesto cut in again,

"They want to stay now they've arrived and get some assistance from the rich islanders for themselves and their families back home."

"Look, Mr Alvarez, I appreciate you're a much respected friend of my employer and this is a 'charity run' of sorts, or so I thought but I cannot leave here, after we've dumped over six thousand souls onto foreign soil. I am responsible for them; I brought them here and I now insist you arrange for them to get back on board our three ships, without further delay. Mr Alvarez, please!"

Ernesto detected real anxiety in the man's voice and felt rather sorry for him and his fellow Captains, too.

"Captain, I fully appreciate the predicament you and your colleagues now find yourselves in, especially since it has been none of your doing. However, there are greater needs involved here than yours, all around you and now we are here, the people we've brought with us hope to materially improve their lot, if they can. I and my friends intend to ensure they succeed in that endeavour.

I suggest you withdraw your ships to a few miles offshore and wait for our venture to succeed. As soon as the Jersey Authorities agree to help us financially and do so, we'll need you to take us all home again."

"But Mr Alvarez, I really must insist this madness stops and right now!"

Ernesto spotted some activity alongside the ferry.

"Oh, Captain, I see you have some visitors; a police launch and a customs boat, seemingly."

"How do you know that, Mr Alvarez?" The Captain asked, as he began to survey the shore from the bridge.

"Because I'm watching matters from the.....the promenade. I have to be with my people at a time like this, of course; don't you agree?"

The Guatemalan saw the Captain's sweep of the bay area drop down to the road level and away from the buildings on the front. Ernesto didn't want to reveal his location just yet, to avoid a premature visit from the police, which could well upset his timetable. He spoke to the Captain again, just as he looked away to address two policemen joining him on the bridge,

"Captain, before you speak to those gentlemen, please take note of my suggestion to move your ships back a few miles out to sea and as soon as we get this matter over and done with, I'll contact you again to arrange the return trip, alright?"

He clicked off, seeing the naval man pointing towards the shoreline, with the officers of the law, straining to see what he was indicating.

There was a knock on their door and Ernesto closed the balcony windows, put away the map of the Island they'd been poring over a few moments before and nodded to Stephen to answer it. He did so and a waiter from Room service trundled in with their breakfast trolley.

After the customary appreciation was attended to, he left and Omah re-opened the balcony windows, as they sat down to have breakfast.

Forty five minutes later, they'd finished eating and Ernesto took up his position again, surveying the scene below.

It was now 9 o'clock and there was near mayhem on the beach, with a massive traffic jam on the main road, visible from his vantage point. The Empress had withdrawn, though and was about a mile offshore, he'd estimated, as he swung around to take another look at the sea front and the beach. There was still quite a bit of jostling going on between his people and about a dozen police officers trying to reason with them. As instructed, though, the 'immigrants' were not fighting back.

As far as the road situation was concerned, there was now a solid line of parked cars along the front, although traffic was moving slowly, in both directions. That would soon stop, once the leader of the 'Enlightened Way' ordered his journeymen to move off the beaches and into the Airport complex and St Helier, proper, respectively!

'That seemed to be about now, giving the men the order to move inland, I would have thought,' Ernesto thought to himself. He noticed, though, a group of three or four policemen trying to isolate the ringleaders of 'Blue' squad, near the sea wall, below him; if they succeeded in confiscating their mobiles, he'd lose contact with his people!

He must alert the squad leaders of that danger, immediately. He 'phoned 'Red' leader, who answered straight away,

"Yes, sir?"

"They're after your mobile 'phones; the police are trying to deny you your ability to communicate. You must get your men around you when you use it, to keep the police at bay, do you understand?"

"Yes, yes, I see what you mean,"

Alvarez saw from his elevated position, 'Red' leader gather a large group around him which ensured the 'long arm of the Law' couldn't get to him, not yet, anyway.

"Good, that's good, 'Red' leader. There are only a few of them but thousands of you, so use your superiority well and tell the other squad leaders with you to do the same, okay?"

"Yes, sir, I'll do that; hold on for a moment." 'Red' rattled off such instructions to those around him in their local tongue, by all accounts and some of his men made their way to the other 'caps,' accordingly.

"Are you there, 'Mr Red'?" enquired Alvarez.

"Yes, sir, I'm still here and the other leaders are now being told to surround themselves with their men to protect the mobile 'phones."

"Well done; you must not surrender those, whatever happens, okay?"

"Understood sir," the squad leader replied.

Ernesto now decided to put the next stage of the 'assault' into action. He told 'Mr Red' that he was about to telephone 'Mr Orange,' 'Mr Grey' and Mr 'Purple' on St Brelade's Beach, the next cove west of him, to move up onto the road and march towards St Helier. As soon as 'Mr Red' saw his fellow journeymen coming along the road from their left, he was to move his people up to the road to join them. The other squads with him, 'Blue' and 'Green' would join him up onto the road, too. Once united, the entire group of some four thousand five hundred souls would march into the town, heading for Royal Square in the centre of it.

Alvarez duly telephoned the other squad 'leaders,' in turn and did the same with those groups on St Brelade's beach. He got the confirmation from them that they were now on the move onto the road by the L'Horizon Hotel there and anticipated being adjacent to St Aubin's Bay in fifteen to twenty minutes.

"And now for some major disruption, my friends," he said to his cohorts, standing beside him in the hotel room. He dialled 'Mr Yellow,' Mr 'Pink,' and then 'Mr White,' the leaders in charge of the two thousand odd journeymen on St Ouen's beach and told them to move inland and make for the airport runway which lay ahead of them.

The end of the runway was approximately one hundred feet above the highest part of the scrubland between the sandy beach and the installation itself but was readily scalable.

If there were difficulties in climbing the hillside, access to the apron of the airport could be gained from La Moye golf course, where the two fairways above the beach were more easily reached. These were only a few hundred yards from the runway and ran almost parallel with it.

He heard 'Mr White,' shout his instructions to his men,
"Come on, then, let's go and join the others, up there; we're to sit down on the runway!" The leader of the 'white' group came back on the line to him,
"We're all on the move now, sir and we should be up there, duly installed, in fifteen minutes."
"Right, very good, Mr 'White'; let me know when you've achieved your objective, will you?"
"Yes, sir, we will." Mr 'White' duly clicked off and Alvarez put his mobile down on the coffee table in front of him.
There was a knock at their door,
"Room service, gentlemen, may we come in and clear away the breakfast things for you?"
"Just a moment, please," Ernesto called out as he closed the French windows onto the balcony once again and nodded to Stephen to let the man in.
A few moments later, the waiter retired with the trolley of dirty dishes and closed the door behind him. Ernesto opened the balcony windows once more, stretching as he did so,
"My, my, what a beautiful day it is, gentlemen; the sun's shining in a clear blue sky, it's nice and warm, the sea is calm but it's a pity about all the noise, though, from the seafront, I mean!"

The other two came out onto the balcony to join him. Other guests in their hotel were doing the same, staring in disbelief, from their balconies, at the scene below. Most residents in other establishments, up and down the front, were agog at the spectacle on the main road into town.

Car horns were blaring and lorries and buses honking their horns in remonstration at the 'army' of black men marching along the road into town. They were ten or more abreast right across the wide road along the front but they'd have to close up into half that number as they approached the narrower streets ahead. Drivers were shaking their fists at them, from their stationary vehicles, along with numerous pedestrians and bystanders shouting abuse at the 'invaders,' too! Only the black journeymen seemed to be moving; everybody else was staring in blank amazement at them.

Several police on motorbikes tried to bar their way but it was no good; the black 'army' simply marched around them and seemed to swallow them up into their midst.

Ernesto's mobile rang on the coffee table. He picked it up and responded to the call,

"Hello?"

"Oh, sir, 'Mr White' here, at the airport. We've all arrived and have sat down on the runway. Some of us have peeled off into the Airport buildings to look around, buy some bottled water, snacks, etc., ..is that alright?"

"Have you stopped the flights in and out, satisfactorily?"

"Oh, yes, there's nothing going on here, now; everything's shut down and a couple of uniformed people, airport officials, I would think, are talking to 'Yellow cap' but he's just shrugging his shoulders at them! He's keeping a large number of his men between himself and them, to protect his mobile, of course."

"That's very good, Mr 'White,' how is Mr 'Pink' doing?"

"He's being shouted at by several police officers, again keeping his distance from them, with his group surrounding him; they keep asking him 'who is your leader'?

"We've both told these people they'll find out soon enough, that's alright, isn't it?"

"Absolutely correct, Mr 'White,' well done; I'll contact you again soon and in the meantime, just hold your ground there, okay?"

"Very good, sir, we will."

Having finished his 'update' from 'White cap' he turned to his companions, who were still surveying the chaos on the front from their balcony and said,

"It must be much worse now in the centre of the town, given the narrow streets and everything; I think one of us should go down there and take a look."

Neither heard him above the din coming up from below, so he retrieved some notepaper from the writing box on the corner table of the room, tore off the hotel's name and address and wrote the following note to the Leader of the States, (Jersey's senior Government official) in Royal Square. It read:-

Dear Sir,

You and your fellow politicians are, doubtless, very concerned about the present state of confusion surrounding you.

At the time of writing, there are approximately four thousand five hundred very poor people now occupying St Helier and a further two thousand odd, equally poor souls, ensconced at the Airport.

None of these people carry any weapons and this is not a demonstration on their part. The reason for their presence on your Island will be made clear at 3pm today, when I will contact you again.

Meanwhile, no offensive action against these people should be undertaken, bearing in mind they are unarmed and the World's media will soon be upon them and your behaviour towards them.

Signed..................................
Ernesto Alvarez

Founder and leader of 'The Enlightened Way'

The Guatemalan folded the note and put in an envelope. He walked out onto the balcony to join his acolytes. The confusion and noise was quite oppressive by now, so he nodded to Stephen to come back into the room where he could make himself heard, at least.

"I want you to deliver this to the States Parliament building in Royal Square; you remember that quite impressive place we saw there the other day?"
"Oh, yes, sure, I recall where that is, no problem."
"Don't put it in their letter box; give it to an official there and depart; if you can't get through to the place, just make sure you return here, okay?

131

And, oh, you'd better use one of our mopeds in the car park; I suspect it will be a lot easier getting around on one of those, now, eh?"

"Sure, boss…I'll be back in a short while."

Omah came back into the room and Ernesto told him of the errand Stephen was running for him. Omah nodded, in acknowledgement.

It took Stephen over twenty minutes to cover the ten minute walk from his hotel to the Royal Square. Everybody seemed to be jostling with each other; either journeymen keen to move forward or hold their position, at least, while most of the 'locals' were keen to get passed them.

Many had dived into the nearest shop to get out of the crush, it seemed and all the while nothing on wheels was going anywhere; except for a blue and white painted moped, which could be seen weaving its way in and out of numerous stationary vehicles and countless people, heading for the vortex of the mayhem, Royal Square.

The rider of the moped got to the steps of the Parliament building, put his machine on its stand and proceeded to walk up a few steps as two police officers moved down towards him. He pointed to something and the policemen went past him down the steps and pushed their way along the edge of the crowd to the corner of the building.

Stephen walked inside and finding a young lady passing by, he thrust the envelope into her hand, telling her to give it to her boss as soon as possible. As she looked at it, he turned around, hurried down the steps, got back on the moped, pushed it forward off the stand and weaved his way into the crowd, once more.

Having collected her thoughts, she ran after the messenger but he was nowhere to be seen. Turning back into the building, she looked again at the addressee:-

'To the Senior Politician in the building.'

'That must be Sir James, then, I would assume; he's in the Cabinet room, I think,' she thought to herself and promptly made her way there. She knocked on the door and upon hearing a voice say, "Come in," she entered the room.

Inside the large, oak panelled, room, there was intense activity. Most of the occupants were in conversation with each other, or on the telephone and all but one had discarded their jackets.

Spotting 'Sir James' chatting to several people around him, only a few feet away, she moved up to him, saying,

"Excuse me, sir, I have been given this note to give to you, as the senior politician in attendance this morning….I don't know who sent it, I'm afraid, since the motorcycle messenger who gave it to me was wearing a helmet and he ran off too quickly."

Sir James le Marchant was a kindly man and the Patriarch of an illustrious Jersey family going back hundreds of years. He was always impeccably dressed and being in his eighties, was generally regarded as the 'father of the house' by the Deputies and Senators alike. Nothing ever got to him, as the saying goes and he was rarely flustered. He was the archetypal 'sound man' of politics and many had sought his wise counsel, over the years.

"Oh, thank you, my dear, let me get my glasses on….you don't know who gave it to you, you say?" Sir James moved away from the huddle and walked over to the window to get a better look at the note addressed to him.

He read it twice and then looked out across the square, over the mass of people shouting and jostling a few yards beyond him. He read it again and then turned to face the people in the room.

"Ladies and Gentlemen, I have something…." the hubbub subsided a little but not sufficiently for him to be heard, so he raised his voice,

"Ladies and Gentlemen, may I have your attention, please. Will everyone just shut up for a moment?!" There was a pause and then silence rapidly ensued.

Sir James never tells anyone to 'shut up,' so it must be a very important announcement he wanted to make, most of them concluded.

"Thank you,...eh, I have just received a letter from a person or persons unknown, which seems to throw some light on the intolerable situation we now find ourselves in." He looked at the deputy speaker and said,

"John, perhaps you'd like to read the message out loud, so we can all be aware of the implications involved."

John Hawkswood, the deputy speaker, duly did so, to a hushed audience. After that, Sir James said flatly,

"We'd better get onto London, right away, in my opinion."

Chapter Twelve

Between a rock and a hard place!

It was almost noon when Stephen Carvell returned to Room 410 on the top floor of Jersey's Hotel Royale, one of the island's finest establishments, to rejoin his friends.

He told his boss, Ernesto Alvarez, that he'd safely delivered his message, after persuading a couple of policemen who were standing guard at the door of the Parliament building in Royal Square, that a near fatality had occurred around the corner. This ruse had enabled him to enter the building; hand the letter to a woman there and then beat a hasty retreat!

"They'll have three hours, then, to decide what to do; how to prepare themselves for our next contact at 3 o'clock this afternoon? Come, my friends, let's go on a walkabout or a push about, more like and find a nice restaurant for lunch. After that, we'll pay a visit to that newspaper office we spotted the other day at 'Five Oaks,' I think it's called, about a mile, or so, out of town."

"I think it's the offices of the 'Jersey Record,' the island's biggest newspaper," Omah chipped in.

"The more publicity the better for us; Omah, would you close the French windows, then? We'll take a look outside," Alvarez replied.

The lobby was unusually full, Ernesto thought, as he led the trio out into the main road. Everywhere was packed with people, all pushing this way and that, in the hot noonday sun.

They soon gave up on the 'walkabout' idea and decided to have lunch, 'in house,' instead.

Afterwards, they set off for the 'Five Oaks' roundabout on their mopeds and eventually arrived, after numerous hold ups, at the offices of the 'Jersey Record' at just after 2 o'clock.

The girl on the reception desk didn't quite grasp the significance of their visit, until Ernesto insisted on seeing a senior reporter to give the paper a massive 'scoop.' That clearly worked, as they were swiftly shown into an interview room and after tea /coffee and biscuits were provided, a senior journalist and a secretary settled down to hear their story.

He got the journalist to agree to publish the story in that evenings issue, after he was assured Ernesto would only speak to his paper, in the publishing media, henceforth. No contact with outside sources was to be made by the paper, without Ernesto's approval and by way of reciprocation, no money was payable by them for the story.

The journalist and his secretary listened intently to Ernesto's quest, on behalf of some of Africa's poor. He explained why they had selected Jersey, and stated the number of 'immigrants' now on the Island under his exclusive control. The journalist then asked him the $64,000 question:
"What will it take for the Island to return to normal?"
Ernesto re-phrased his question for him,
"What will it cost for the 'visitors' to pack up and go home, you mean?"
"Well, yes, I suppose that is what I'm asking," the journalist conceded.
"For you residents of Jersey, the very wealthy ones at least, very little but for these very poor people I'm shepherding, it will mean everything."
"Could you calculate that in monetary terms, do you think?" The journalist persisted.
"In aggregate…." the newsman said and holding up his hand, added,
"The total cost to Jersey of getting you and the poor people you have brought onto the island today to return home."

The journalist's qualification of his question was tersely put, Ernesto thought, which irritated him. He looked the pressman straight in the eye and said,
"About $65 million, or £43 million…..at the current exchange rate."

"WHAT!" exclaimed the man from the Jersey Record, as the secretary gasped, with her mouth open, in stunned amazement.

"You cannot be serious, Mr,..eh...Alvarez...that's tantamount to an outrageous act of daylight robbery...I mean, no Government could countenance such...." Ernesto interrupted him, this time,

"It's not an act of 'daylight robbery' my friend, it is a 'tithe,' do you know what that is?"

"Well, yes, it's a type of.....what shall I say.... a tax, I suppose, yes, it's an old fashioned form of taxation, isn't it?"

"More like a levy, I'd say," countered Alvarez, sitting back in his chair.

"Well, whatever you call it, sir, it is an unlawful payment request, known as extortion, which for this jurisdiction, at least, wouldn't be countenanced, I can assure you!"

"If the 'tithe' isn't paid over to the people who've journeyed here, then they'll just stay put, I'm afraid. Think of the consequences of that for a moment.

The capital and the airport would remain closed, as they are at present, with limited supplies moving in or out. The finance industry, your precious source of revenue, would be paralysed and deposit money would soon be moving on elsewhere, I shouldn't wonder, after a few days of such chaos.

There would soon be rioting in the streets and you've no police force, in sufficient numbers at any rate, to quell any major unrest, still less, anything resembling an army to restore order.....need I go on?"

"Hmmm, I see...you seem to have done your homework, as to our frailty in such circumstances, I have to agree..." His secretary cut across her boss at this point,

"Can I ask a couple of questions, sir?" She asked him, trying to simplify matters.

"Sure, Sandra, go ahead, I'm stumped for words at the moment," he replied, with a wave of his hand.

"Why $65 million or whatever it is in Sterling, £43 million, I think you said?"

"That's easy. There are six thousand five hundred men now on the Island and I've promised them a personal 'tithe' of $10,000 per man. That's

$65 million or about £43million Sterling, at the current exchange rate of $1.50 to the Pound."

"I'm sure the States, eh, that's our government, by the way, won't agree to pay that, if anything at all. I mean, they haven't got the money to pay over, just like that!"

Ernesto shrugged his shoulders and said,

"The risk is the price going up, if they have to stay for more than a week or two; the economic consequences for you would be truly horrendous by then and Jersey might never be able to recover its 'safe haven' status it cherishes so much." He continued,

"As for the 'immigrants;' well, I mean, if they suffer undue hardship here while their, quite reasonable 'tithe' request, in my view, is delayed or refused, you can imagine what might follow. With the World's media covering every aspect of the story..."

At that moment, a helicopter was heard droning overhead, as if, on cue, his point was rammed home.

"As I was saying, with such aerial scrutiny to contend with, all the reporters fighting to get 'the latest' on the ground, this place would soon degenerate into a circus, wouldn't it? And, quite understandably, they'd demand a bigger tithe, then, I would think; maybe, $15,000 or even $20,000 per man. Now that really would be costly, I'd say!"

"How and when do you expect all this money to be paid over, assuming the States agreed to pay it?" The journalist asked.

"In gold; each man to receive a one kilogram bar of gold, which equates to 32.15 ounces and is worth about $10,000 with gold around $315 per ounce at the moment. On payment; that should be as soon as possible, for all our sakes, I'd suggest."

The exasperated reporter through his pencil down onto the desk in front of them and declared,

"We don't have six thousand five hundred 1 kilo bars of the stuff here, I'm sure, we don't!"

"Then you'd have to buy them on the market, like anybody else, wouldn't you?"

"That's if we had the money, of course!" The exasperated newsman retorted. The secretary piped up again,

"Well, there is the 'Rainy Day' Fund, isn't there? That's readily available to the Government to meet emergencies, although they've never seen fit to draw upon it, as yet. There must be that sort of figure in the fund, by now, surely…"

"And it's starting to piss down with rain now, it seems to me…" his riposte to her being quite humorous in the circumstances!

Sandra smiled at him as she turned to Ernesto and said,

"I have another question, if I may, Mr Alvarez and that is,

"Let's assume we got the ransom…eh…sorry, the 'tithe' together and paid you the 6500 kilo bars you've mentioned, how would we know you would honour your part of the deal thereafter and go home?"

"Yeah, that's a damned good question, Sandra," her boss added, with both now looking directly at the leader of 'The Enlightened Way.'

"There's no difficulty on that score; the men only take orders from me and if I tell them to get back aboard the boats and go home, they will."

"And we'd just have your word about that, would we? You'd have to give the authorities more than that, Mr Alvarez, if you're to be taken seriously," the angry journalist insisted.

"Surely you can see that?" added Sandra.

Ernesto thought for a moment and then said,

"That's fair enough; I'll give you a demonstration of my authority over the 'immigrants' in St Helier, right now. How far away from the town are we?"

"About two miles," the journalist volunteered.

"And there aren't any black men walking around here at the moment are there? All the disruption is in town and at the airport, right?" asked Alvarez.

Both the journalist and his secretary got up and looked out of the window onto the 'Five Oaks' roundabout and along the several roads leading off it.

"No, nothing unusual outside at all," the newsman confirmed.

Ernesto looked at his watch and saw it was almost 3 o'clock. He said to the reporter and his secretary.

"I have to make an important telephone call to your senior government people in a minute, so may I make it from your office here, in a private room somewhere?

I will also issue instructions for all the 'immigrants' who are presently strangling St Helier by their presence there, to move away, passing this junction, for a trip up to the North coast of the Island, okay? Would that satisfy you that I, and I alone, am in charge of these men?"

"Yeah, that would be convincing enough, for sure; don't you think so, Sandra?"

"Certainly, if he can arrange for that to happen, I'd be totally convinced, that he is the man in charge," concurred his secretary.

"Right, then, if you show me where I can telephone privately, I'll get them to move past here; they should be coming by in, say, thirty minutes or so. Certainly by 3.45pm, you should see them going by your office."

The journalist showed Ernesto into an interview room, while Omah and Stephen waited outside. Alvarez got to work.

As it was right on 3 o'clock, he telephoned the States Parliament building in Royal Square. After introducing himself, he was immediately put through to Sir James Le Marchant, who was chairing an emergency meeting of the Cabinet, along with several experts in emergency operations, anti-terrorism and riot control being present. There was also an open line to Special Branch in London in operation.

"Mr Alvarez, is it?" Sir James enquired, putting the receiver into the cradle of a 'squawk box' for all in attendance to hear the caller.

"Yes, that's right: To whom am I speaking, may I ask?"

"Sir James Le Marchant, I'm the senior politician here, as you requested. I've put the telephone on 'conference call' so all of us present can hear the conversation, Mr Alvarez, just so you know.

Now what the hell is this all about? How do I know you are who you say you are? And more importantly, what do you want?"

"Well, first of all, tell me what the situation is outside in Royal Square, would you?" Ernesto asked.

"It's total chaos here and if you're responsible for all..."

"Utter mayhem, more like," muttered another politician in attendance, prompting various nodding of heads from others around the table.

"Yes, yes, we only need one to speak at a time otherwise..."

Ernesto cut in,

"What if I got the mob outside to move away from you, to, say, somewhere up North, to give you a bit of a breathing space for a while, would that convince you that I had full control over the men there?"

"Well, certainly, it would…"

"I'll believe that when I see it!" muttered a Senator at the end of the table, prompting Sir James to hold his hand up to silence him.

"I and I alone, have these men under control and I will show you that that is so; look out of your window and they'll all start moving away from you towards 'Five Oaks,' towards the North of the Island, in about five minutes. I need to call someone on another line and I'll 'phone you back shortly."

Ernesto put the telephone down and picked up his mobile and rang Messrs' 'Red,' 'Blue,' 'Green,' 'Orange,' 'Purple' and 'Grey' in quick succession. His message to each of them was the same;

'Move your men away from the Square now and head north. Take the road towards 'Five Oaks,' you'll see the road signs for it as you leave St Helier.

When you get to the roundabout at 'Five Oaks,' go straight across heading towards the North coast. Stay around that part of the Island in your groups for a few hours and then return to the Royal Square by 11pm. I will address you all and the press, on your behalf, at midnight. Do it now!" All the 'Caps' replied in the affirmative.

Those in the Cabinet room had moved over to the three windows overlooking the Royal Square. Somebody called out,

"You know, I think they're moving; there's certainly a drift away from here."

"Yes, I think you're right, they do seem to be on the move, towards the upper end of town, towards 'Five Oaks,' as that chap stated," said another.

Ernesto got up from his desk, opened the door and asked Sandra if he could have another cup of coffee brought into him and,

"I suggest your boss starts to write the headlines for this evenings edition: They're on the move now and will be passing your offices within the next twenty minutes, I would think!"

"He's already doing that, don't you worry; he knows an important story when he sees one!"

Ernesto returned to his desk and rang for Sir James again on the Record's landline. Upon hearing his cultured voice, Alvarez asked him,

"What's it like outside your window now, Sir James, eh?"

"Amazing, quite amazing, I have to say; it's almost like normal outside now, a blessed relief, I can tell you."

"So, what now, then, Mr Alvarez?" the politician intoned.

"Well, don't get too excited there; they'll be back around 11pm as I would like to address them, and the media, at midnight, after I've discussed matters with you and your colleagues, if that's alright?"

"Why so late?" Sir James asked, adding,

"Only most self respecting people are in bed by then, aren't they?"

Ernesto's response to that, rather flippant, remark, visibly chastened the old man, as all present in the room could see, when he said,

"The future of your Island, as a credible 'safe haven' in which to do business, hangs in the balance, as we speak, Sir James, so I wouldn't make light of it, if I were you!"

Silence descended upon all present. None had really considered that bleak prospect at all.

A note was passed to Sir James by one of the Special Branch officers monitoring the telephone conversation and trying to trace its origin. It read,

'It's a local call coming from 'Five Oaks' it appears - should have it nailed very shortly.' Sir James nodded to the officer but their 'advantage' over Mr Alvarez was nullified, when he spoke again,

"Sir James, let me tell you, I'm speaking to you from the offices of the Jersey Record and I've given them much of my story, which should be hitting the streets in about three hours time. I've given them exclusivity on it, so the publishing media, at least, can be contained for the time being.

I need to come down to speak with you all, before the paper is distributed later on, so if your security people are planning to arrest me and my friends, you'll lose your only contact over the control of the men, during these crucial hours left to you. That would be really silly, don't you think?"

"Yes, you need to come down and see us all and maybe we can reach an agreement of some kind. In the meantime, I give you my word, my solemn word, that you'll not be arrested. Not any of you."

"Very well, Sir James, we'll make our way down to you and we should be in Royal Square around 3.45pm. Goodbye."

Sir James turned to his police chief and told him,

"Under no circumstances are you to arrest that man or his associates, not until this mess is cleared up, in any event: Do you understand?"

"Sir, I must protest… this terrorist amongst us can wreak any amount of damage, with all those men under his command and we need…" Sir James cut him short,

"Chief Constable, what part of my instructions to you did you not understand?" The police chief was about to reply, when the older man, added,

"You and your men are public servants, may I remind you and as such you are answerable to the Civil Power on this Island, like any democracy and I insist you obey the instructions of your Government.

Are there any dissenting voices to be heard, gentlemen?" The elder Statesman asked his peers, looking slowly around the table at each one in turn. Only nods of agreement or bowed heads were seen, so he turned to the humiliated Chief Constable again,

"Well, there you have it, Michael; complete agreement to leave this fellow alone until we've had a chance to hear what he has to say. If there's any need to arrest him, subsequently, you'll have the instructions to do so from your Government and no-one else, is that clear?"

"Yes, Sir James, unequivocally, so."

"Very well, then, you'd better arrange to stand your people down for the time being and we, gentlemen, need to put our heads together in preparation for our meeting with this Mr Alvarez, shortly."

Back at the 'Five Oaks' offices of the Jersey Record, a distant rumble of sorts was heard, as Ernesto vacated the office he'd been using.

"Here they come, I think," stated the Guatemalan, winking to his two cohorts, as the sound of something mighty approaching, grew.

Several office workers moved towards the windows, along with Sandra and her boss. All were speechless as the noise developed into a din, as the first ranks of the black 'army' filed past, over the roundabout and up the road, heading North.

After ten minutes or so, with the mob still shuffling by their office making a loud noise, as they did so, Ernesto said to Sandra and her boss,

"Well, convincing enough?" They just looked at each other, still disbelieving what they were witnessing.

"They'll be back this way again, in a few hours, so you'd better enjoy the peace and quiet after they've gone, while you can. We're going to hold a sort of rally in the Royal Square at midnight; I'll address the crowds there and the media at that time and hopefully, we'll have some good news to tell everybody. If we can't reach an agreement with your Government, though, I daren't think what the consequences might be!"

Ernesto suggested to Omah and Stephen that they'd better be going but he asked the reporter and his secretary,

"Will you get the paper out later, alright?"

"Oh, yes, we're beavering away at it now; it should hit the newsstands and the shops on time, around six o'clock or so."

"And will we see you later on at the rally etc.,?"

"Oh, sure, we'll be there, in force, I shouldn't wonder but tell me, why hold the event so late?"

"It's the midnight hour; things are gained or lost at the midnight hour, are they not?" Alvarez philosophised, adding,

"I hope for all our sakes, I'll be able to announce something positive to ensure we all gain something but there are always losers, too, one has to say. We'll see you later on then - goodbye."

With that, the trio walked out into the brilliant sunshine, got astride their mopeds and drove off towards town, quite slowly and with much weaving in and out of the columns of men still moving northwards.

Sandra's boss turned towards her and said,

"Phew! That's the most formidable guy I've ever met. He seems utterly serious in what he believes, I'd say. Not one to be underestimated in my opinion. Wouldn't you agree?"

"You can say that again, for sure!" She replied, as they returned to their desks.

On their slow return journey to St Helier, Alvarez and his acolytes noticed several helicopters overhead, most of them were being used by the media, seemingly, as *BBC, ITV and CNN* logos on the sides of them were clearly visible. They appeared to be filming the long march north.

As they got back into town, their journey was much easier, with fewer people about. They left their mopeds in the hotel car park and proceeded to walk the short distance to the, near-empty, Royal Square.

Upon entering the historic quadrangle, the scene of the '*Battle of Jersey' in 1781,* Ernesto noticed that the two policemen on the door of the Parliament building were now armed, with machine pistols across their chests. '*Such bravado on their part,*' the Guatemalan thought to himself, as the trio approached the steps to the portico.

A woman appeared in the entrance at that moment to greet them, saying to the officers on the door,
"It's alright, constable, these gentlemen are expected." They stood aside and let them pass, accordingly.

They followed the woman upstairs and were ushered into a huge room where, either side of a long table, the 'Emergency Committee' was seated. They all looked up at the 'interlopers' with a considerable degree of disdain on their faces.

An elegant gentleman at the far end of the table arose and introduced himself first and then the assembled company.
"Mr Alvarez and…eh…gentlemen, I'm sorry but I don't know the names of your colleagues, I'm Sir James Le Marchant; we spoke on the telephone earlier and these gentlemen are all members of the Islands 'Emergency Committee.' How do you do?" Ernesto shook his hand.

Few of the Committee members bothered to look up at the trio and those who did, scowled at them. The hostility towards them was palpable!

"Thank you, Sir James…eh, could we have a word outside, do you think?" Ernesto requested.
"Well, ..eh…yes, I suppose so; would you all excuse me for a moment then, gentlemen?" and the elder Statesman moved away from his chair and followed them outside.
"What is it?" Sir James asked when he joined them outside the room.

"Sir James, I thought we were to have a meeting to discuss matters. To see if we could reach an accommodation of some kind; not be subjected to some sort of an interview. Your colleagues overtly hate our guts; that's obvious for all to see and they cannot be capable of considering, objectively, the serious matter in hand, as a result."

"Well, they're all pretty 'pissed off' shall we say, that's true, as am I but…" Ernesto interrupted the old man,

"Sir, we'll get nowhere in there with that lot; they're obviously going to defend the 'status quo' at all costs, so any discussions with them will be a complete waste of time. I'd suggest you and, perhaps, just a couple of your most senior people have a meeting with us, in another room; you can always report back to your Committee from time to time, if you wish."

The politician was hesitant about that,

"Mr Alvarez, I cannot speak on their behalf; they're the people who'll decide the outcome, from our side, in all this, so it's necessary that all…"

Ernesto cut across him once more,

"Sir, you and your Committee don't appear to sufficiently appreciate the gravity of the situation. I mean, if you cannot, or will not, move to quickly resolve this predicament you find yourselves in, then Jersey's finished.

I mean, the Institutions here would have been liaising with their head offices in London all day, about what to do if there's no respite from today's chaos. They won't wait on you for long; they can't afford to and once the money starts to move out, well, I don't need to tell you…"

"Wait here a minute," Sir James replied, as he went back into the big room. Quite a hubbub ensued, as Ernesto and his cohorts waited.

Five minutes later, a dozen, or so, people traipsed out of the room, ignoring the trio, as they walked passed them.

Sir James called to them from inside the room,

"Gentlemen, would you please come in again," and they duly did so.

There were only four of them now, which seemed to even up the odds, to Ernesto's satisfaction and so the three of them sat down opposite the 'home' team.

It took Ernesto, who was the sole 'spokesman' for their side, an hour to explain his philosophy to them, the reason for their visit to the Island

and why the Jersey Government should pay the 'tithe' to his followers, to save the wealthy enclave, while there was still time.

Upon learning the cost of the 'tithe' or 'levy' as the 'home team' preferred to call the charge, there was stunned silence.

"We cannot possibly pay them that sort of sum, Mr Alvarez, that's completely out of the question and anyway, we haven't got the money!" Sir James insisted.

"What about your 'Rainy day' Fund, Mr Chairman; that is expressly retained for emergency purposes, isn't it?" Ernesto countered, adding,

"And this is just such an emergency, a really dire one, wouldn't you say?"

"What do you know about our 'Rainy day' Fund, Mr Alvarez?" retorted the elder Statesman, seemingly irritated that an 'outsider' would have knowledge of such a thing.

"Well, Sir James, it's noted in your Treasury accounts and also referred to on your website (Ernesto guessed on both counts, hoping nobody present would be immediately able to refute his assertion) but not how much is held therein, of course."

"Well, yes…hmm… I'd best go and report to the Committee outside, of the progress, so far at least, I think, if you'll excuse me?" and the likeable Sir James got up and left the room.

Alvarez also got out of his chair to stretch his legs and wandered over to the window. The sun was still shining brightly outside and there were quite a few people walking back and forth, probably a near normal level of activity, he assumed, although he had no way of knowing that, of course.

Those left in the room, three on each 'side,' didn't chat to each other or their opponents, until Ernesto asked one of the 'home' team, if there was a chance of any refreshments at all?

The absence of even a cup of tea for everyone was probably deliberate, he surmised; not showing the slightest courtesy to such an unworthy foe seemed to be part of the psychology of undermining their resolve. That had the reverse effect, as far as the Guatemalan was concerned.

Without any enquiry about who'd like what to drink, not even a word, in fact, one of the Committee members telephoned somebody and requested trays of tea and coffee be brought into them! He returned to his seat and resumed 'doodling' away on his blotter.

A few minutes later, two waitresses entered the room, each carrying a tray of refreshments for them; although neither woman smiled as they put down their trays onto the table in front of them, there wasn't any discourtesy shown them; just a neutral disposition, seemingly. They turned around and left the party to it.

Before anyone offered to act as 'Mother,' Sir James walked back into the room, looking quite sombre. He sat down and, ignoring the provisions just placed on the table, he declared,
"I'm sorry, Mr Alvarez but the decision of the 'Emergency Committee' is to ignore the, so called, 'tithe' request you've proposed to us and that's that!"
Ernesto looked at his wristwatch. It was 4.25pm. He glanced at Omah and then at Stephen. Finally, he looked at each member of the opposition in turn, finishing with the congenial, Sir James.

The silence in the room was 'deafening' for all were on tenterhooks, as they awaited the response from the leader of 'The Enlightened Way.'

Ernesto rose from his chair and walked over to the window overlooking the Royal Square. Finally, he spoke,
"Sir James, as the Chairman of this meeting, I would like you to answer one question, on behalf of your colleagues, before we leave you to your fate."
The old man turned around and looked at Ernesto, apprehensively.
"How much do you think Jersey is worth to you all?"
"I don't understand the question, I'm afraid," pleaded the old man.
"Well, let me put it this way," Ernesto replied, pacing slowly back and forth by the window,
"We've spent a lot of time drawing up this plan of ours to get a modicum of justice for these poor people. We've been over here many times before today, to test your strengths and determine your weaknesses."
Alvarez stopped and moved alongside the politician, bending forward slightly and in almost a whisper to the old man, he said,

"Let me tell you, Sir James, your Island is sadly lacking in its ability to defend itself. It is woefully vulnerable and you politicians are all culpable in ignoring that fact. Believe me; we've done our homework on this place. In such circumstances, don't you think that we would have made an allowance for your initial refusal to help us?"

The leader of 'The Way' straightened up and resumed his perambulation by the window, as he continued,

"Instead of bringing over three boatloads of refugees today, suppose I'd come into your office this afternoon and told you there was a nuclear device, already on this Island! That it had been brought over a few weeks ago, as a safeguard against our failure to get you people to dip into your pockets, just for once. Would that change your collective mind? Would an atomic flash be preferable to the slow demise of Jersey through Institutional abandonment, as things now stand?

The clock is now ticking through your stubbornness, your refusal to help others, even to donate a fraction of the wealth you have here. You guys preside over everything on this rock, don't you? Is it worth £43 million to preserve it? You decide - it's your Island!"

Sir James was speechless, as were the others around the table. His hand was shaking visibly, as he tried to pour himself a cup of tea. He coughed a few moments later and said,

"Are you saying, you've installed a nuclear bomb on Jersey?"

"I'm saying anyone could bring anything into this 'Croesus Cave' of yours and you wouldn't be any the wiser. If you think I haven't got a plan 'B' at my disposal, if you refused to help these poor people, bearing in mind the control over them I've already demonstrated to you, then call my bluff, Sir James. Refusing to help them is tantamount to the same thing.

Finally, let me just say this: I regard the miser as the lowest form of life on this Earth and my hatred of miserliness is extreme. Death becomes them, whether by vapourisation or execution, it matters not to me. I know of one man who refuses to co-operate and who will die tonight, because of it!"

"Are you threatening me, Mr Alvarez?" a much shaken politician asked the figure towering over him.

"No, no, of course not, Sir James. I said I know the man who won't be around after midnight; I don't know you at all and anyway, you and your Committee haven't finally decided yet, have you? No, I'm just telling you how it is, that's all."

Turning to his acolytes, Ernesto said,

"Come, gentlemen, there's nothing more to do here, not for the time being, anyway."

As he walked towards the door, he looked at his watch again, showing it was approaching 5 o'clock. He looked back at them and said,

"Oh, by the way, Sir James, the Record is running the story about all this tonight, so you and the Committee have about an hour to ponder what to say to the public later on. And don't forget, either, the 'immigrants' are back here at 11pm for the midnight rally I mentioned earlier. See you then, possibly, eh? Good afternoon, gentlemen."

The trio filed out of the room, looking straight ahead, as they passed the, temporarily redundant, members of the Emergency Committee who'd congregated in the corridor outside. The disdain was mutual.

A few moments later, Sir James emerged from the room and beckoned them to return. When they'd all settled into their seats, he gave them a summary of the conversation with Alvarez and his friends. There was uproar when the nuclear prospect was mentioned but Sir James held up his hand, telling them to remain focussed on 'keeping their heads,' while contemplating their response to the gravity of the situation.

He spoke to his security chief, Philip Marquand, first of all,

"Well, is it possible, Philip, that a nuclear device could have been smuggled in here, do you think?"

"Highly unlikely, I'd say...I mean..." One of the Special Branch officers cut across him, though,

"Yes, it is certainly possible, I'm afraid, unless your customs people check every lorry, truck, van etc., coming in here, with geiger counter equipment, very thoroughly. Do you? I doubt it from what I've seen...."

"Well, do we?" Sir James asked Philip Marquand again, fearing he knew the answer to that one, already.

The security chief shuffled uneasily in his chair,

"Well, I don't think everything is examined with radiation detection equipment, as it comes ashore, I have to confess but..." The man from London interrupted him again,

"I doubt whether you've installed any such equipment yet have you? To my knowledge, we're still waiting for you to agree to it, as part of the defence of the U.K. Am I right?"

More uneasy shuffling by the security chief, who finally acknowledged the shortcoming,

"The question is still being considered by the States, I believe, that's true and, therefore,..."

Sir James cut in this time,

"So, it is quite possible, then...that we may have a genuine nuclear bomb threat on our hands, gentlemen. We must now give our undivided attention as to how best to respond to it. Nothing else matters!"

As Ernesto and his cohorts sauntered across Royal Square, two, casually dressed, 'tourists' moved away from the Parliament building and fell in behind them, maintaining a discreet distance. Alvarez sensed they might have been followed out of the building, so he wandered towards a jewellers shop window to verify it.

He saw the two 'tourists' in the reflection, both wore jeans and tee-shirts, some twenty yards behind them. They stopped walking, too, making out they were trying to get their bearings towards somewhere else.

"It doesn't matter that they've put a tail on us, my friends; I'd be surprised if they hadn't done so. Let's hope they are taking us seriously back in the Committee room. Come, let's return to the hotel and have a nice Jersey cream tea; I'm told they're pretty good."

They moved away from the jewellers and continued ambling towards the Hotel Royale, a few hundred yards along the promenade. The 'tourists' resumed their walk and seemed to be going that way, too!

Back in the Committee room, Sir James was struggling to maintain order amongst his irate peers. With only half an hour to go before the Record hit the streets, he asked a deputy to 'phone the editor and get an idea of what the Paper would be publishing in their evening edition.

"See if they make any reference to the bomb threat; hopefully, they haven't been told of it by Alvarez, not yet anyway. That's the last thing we want now; the Public panicking to get away from the Island!"

The deputy returned some ten minutes later. He coughed and then told the assembled company that the headline the paper was running was going to be :- '£43 million 'tithe' demand!'

"They're obviously against meeting the 'ransom' demand, as they're calling it but equally stressing the Island is pretty well stymied, if the 'immigrants' don't go away, as things stand," concluded the deputy.

"Yes, that's a good summation, I suppose; at least they don't seem to know about the bomb threat, which is something!" Sir James intoned.

After a short pause, he asked the obvious follow-up,
"So, Gentlemen, what do we do? Do we call their bluff and hope they'll go away or do we pay this 'tithe' of theirs and opt for damage limitation, instead? We have until midnight, it seems, to make our decision, although I, for one, see little point in prolonging the agony, so can I ask for a show of hands, at least, initially?"

"How many in favour of bluffing it out and saying, 'No'?" He went around the table, with his finger, counting those in favour. He wrote down the figure on a sheet of paper in front of him.
"And those in favour of paying the 'tithe' and seeing things return to normal, as soon as possible?" Again, the elder Statesman's finger pointed towards the raised hands, as he canvassed the 'expedient' vote. He wrote that figure down and then declared the result.
"Nine in favour of calling their bluff, four in favour of buying them off and one abstention. That's pretty decisive, I have to say but Cyril, you cannot hide behind an abstention on something as serious as this, please!"

Cyril Le Seulleur, the oldest member of one of Jersey's most illustrious families, insisted the whole question had to be properly debated in the 'House' rather than be decided in this 'ad hoc' manner.
"Yes, yes, of course it should, Cyril, in normal circumstances, I quite agree but there just isn't time; a few more days like today and Jersey's

reputation will be history. We'll be relegated to being the occasional 'weekend stay' little Island before we know it and that'll mean bankruptcy for us; everything is paid for by the Finance Industry here, as we all know."

He took off his glasses, ran his hand through his hair and called to a secretary to come over to him and whispered something to her. She scurried off out of the room.

"Gentlemen, let me re-phrase the questions and their consequences, so we all know what we're dealing with here and there's no misunderstanding over what our votes indicate. I'm thinking of the electorate, in saying that, to whom we're ultimately accountable.

"We have but two choices; doing nothing about this man and his threats is not an option, since many more days of the present chaos will ruin our reputation, anyway. Those choices are :-

1. Refusing to pay the 'tithe' and to hell with the consequences by calling his bluff or :-

2. Paying the £43million 'tithe' to return to normal, as soon as possible.

Those are the two realistic considerations, it seems to me. If we opt for the bluff and get it wrong, the miscalculation could be too horrendous to contemplate and we wouldn't know anything about it, in all probability!

If there isn't a bomb and we won't know that for a while, supposedly, there is still the major question of what to do with all these 'immigrants' and how to get rid of them. And that assumes their co-operation to surrender their hopes and go back home, peaceably. That could be difficult to achieve, given their unusual loyalty to this man, Alvarez.

While all this is going on, stretching over several weeks, I imagine, the Finance industry would be making alternative arrangements to prosper elsewhere and Jersey would be haemorrhaging its life blood, almost certainly. And the delay probably invites a higher cost to end it, too.

The second option, although very unpalatable, does offer a more pragmatic solution, I think."

At that moment, the secretary returned to the Chairman of the meeting and passed him a note. He looked at it cursorily, put it down on his blotter and took up from where he left off,

"Paying the 'tithe' to these impoverished folk, would achieve three things, it seems to me. Firstly, it removes, at a stroke, the bomb threat, secondly, it sets in train the fastest removal of these people from the Island, enabling us all to get back to normal, as quickly as possible and thirdly, doing so would put Jersey in a very favourable light, with the media, I'd say…compassion for the underprivileged, empathy with the less fortunate and so on. Quite a bonus, that; a definite 'P.R.' coup, I would suggest.

Finally, Gentlemen, I would remind you of the question that nasty man, Alvarez, asked me earlier; the one I didn't, initially, understand. You'll recall he asked me; 'How much is Jersey worth to us all?'

I now know what he meant by it; is it worth £43 million to us? Well, is it?" That is the only question we have to answer today - now!"

He glanced down at the piece of paper on his blotter and said,
"Oh, before I forget, Gentlemen, I'm told there is just over £70 million in the 'Rainy day' Fund, give or take a bit, as we speak.

So, Gentlemen, I think you might have gathered which way I am leaning but I will ask you for your decision for the second and final time." He paused for a moment, looking around the table at them all and then declared,
"On the first question, then:-
Do we call the man's bluff in refusing to pay? Please show…..that's one in favour, I think, thank you, Cyril…
And then onto question two:-
Do we, albeit reluctantly, pay this 'tithe' to preserve the Island's reputation……Please show…that's thirteen in favour and one against.

That's very decisive, I think, so thank you gentlemen. Shall I now convey our decision to Mr Alvarez and get things underway with him? You can rest assured, I'll insist on certain guarantees, chiefly that his 'invasion' of our territory will never happen again!"

All but one nodded their approval for Sir James to proceed on the Committee's behalf.

"Right, then, Gentlemen, thank you for that vote of confidence; I'd better now get on with it, I suppose…eh…Chief Constable, do we know where this Alvarez character is, I mean, how to get hold of him?"

"Oh, yes, sir," Michael Beauchamp, the Chief Constable, confidently asserted, as the others filed out of the room,

"He's staying at the Hotel Royale, room 410, under the name of Ernest Ravel, apparently, with one of the others in 412; we have them under close surveillance, of course."

"Right, I'd better ring him to go around to see him and then arrange to have a word with Treasury about acquiring all those gold bars for his people; I can't imagine we've got many lying around over here!"

Chapter Thirteen

Arrivederci.......ROMA!

Having rung Ernesto Alvarez and informed him of his desire to meet with him again, Sir James Le Marchant set off for the Hotel Royale.

As he stepped out of the Parliament building, he was surrounded by a number of reporters and media people, clamouring for him to give them a statement. He wondered how the news had got out so fast, until a zealous fellow, microphone in hand, thrust a copy of the Jersey Record at him. He took hold of it and glanced at the dramatic headline shouting at the reader:-

'£43 million 'tithe' demand!'

He was immediately engulfed by the scrum, as he handed it back to the individual. They quietened down as he said,

"We have the matter in hand, ladies and gentlemen, I can assure you; we'll be making a proper and fuller statement to the media later on this evening. That's all I can say at this stage, I'm afraid. Now please, let me through,…thank you…thank you," as he pushed his way through the throng and into the middle of the Square.

He walked purposefully towards the promenade, with the Hotel Royale coming into view. He was approached by a policeman at the door, who offered to accompany him up to the fourth floor but he declined,

"Thank you, constable, but that won't be necessary."

He knocked on the door of Room 410 and recognised Omah, as he opened it and saw Ernesto reading the evening paper in the background. His aide, Omah, turned back towards the Guatemalan, saying,

"Ernesto, it's Sir James to see you."

"Oh, yes, Sir James, do come in, won't you?"

156

"Thank you, Mr Alvarez, or is it Mr Ravel? That's what your passport says, I believe," as he walked into the short hallway. Ernesto smiled awkwardly,

"No, it is Alvarez, Sir James; it's just that sometimes one has to be mindful of the security needs these days, as I'm sure you'll appreciate."

Stephen hurriedly swept off the table a map, several papers and other notes he'd been working on and disappeared into a bedroom, as Ernesto, Omah and Sir James sat down in the lounge area.

After declining a drink, the elder Statesman got down to business.

"Firstly, Mr Alvarez, I must tell you that the committee has fully discussed the options open to us, given the situation we find ourselves in and they have decided to meet your request and pay the 'tithe' of some $65 million or £43 million or so, to your people. We are, at this moment, speaking to London about purchasing the six thousand five hundred, one kilo gold bars, you mentioned to us, in this regard.

I am informed the bullion might be here late tomorrow or by the following morning. You'll have to clear the runway, for the plane to land, of course."

There was a trace of a feint smile on Ernesto's face, as Sir James paused and Alvarez looked over towards Omah and Stephen, who'd just rejoined them.

"There are two conditions, though, upon which I require your agreement before we go any further."

Ernesto's expression changed somewhat, as he waited to learn what the provisos were. Sir James continued,

"We would expect to complete this exercise in a spirit of co-operation with you, each side helping to bring this unfortunate state of affairs, for us, at least, to a swift and amicable conclusion.

Secondly, your guarantee that we'll never be invaded again; your word on it will be good enough, Mr Alvarez."

Ernesto's smile immediately returned, augmented by his outstretched hand,

"You have my word on both counts, Sir James; once my people receive their 1 kilo bars, they'll set off again, as speedily as they arrived. In the meanwhile, I will inform them of this agreement at tonight's rally and make arrangements for Jersey's disruption to end in the morning, pending receipt of the 'tithe,' is that acceptable to you, Sir James?"

"Eminently so, Mr Alvarez and thank you," the older man replied.

The two men shook hands, as Sir James said he'd make arrangements, on the co-operative side of things, for a worthwhile platform to be in place for Ernesto to address his people and make his announcements, at the forthcoming rally.

"Thank you, thank you so much; that would certainly be appreciated!"

Sir James left the room a much relieved man, some ten minutes later but not as much relieved as one, Ernesto Alvarez, the leader of 'The Enlightened Way!"

In Room 410, the trio looked at each other for a brief moment and then all cheered, with Stephen punching the air, in celebration. After a quick, congratulatory, embrace, they sat down and Stephen exclaimed,

"You're obviously a very good poker player, Ernesto; it looked for a while, after the first 'No' vote by the committee, that we weren't going to get anywhere with them, didn't you think?"

"It was touch and go there for a moment, I agree but we clearly had them 'by the balls' after the nuclear bomb notion took hold; they couldn't take the risk that there wasn't one already installed here and ticking away. If I'd have been in that dilemma, I would have paid up, too, without any hesitation; a smouldering rock in the channel might have been the residual cost of misplaced bravado - a no-brainer, really!"

After they'd all had a shower and ate dinner in their room (the restaurant and lobby were packed to capacity with reporters and media people apparently) Ernesto made five 'phone calls on his mobile.

The first three were to each of his 'caps' heading the squads at the airport, wherein he told them to bed down for the night but they might need to clear the runway to let the 'gold delivery' plane land there in the morning. He'd confirm that tomorrow but, in the meantime, things were going well and they were to encourage their people, accordingly.

The next was to Arnold Fleischer in Managua. With it being ten o'clock, Greenwich Mean Time, in Jersey, it was 4 pm in that South American City. Arnold told Ernesto that the first reports of the Island being held 'hostage' were just coming through there and when the payment in gold was mentioned, the price of the yellow metal appreciated to $330 per ounce.

That was some $15 per oz higher on the day, so far, largely due to first reports of the gold requirement being $650 million to cover the 'tithe' demanded and Arnold had unloaded half their gold options very profitably already, before any correction was reported!

He also mentioned that other 'tax havens' were bolstering their defences against the risk of similar incursions, notably, The Cayman Islands, The Isle of Man and Monaco, according to reports.

"The speculators are getting into gold, as we speak," chortled the American, as Ernesto thanked him for the update and reminded him to watch the six o'clock news there in a couple of hour's time. He said he hadn't forgotten.

His last call was to the leader of his 'hit squad' who was mustering his men some thirty miles north of Managua. His 'unit' comprised one hundred, heavily armed, 'soldiers' who were about to board four army trucks, recently purloined from the Nicaraguan military. He anticipated being 'on station' outside the boundary of the target, just before the 6pm deadline, as instructed.

Ernesto reminded the man to ring him on his 'mobile, when they were finally in position and ready to 'Go.' He confirmed he would.

An hour later, the trio made to leave their room to go to the 'rally' in Royal Square. The telephone rang and it was the police chief, informing Ernesto that it was necessary for him to provide a police escort for them; the crowd outside the hotel was barely controllable, apparently!

"Well, gentlemen, shall we go?" Ernesto said to his cohorts and they left their room and took the lift down to the lobby. The doors opened to a mass of people confronting them; mostly media folk, it seemed, although quite a few irate 'locals' were also present, judging by the angry looks.

They got outside where a massive crowd started to press in on them but a police cordon, of sorts, managed to provide an exit for them, otherwise, they wouldn't have gone anywhere.

They were at the front of the mob and being almost carried along by the front row of it, as they neared Royal Square. Fortunately, the police had had the foresight to put barricades across the several streets leading into it and they were allowed to pass through. There was much confusion behind them, though, as the 'thin blue line' struggled to close the barricades again and keep most of the angry followers at bay.

The noise of the crowds was deafening and the near isolation of the trio in the Square and the few police officers escorting them, made for a near surreal situation.

Ahead of them was a sizeable rostrum, supported by scaffolding, with a battery of microphones in place. Their wires led to an array of loudspeakers situated on the top steps of the Parliament building. Had it not been for these electronic accoutrements, they could have been forgiven for thinking they were approaching a scaffold: the crowd certainly seemed to be baying for their blood, if not a public hanging!

Adding to the cacophony all around them, were several helicopters circling overhead, their spotlights trained on the quadrangle and its boundaries; quivering shafts of light to augment the, already floodlit, arena.

As the trio got to the bottom step of the august edifice, the tumult slowly died away, as another sound was becoming discernible, a sort of 'hum'; it seemed some way off but it was becoming louder.

Three overhead shafts of light suddenly changed direction, all concentrating on one entrance to the Square from the North: the road from 'Five Oaks,' in fact. The helicopter spotlights now seemed to 'zero - in' on that entrance, with the 'rumble' louder now.

Then, all of a sudden, those people who'd been watching the, near - deserted, Square from that position, many of whom had been cat calling a few minutes earlier, were brushed aside by the appearance of a sea of black faces, all smiling and chanting, as they marched, in columns of four, into the heart of the quadrangle. Ernesto's army had returned!

At the head of the first column, which alone stretched back almost half a mile, was 'Red cap' who promptly walked up to the leader of 'The Way' and saluted.

"You're five minutes late, Mr 'Red,' " stated Ernesto, with a smile.

"Sorry, sir, we'd have been on time, if we'd pushed the 'locals' out of the way but we didn't do that, as you ordered, sir."

"Quite right, Mr 'Red,' line your people up properly, as they file into the Square, would you?" requested Alvarez, rather proudly.

"Yes, sir," responded his chief squad leader, just as a phalanx of media people surged forward to the bottom step of the Parliament building to secure the best positions for covering the proceedings.

Five minutes later, Mr 'Red' had his 'troops' smartly lined up and then into the square came Mr 'Blue' with his contingent and he 'followed suit' as did all the other squads, behind their respective 'commanders.' Forty five minutes later, the entire 'army' from the north of the island, numbering some four thousand souls, had filled the quadrangle to capacity.

The leader of 'The Enlightened Way' was impressed, very impressed, by the manner in which his people had behaved as they'd entered the Square, especially their courteous approach to the 'locals' around them and their punctuality.

It was 11.45 pm by his watch and as he turned to mount the steps with his acolytes, he saw several 'notables' were already on the rostrum. Amongst them was Sir James Le Marchant, who beckoned them to come up and join him. As they did so, there was a tremendous, ear splitting, roar of approval, from his 'army,' easily drowning out a few cat calls and noisy dissenters from the edge of the Square.

Ernesto acknowledged the cheers of his people but then assisted Sir James in calling for everybody to quieten down. As the hubbub subsided, the elder statesman prepared to give a short speech to the huge crowd.

As the reporters' cameras flashed and the TV people pressed in on the rostrum, Ernesto's 'phone rang.

He looked at his watch; it was five minutes to midnight. He answered it, to be told that his 'soldiers' back home were now in position and a 'Go' situation was confirmed. He told the leader of his 'hit' squad,

"Very well, then, destroy them, destroy them all! But don't kill their leader, until you hear the code words from me on the TV; got that?"

"Yes, sir, will do."

"Good luck to you and do a thoroughly good job for us all, then."

"We will, sir; Go! Go!" he heard the commander shout to the assault unit, just as he clicked off.

All was now quiet in the Square, as Sir James had finished his introductory comments and he again invited Ernesto to take over.

"Sorry about the call; I hope I wasn't rude in keeping you and all the people waiting, Sir James."

"Nothing important, was it? I mean, there isn't any change in plans, is there? Sir James enquired, quite concerned.

"No, no, everything's as agreed. It was just about that fellow I mentioned earlier; he's at death's door, I'm told."

"Oh, I see…oh, dear, that's a shame, I…" Ernesto interrupted him,

"I'd better get on with my address, hadn't I? They've been waiting long enough, I think…."

"Oh, yes, yes, of course, please go ahead," Sir James replied, inviting him onto centre stage and stepping back a couple of paces, himself.

Another huge roar went up from the 'army' below him, again drowning out the detractors, as he took off his wristwatch and placed it on the table in front of him. *'I'll give them ten minutes to be inside watching TV with him, I think'* he thought to himself, as the noise fell away and he began his address.

"Members of the government of this island, Lords, Ladies and Gentlemen of Jersey, I stand before you tonight…."

Every so often, he would glance down at his watch to check his timing and at ten minutes after he started talking, at 12.10am, he suddenly brought the opening of his address to a swift conclusion.

"….And so, I say to the good people of Jersey, that there are others elsewhere in the world, even more surprised than you, to see me standing here talking on T.V." And, having earlier spotted a CNN cameraman in the front row of the media below him, he looked directly at him and said,

"And to them, I say….. *"Arrivederci ROMA!"*

He had smiled and given a wave, as he uttered the first word but then scowled as he spat out the second.

Six thousand miles away in a hilltop property overlooking Managua, a short burst of sub-machine gun fire was heard, as the leader of Ernesto's 'hit' squad, emptied the rest of his AK47 magazine into a dying man, sitting on the floor, watching the news on television, in utter amazement! At that moment, Ronaldo Martin, nicknamed *Roma* by his close friends, was no more!

Within seconds of his, seemingly impromptu, greeting to someone, Ernesto turned back to the audience looking at him and with a generous smile on his face, he continued explaining the reason for his visit and what he had managed to achieve.

Another fifteen minutes elapsed before he drew his moving and, at times, quite tearful, plea to a conclusion.

"And so finally, Ladies and Gentlemen, I say to you, the fine, warm - hearted and generous people of Jersey, thank you. Thank you for listening so patiently to our plea for assistance. Thank you for your swift response of exceptional generosity towards us. Thank you for sharing, so readily, just a little of what you have with these people in front of you. Your example is a beacon to the World, of that you can be justly proud. Thank you again and goodnight."

Ernesto Alvarez waved to the huge crowd, as he stepped back a few paces, taking it all in. The adulation was quite intoxicating and so he moved forward again and shouted into the microphones, extolling his 'army' to give the great people of Jersey a hearty Three Cheers which they did. As the crescendo of gratitude towards all the 'locals' gradually fell away, he withdrew again and waved once more.

"That was very moving, Mr Alvarez, and thank you for explaining so lucidly, to everybody out there, the reason for our assistance to you," a grateful and chirpy Sir James said to him and added,

"Perhaps you'll come over here tomorrow and we'll finalise the payment procedure and also the evacuation arrangements, yes?"

"Yes, Sir James, that'll be fine; I'll call you in the morning before I come round and thank you again - goodnight!"

He went down the steps and into a scrum of media people, amid a battery of photo flashes and mounted camera lights upon him, as Omah and Stephen tried to open a path to his 'troops' for him.

After much backslapping by them, he was carried, shoulder high, in a triumphal surge towards the edge of the square.

Most of the 'locals' on the periphery of the quadrangle didn't quite know what to make of it all. They'd been feted by this man as the most generous of peoples in so rapidly coming to the aid of these impoverished souls in front of them.

'That was great; with the World watching, too! It felt good, really good, to be so highly regarded, all of a sudden.

Yet, hadn't they just agreed to pay over £43 million for the privilege?

Had that 'donation' been properly discussed by their Government beforehand?

Or had it just been sprung on them?

And if so, why had the Authorities so readily agreed to help these, albeit worthy, supplicants?

We only learnt of this business in today's paper, didn't we?

It feels like we're being duped, somehow but then….these people in front of us are clearly genuine refugees, so…'

Such thoughts were probably universally felt amongst the 'locals' attending the rally and by those watching it all on television. There was no doubt the detractors were now much in the minority, as the 'scrum' shouldering the leader of 'The Enlightened Way,' surged towards one of the exits from the Royal Square.

At that point, he was gently lowered to the ground and the noise of his 'army' lessened considerably. He moved slowly forward, with Omah and Stephen either side of him, as the huge crowd gradually gave way, allowing him to pass by.

One, obviously unconvinced, Jersey man, shook his fist at Ernesto, as he was alongside him and shouted,

"It's all a big con! You're robbing us, you are!"

The Guatemalan stopped to answer him, being aggrieved at such a suggestion. The crowd behind him stopped suddenly, too, as if on cue, enabling him to do so. Strangely, the hubbub also fell away, with everybody straining to hear his reply.

"It is their future, as well as yours, my friend; would you have it that it was only theirs?"

The man was perplexed by the riposte, as was anybody within earshot of the utterance.

'What did he mean by that, do you think?' Asked several people closest to him but as he moved on, the hubbub resumed.

A few minutes later, the trio was being pushed down the promenade but once outside the Hotel Royale, they turned into the foyer, being much relieved to get out of the crush behind them.

It, too, was packed with people, all wanting to get a look at this 'newcomer' who was causing all the upset to the tranquillity of the island. Another battery of photo flashes erupted and with camera 'floods' trained on them, as well, it was difficult to see very much.

They managed to get to the lift eventually and shortly afterwards, they were outside their room, No 410, on the top floor. The two 'on duty' policemen outside the door, moved aside to let them enter their abode, which they did.

Once safely ensconced within, they went to the balcony window to spy the scene below them.

"No, don't open it, Stephen, you'll only encourage them the more," stated, a near exhausted, Alvarez. He sat down on the settee in the lounge, while the other two stood at the window, staring in disbelief at the scene beneath them.

"Could you get me a beer from the mini-bar, Stephen? I'm shattered, right now, aren't you?" Ernesto called out to his acolyte. Stephen brought the drink over to him and they all sat down and discussed the evening's events. An hour or so later, both Omah and Stephen turned in, leaving Alvarez to ponder upon things a little more.

It was now almost 3 o'clock in the morning, noted Ernesto, looking at his watch. *'It would be, therefore, around 9 pm in Nicaragua right now, time to call Arnold again, I think,'* he thought to himself.

He retrieved his mobile from his jacket and rang the American's number in Managua.

"Hi, Arnold, how's everything with you, now?" Ernesto asked his partner in crime, some six thousand miles away.

"Oh, hi, Ernesto, I've just closed off our last positions in the gold market for us, as it was closing for the day."

"So how much have we made, then?"

"I haven't worked it all out yet but with bullion finishing at $340 and one kilo bars especially strong, I reckon we've probably made around five times our money; that's about $25 million each, not bad for a few days work, eh? How's it with you over there, more importantly, my friend?"

Ernesto gave Arnold a potted version of the way things had gone on this, truly memorable, day in Jersey; a day nobody on the Island would forget in a hurry, he reckoned.

"No, I bet they won't, nor you and your friends, that's for sure!" Arnold replied, supportively.

"Did you watch it on T.V. over there, Arnold? I mean, was the event well covered?"

"I should say so; CNN ran a half hour 'special' on the whole thing, with good pictures of you on it throughout: Everybody here must be talking about it, I'm sure...eh hold on, my friend, there's something else being reported now....let me just turn the sound up...hold on for a moment."

'I wonder what he's going to tell me in a second or...' Ernesto thought to himself, as the American came back onto the line, shouting excitedly and interrupting his train of thought,

"Hey, Ernesto, you'll never guess what!"

"What?" said the 'Way' leader, obliging him.

"Ronaldo Martin has been murdered; it's just being reported that there was a major 'hit' on his place this evening, around 6 o' clock, apparently and he and all his people have been killed. Some sort of drug war reprisal, they reckon. Blimey! What do you make of that? I was only chatting to him the other day, too!"

"Were all his people killed? I mean, were they all wiped out, do you know?"

"Yeah, it seems like it…it must have happened while we were all watching you over there!"

"It would seem so, wouldn't it?" Ernesto replied, nonchalantly, adding,

"I will not lose any sleep over it, though, since I hated the man and his business, enslaving people and killing so many through his dreadful activities. I'll sleep better for it, actually, now!"

"Well, you'd better turn in and have a good nights sleep, then; I'll call you tomorrow with the final tally on our gold option dealings, okay," Arnold replied, wishing him,

"Goodnight, my friend, or should I say good morning, for you over there, eh?"

"Yeah, okay, Arnold -'bye." Ernesto whispered to his gold dealer, as he switched off, with the mobile slipping from his hand, as he fell asleep.

Later that morning, around 10 o'clock, on the 2nd May, Ernesto Alvarez was woken by Omah shaking him. Bleary eyed, the Guatemalan squinted at his henchman, sat up on the settee he'd dozed off on, yawned and stretched his arms. He was dazzled by the mid - morning light which suddenly filled the room, as Omah drew back the heavy drapes and opened the French windows on their balcony.

It was again a glorious, sunny day with not a cloud in sight. Another scorcher was clearly in prospect.

Ernesto's Number two, picked up the binoculars from a side table next to the television and walked out onto the balcony. He focused upon the promenade and saw the thoroughfare was still thronged with people with few vehicles on the road. Such traffic as there was, moved very slowly, as the crowds, almost grudgingly, gave way to let anything pass.

The absence of car horns, or any remonstrating by frustrated drivers, seemed odd, almost eerie, somehow, as if the public was having to accept that life was changing for all of them, post yesterday's midnight rally in the Royal Square.

Omar turned his gaze out to sea, re - focusing, to get a look at the ferries. He thought for a moment that they'd gone but then he caught sight of the three of them, anchored some way off, possibly three or more miles offshore. He fine tuned the focussing of his glasses and tried to see what was happening on the bridge of the largest ship, the Makmar Empress.

He could just make out the Captain on the bridge but it appeared he had several others with him in the control room of the vessel. They appeared to be policemen, or were they military personnel? It was difficult to be sure from that distance.

He then spied a fourth ship on the horizon, some distance away from the ferries. '*What is that, I wonder?*' He said to himself, as he tried to make it out. Adjusting his binoculars once more, he 'zeroed' in on the mystery vessel. '*It's a warship, I think…seems to be a frigate, possibly; it has a gun on the foredeck, anyway.*'" He said to himself again.

He turned back into the lounge and said to his boss,
"Well, the front is still jammed with people and the traffic is hardly able to move but the ferries are still anchored some way out and it seems a warship is now guarding them. What do you make of it, Ernesto?"

Alvarez got up from the sofa, took the binoculars from his deputy, saying,
"Let me have a look," and strolled out onto the balcony and repeated the observation exercise. He spent a good few minutes surveying the situation out to sea. Finally, he turned back into the room and declared, somewhat ruefully, that,
"Well, I suppose that was to be expected; I mean, I imagine they're just guarding against another influx of refugees…just in case we need reinforcements but as we've reached an agreement with the Authorities… which reminds me, I need to ring Sir James about our meeting today."

The leader of 'The Enlightened Way' strolled off into the bathroom, handing the binoculars to Omah, as he did so.

Half an hour later, he was dressed and eating breakfast, courtesy of room service, with his acolytes. He told Omah to dress smartly as well, since this meeting was going to be an important day to remember.

"Stephen, I want you to stay here and 'man the 'phone' and ring me if there are any problems, okay?"
"Sure, boss, I understand," replied Stephen, dutifully.

After the dishes were cleared away, he got up and telephoned Sir James to arrange a time for their meeting.

This was then set for 11.30 am and as he'd decided to take only Omah with him, he gave Stephen strict instructions for any of his 'cap' leaders, if they called in.

Ernesto and Omah were escorted to the Parliament building in Royal Square by a couple of policemen. It was quite strenuous getting there, having to push through the crowds en route and even in the square itself, there was little respite. Hundreds of 'locals' hemmed them in most of the time but they eventually got to the steps of the edifice.

At the top of them, he looked around to survey the sea of faces looking up at the duo. It was difficult to know whether they were perceived as rogues by the mob or were still regarded in an heroic light, on balance, as seemed to be the case the previous evening. The noise level wasn't as raucous as before, so, perhaps, a mixed response was a fair assessment; certainly there was expectancy in the air, though.

Having waved to the crowd, (he didn't wait to see how they would react) he turned around and entered the building, with Omah following him.

They were met by a pleasant young lady in the vestibule, who greeted them with a smile of sorts. *'Her reception broadly reflects the mood of the crowd outside,'* Ernesto thought to himself and also that, *'apprehension seems to be the overriding feeling at this juncture.'*

"The meeting room is just along the corridor, gentlemen, if you'd care to follow me," the pretty brunette indicated, with a gesture of her hand, as she turned to her left.

Ernesto and Omah followed her, the latter a couple of feet behind his superior. She stopped outside a large oak door, knocked gently and upon hearing a muffled grunt from within, turned the handle and bade them to enter. They did so, as she engineered a smile towards them again and closed the door behind them. It was precisely 11.30am.

Inside the large, Georgian room, they recognised the amiable Sir James and his Police Chief, Michael Beauchamp. Both got to their feet and shook hands with them, although their smiles were rather guarded, too. *'Still, that's a major improvement on the courtesy front, compared to our first meeting,'* Ernesto thought to himself, as he shook their hands, to reciprocate.

"Gentlemen, do please sit down and take off your jackets, if you wish, as it's so hot today and even in here, too, somewhat unusually," said the elder Statesman, looking to the Chief Constable for corroboration, which he got, via a sympathetic nod from the officer of the Law.

As Alvarez and Djesturi both discarded their smart jackets onto the backs of the two chairs in front of them and sat down, Sir James extended his measured welcome to them.
"Would you like tea or coffee or anything stronger, perhaps, before we start?"

The two outsiders both took in the noticeable array of 'goodies' set out on a large, silver, salver in the middle of the table, around which were tea and coffee sets, of comparable quality.
'My, these people seem determined to clear up this mess we've created for them, as soon as possible!' Ernesto further thought to himself, as he responded to the kindly gesture from the older man,
"Oh, thank you, yes, tea would be most welcome, Sir James, thank you." Omah indicated the same, with equal gratitude to their host, as they settled into their seats, in anticipation of the refreshments.

Sir James seemed to simply nod over their shoulders and, as if from nowhere, two waitresses appeared before them. The older one attended to the teas, while the younger lass, picked up the silver salver and invited them to choose from the 'goodies' thereon.

Ernesto chose three canapés and two, carefully selected, sandwiches from the tray, one ham and one egg, to augment his cup of tea and Omah did the same, although taking the first pair of beef sandwiches nearest to him.

After the two from the 'home' team did likewise, Sir James nodded again and the two ladies withdrew, unobtrusively as before, this time leaving the room.

After a few minutes elapsed, Sir James declared the meeting was now 'in progress' and at 11.45am it got underway.

Back in Room 410 at the Hotel Royale, Stephen was using the binoculars on the balcony, trying to determine who was on the bridge of the Makmar Empress with the Captain, when the telephone rang. He came back into the room and answered it.

He heard an American voice on the line and didn't immediately 'twig' that it was Arnold Fleischer calling from Managua.

"Hi, is Mr Ravel there, please?" He paused and then it suddenly dawned on Stephen, that it was his boss's man in Nicaragua, handling their gold option deals for them.

"No, he's not here right now; he's having a meeting with some Government people currently but I can take a message for him. I am one of his people over here, his 'minder' in fact, helping with the operation we're all involved in."

"And your name is, might I ask?" The American enquired, warily.

"Stephen Carvell, Mr Fleischer."

"Oh, yes, Ernesto has mentioned you to me; say, are you involved in this gold thing we've got going?" Arnold now convinced he was, genuinely, talking to an 'insider,' especially after Stephen knew his name before he'd mentioned it.

"Yes, sir, I am; I know Ernesto is keen to know how much you've managed to do for us in the gold market. I'm in for 10% of the profit, too!"

"Oh, is that right? You should be a happy man, then, since your share is worth about 2.5million bucks; tell Ernesto we made just over five times our money on those options, about $25 million apiece, will you?"

"That's amazing, Mr Fleischer, thank you very much; I'm sure Ernesto will be delighted with the final result. I'll tell him the moment he gets back from the meeting."

"Yeah, a good few days work, for sure; I'll await his call as to what he wants done with his share, where to send the money etc., you know."

"Okay, Mr Fleischer, I'll get him to call you shortly."

"Fine, fine, no rush, in his own time, since I know you're all so busy over there," chuckled the American, as he rang off.

'Phew,...... $2.5 million bucks I get out of it; I never thought it would be this good. I'd better write the numbers down before I forget; as if I'd forget anything this big, though!'

Stephen duly wrote out his note to give to his boss when he returned and was looking forward to telling him the good news.

Meanwhile, back in the prestigious meeting room in the Parliament building, things were finally progressing, after some initial reticence on Michael Beauchamp's part, the Chief Constable. To get passed this difficulty, Sir James had to call a short 'time out' with his man and when they were outside the room, the elder Statesman was none too happy with him!

"Look, Michael, it's all very well you questioning various legalities about things, as we go along but we're in a right pickle here on this island. We've had a number of institutions on to us already, asking how long will this thing take to overcome? One or two are known to be making arrangements to move elsewhere, as we speak, thinking we might not be able to retain our reputation, even if we do return to normality fairly quickly."

"I'm just trying to ensure we don't countenance, even unwittingly, any wrong doing on our part, I mean..." Sir James interrupted him,

"You don't seem to have grasped the fact and it is a fact, that this guy and his army, has got us 'by the balls,' Michael and he knows it. Dammit, man, you don't start ducking and diving when you're in that position; he needs only to squeeze a little more and we're done for!"

"Yes, but…" The older man cut across him again,

"And that's without this nuclear bomb threat; I mean, what on earth would happen, if news of that got out, eh? People wouldn't get away from this place fast enough!"

Not yet fully convinced, Michael said,

"I don't really believe they've managed to smuggle a nuclear device onto this island, do you? I mean…"

"They might have done, since we have no security arrangements in place to identify such things, no means of protecting ourselves, do we?… we're still damned well talking about it, on cost grounds, efficacy and all that; well I bet we all wish we had done something about that now!

No, we'll just have to accede to their demands, in as dignified a manner, as possible, I'm afraid and that's all there is to it. If rumours of that bomb start circulating, well, we're history; reputation in business is everything and if you lose it, you're dead; almost as bad as if they have installed one and the damned thing went off."

Not having an immediate answer to that dramatic assertion, the Chief Constable sighed and said,

"Yes, if you put it like that, Sir James, I suppose…"

"Come on, let's get back in there, before the price goes even higher!"

The two Jersey men returned to the discussion table and apologised to Ernesto and Omah for keeping them waiting.

In their absence, Omah had asked his boss whether he thought they were going to change their minds, after earlier agreeing to their demands.

"No, they can't afford to, in my opinion; it's the policemen, Sir James is having trouble with, I'm sure. I mean they need to do everything 'by the book' and when something comes up that's not covered by it, they're flummoxed. They cannot easily move away from their fixed 'mindset' in my experience. So don't worry; let me handle everything, as before."

"Sure, boss, sure, of course," Omah had replied, as the politician and the policeman came back into the room.

"I'm sorry about that, gentlemen, I…eh,..or rather we, I should say, wanted to be assured on one point before we move to wrap everything up to our mutual satisfaction," Sir James enquired, forcing an anxious smile, as he did so,

"What clarification do you seek, Sir James?" asked Ernesto, relaxing a little and inferring the question suggested the momentum was still with the 'away' team.

"The bomb threat: I mean, have you told anybody else about it yet, may I ask?"

"Not yet, Sir James but…" The politician quickly cut across him,

"Not even the Jersey Record, yet?"

"Not even the Jersey Record, so far."

" I ask only because the tacit agreement we've reached so far would be wholly nullified, if you or your people mentioned such a threat existed and as we have reached our, shall we say, our 'accommodation' in a spirit of co-operation for humanitarian purposes, we'd like to keep it that way, of course. Consequently, gentlemen, I have to ask you to promise us that you will not divulge that threat to anyone outside this room. Do you agree?"

"You have my word on it, Sir James," Ernesto replied, adding,

"There are a couple of assurances we need, too, in giving you that peace of mind, though."

"And what are they, Mr Alvarez?" Sir James asked, hesitantly.

The Guatemalan continued, sitting well back in his chair.

"That neither the police, nor the security people here, or those from London will interfere with us, or try to arrest any of us, while we're here and, once the one kilo gold bars are distributed to my people, they will be allowed to leave immediately and the same goes for me and my men. The same freedoms are to be extended to the UK, too. Do you agree?"

"Well, as far as Jersey is concerned, I give you my word, and Michael here will do the same, won't you Mr Beauchamp?" Sir James stopped momentarily to allow his colleague to assent, as well, which he did with a nod of his head.

"However, I cannot, of course, speak for the United Kingdom on such matters…."

Ernesto sat up and leant on the table, as he replied,

"Sir James, need I remind you that disclosing a nuclear bomb risk on Jersey from London, is tantamount to the same as mentioning it here, so I suggest you bring all your persuasive powers to bear upon your friends on the mainland, otherwise…"

"Yes, yes, of course, I quite understand; you can assume that will be the case, since I will speak to the Home Secretary immediately after this meeting."

"Not good enough, Sir James, I'm afraid; there's no point in our arrangements being worked out between us, if you cannot meet one of my most important requirements, beforehand. Surely, you can get their vote by proxy, here and now. We are prepared to wait for it."

"I'll do it right now," replied Sir James, getting out of his chair with a determined expression on his face.

"Eh,..with a tape of the conversation, if you'd be so kind," Alvarez added.

Sir James hesitated at that, with a rather quizzical look on his face.

"I'm happy to trust you, Sir James, since we've now met a couple of times and I believe you to be a man of your word but I don't know this Home Secretary in London, at all, of course…"

The politician acknowledged the point by an understandable but awkward, smile, as he opened the door.

The Chief Constable got out of his chair, at that, too and followed him outside.

Ernesto turned to Omah and said,

"It's better to get these points cleared up before we go any further, don't you think, Omah?" "Yes, good thinking, boss."

Ernesto smiled at his Head of Operations, as he reached forward and helped himself to another, carefully selected, sandwich - a cheese and pickle one, this time.

Chapter Fourteen

Liberation Day.....again!

Almost half an hour passed, before Sir James and Michael Beauchamp returned to rejoin them. The amiable parliamentarian had a beaming expression on his face, as he sat down opposite the pair again. He put a mini-cassette down on the table in front of Ernesto and declared,

"There you are, Mr Alvarez. That will provide you with all the assurance you require," tapping the device with his forefinger.

Ernesto picked it up, held it in the palm of his hand for a few seconds and then looked up and asked him,

"Are you sure?"

"Yes, definitely," Sir James stated, emphatically.

"Well, thank you; I'll take your word for it, Sir James, of course," replied Ernesto, putting the small tape recording into his pocket.

"Right then, gentlemen, let us proceed with the details of, firstly, how all the individual donations might be distributed to your supplicants, shall we say, followed by their departure date from Jersey. After that, perhaps we could agree how and when, you and your colleagues might also bid us farewell. Without sounding rude, the sooner the better for us, as you'll appreciate!"

"Yes, let's do that, then, Sir James," a smiling Alvarez replied.

An hour later, all issues had been agreed between them. It would take a few days to arrange everything but it would be properly organised this time, to minimise disruption of the island and inconvenience to its inhabitants.

There was to be an 'official' ceremony in the Royal Square to distribute the one kilo gold bars to each of the supplicants, in order to ensure all the 'journeymen' benefited from the 'tithe.' Moreover, the Island would be seen by the media to be dispensing its largesse to some of the World's poor, as a magnanimous gesture of the first order, for all nations to emulate, henceforth, it was to be hoped.

The date set for this 'award ceremony' was the 8th May.

After that, Ernesto and his black 'army' would 'ship out' on the three ferries which had brought them over to the Island and the Guatemalan and his cohorts would then fly away to London and Island life would begin to return to normal. Hopefully, rapidly so, although it could never be quite the same place as before, alas.

The next few days, therefore, would involve Ernesto and his acolytes liaising with his 'army' to make ready for the 'great day' in Royal Square and subsequent departure, with minimal upheaval.

In the meantime, the 'home team' would arrange for all the gold bars to be purchased and brought over to the Island, attend to all the ceremony preparations, inform the media etc., and ensure there wasn't any harassment of Ernesto, his associates, or members of the black 'army' prior to the conclusion of these events. They'd also arrange for temporary feeding depots to be set up, along with sanitation facilities and medical stations.

Just before 2 o'clock, Ernesto and Omah arose from their chairs, shook hands with Sir James and Michael Beauchamp and left the building.

As they departed from the meeting room, the elder Statesman turned to his Police Chief and said,
"You know what day it will be when they've finally gone, don't you?"
"Oh, yes, Sir James, it'll be the 9th of May, Liberation Day."
"Yes, it will; the day the Germans left this Island, fifty five years ago to the day; rather ironic, don't you think?"

On the way back to their Hotel, Ernesto ducked into an electrical retailer, catching Omah by surprise, who had to retrace a few steps to rejoin him. He found the leader of the 'Way' at the counter, surveying some electrical goods.

"What do you need, sir, some batteries for your mobile?" Omah enquired of his boss.

"No, no, I want to buy a cassette recorder, so I can listen to this," getting the mini-cassette out of his pocket, adding,

"Apart from establishing, unequivocally, that we have the amnesty from the British Authorities on here, it will also reveal how desperate Sir James was, on behalf of the Jersey Government, to get us off this Island."

The salesman returned to them, showing Ernesto a suitable machine for his consideration. He popped into it the mini-cassette and it fitted perfectly.

"I'll take this, then, thank you very much," the 'Way' leader said to the man, as he put the cash down on the counter for it. A few moments later, the boxed cassette recorder was put into a carrier bag and they walked out of the shop.

Although there were quite a few people about who were staring at them, there was nothing like the crowds jostling them, hitherto and the Hotel Royale was only a few yards further on.

Once back in their room, they played the tape and the three of them sat spell bound listening to it. After twenty minutes, it was abundantly clear Sir James hadn't let them down; the Home Secretary had agreed, unconditionally, to grant them a pardon, if they ever set foot on British soil again.

What was even more revealing was how desperate the Jersey Government was to get that agreement from Whitehall. Sir James was pleading with the Home Secretary not to underestimate the gravity of the situation, as far as the Islanders were concerned.

'A few more days like this, sir and we'll be done for! Our reputation is draining away as we speak. You must accede to their request for an amnesty, as we have done; otherwise, frankly, we've had it!'

There was quite a long pause and then the British Government official agreed to grant what Sir James was virtually begging for,

'Yes, I can quite appreciate your dilemma, Sir James and fully understand the rapidly deteriorating conditions there and, especially so, the reputational risk involved, so I will agree to your request, forthwith.

You may convey that to the people you're negotiating with, ie, that they will not be challenged, still less, apprehended by the British police about this matter, should they decide to return to these shores.'

When the tape ran out, the machine was switched off and they all looked at each other.

Stephen was the first to speak and was visibly animated by it.

"Blimey, we could have taken them for more, substantially more, than we've got out of it, couldn't we? The guy was desperate, almost wetting himself, if he couldn't pull it off, that was obvious from the tape," he declared, looking distinctly disappointed, at the others.

Ernesto got up and moved over to the mini-bar and poured himself a beer. He took a long sip of the drink and then, turning around, said to Stephen,

"What do you mean; we could have got a lot more out of it, for whom? That one kilo bar of gold all the 'journeymen' will receive in a few days time is worth $10,000 or so; that's a massive fortune for them!

Another few bars wouldn't have made the slightest difference to them; just the prospect of breaking free from their wretched existence is all they care about!"

Stephen sat sullenly, looking out of the window.

"Yeah but the guy would have paid almost anything to regain his Island and we could have got some of those gold bars for us, too, quite easily and they would have agreed to that; we had these people over a barrel and he knew it. We could have got a lot more, that's all I'm saying..."

"But, Stephen, the whole point of the exercise was to get this fabulously wealthy enclave to give these poor people just a little of what they've got, just to get them started on a better way of life; not rob these islanders blind, just for the sake of it."

There was a short pause, before Ernesto finished his riposte,

"And, anyway, we're getting paid, quite handsomely, through Arnold's dealings in the gold market for us..." Stephen interrupted him,

"Oh, while you two were away negotiating with Sir James and all, Arnold telephoned to confirm the extent of your profit on the gold trading activities…eh, here you are," Stephen handing Ernesto his note of the figures, Arnold had given him.

Ernesto looked at it and said,

"My! $25million profit we've made apparently; that's extremely good news, eh?" Ernesto exclaimed, looking at Omah, who responded with a big grin and then he looked at Stephen for his reaction but he was still looking out of the window, disconsolately.

"That's $2.5million for you Stephen; we agreed to paying you 10% of any profit; what more do you want for a few weeks work?"

Stephen looked back at his boss in a surly manner, stating,

"We could have had a lot more; not your 'down and outs' but us, that's what I'm saying."

The Guatemalan was now becoming angry with the man.

"Of all of us, Stephen, you have had to do the least work and yet you're the one complaining your reward is not enough.

If you knew how much I've put into this project, not only money but planning, arranging this and that, going here and there, just to get this thing into being and all I want is just a modicum of justice for these people, that's all…"

The ex-marine cut across him again, still 'sore' about their efforts,

"Well, we could have all got more out of it, though, couldn't we? A lot more for ourselves; Jersey's hugely prosperous and they would have paid up, that's for sure."

There was another pause before the 'Way' leader spoke again,

"Your heart's in the wrong place, my friend; you've got $2.5million coming to you and all you want is more. There'll be no satisfying you…"

"Look, Ernesto, I'm not a wealthy bloke like you, I mean…" Omah interjected this time,

"But, Stephen, you're now a millionaire…."

"Shut up, Omah, this doesn't concern you…"

"But it does concern *me,* my friend, I have to tell you," Ernesto stated, flatly, adding,

"Those whose sole concern is enriching themselves, at the expense of others, or even regardless of those around them, are pitiful human beings…"

"Oh, we're going to be lectured now are we? Money is the root of all evil and all that, eh?" retorted Stephen, moving up to the mini-bar to get himself a beer.

Ernesto thought, momentarily, that the burly ex-marine was going to threaten him but he simply moved aside, so his aide could get his drink.

"It isn't money that is the root of all evil, since the stuff is inanimate; it is the **love** of money that's the root of all evil. That's the problem, my friend."

"Are we through with all the moralising, yet?" Stephen asked, facetiously, adding,

"Only, I was worried there for a moment, that you might ask me for a donation from my share of the profits made, to help your precious 'down and outs' and I'm glad you didn't."

"They're not 'down and outs' or tramps, as you seem to think, they're genuinely poor people who work damned hard to scratch a living for themselves and their families. They work a hell of a lot harder than you, my friend, that's for sure and get precious little reward for it all. Until now, that is, I'm pleased to say and unlike you, they'll be eternally grateful for what they receive from this project."

Omah, who'd sat passively throughout most of this argument, noticed how Ernesto was now referring to Stephen as 'my friend' all the time.

Not using his name at all - this was an ominous sign; he knew his boss and his demeanour extremely well, whereas Stephen didn't or wasn't bothered, given the mood he was in.

'Our military friend needs to be careful, if he carries on like this, I think,' Omah thought to himself.

In an effort to diffuse the situation, the Head of Operations, stood up and declared,

"Well, who's for a late lunch, then? I'm starving, even if you're not. Ernesto shall we try downstairs or outside, or call room service?"

The Guatemalan put his empty beer bottle down on the coffee table and said to his deputy,

"Let's try outside for a change; it wasn't too crowded, earlier. Are you coming along, or do you want to stay inside? Alvarez asked his truculent 'minder.'

'*Still no name at all,*' Omah observed again, as Carvell got up and replied,

"Yeah, okay, might as well; being cooped up in here is beginning to get to me, I think."

Ernesto held the door open for the Englishman and as he walked through, he followed him, looking at Omah; he was angry, very angry with the man, that was plain to see!

Outside, they walked along the front, with the sunshine and the modest number of people about, making for an enjoyable stroll. They spotted a hamburger parlour a few yards further on and went inside.

As they settled down to enjoy their burgers and French Fries, Ernesto received a call on his mobile from the Jersey Record Journalist, asking him if there were any further developments to report? He referred him to Sir James, who'd bring him up to date, for sure.

Afterwards, Alvarez and Omah decided to walk the couple of miles to where his people were encamped on St Aubin's beach. Stephen, though, declined to go with them, preferring to 'hold the fort' back in their hotel room.

As the leader of the 'Enlightened Way' and his deputy strolled along the front, Ernesto expressed his annoyance over Carvell's attitude, especially his preoccupation with money and his concern that he probably wasn't a suitable character to be involved in all this. Something needed to be done about it, too, Ernesto told his deputy, with a set expression on his face.

As they approached the far end of St Aubin's beach, the contingent of the black 'army' that was encamped there, began to get to its feet and a growing cheer was heard. 'Red' cap approached him, with a big smile, smart salute and warm handshake. Many of them surrounded the pair within seconds, all jostling to show their appreciation.

Ernesto gestured to all of them to relax and sit down again, as 'Red' cap turned about and barked out a stream of orders to the same effect.

Their ready compliance would have met with approval from any rigorous Sergeant Major in the British Army!

Alvarez took 'Red' cap to one side and explained to him the agreement that had been reached with the Jersey Authorities, the anticipated arrival of the bullion plane in a day or two and the distribution ceremony to be held in the Royal Square on the 8th of May.

They were all to assemble on the beach the following morning, around 9 o'clock, to re - board the ferries and start their journey home. In the meanwhile, the 'army' was to continue quietly occupying this part of the beach, in the exemplary manner displayed so far and wait patiently for the distribution ceremony on the eighth - just a few days hence.

They then walked along the south coast road to the next beach, St Brelade's Bay, which was a couple of miles further on and received a similar reaction from their 'journeymen' encamped there.

Ernesto relayed the same message to Mr 'Orange,' the senior 'cap,' for this contingent but told him to move his people around the south west corner of the Island to link up with the division at St Ouen's Bay.
The beach there was much bigger and even the combined grouping could be easily accommodated.

Finally, Alvarez and Djesturi continued on towards the encampment on St Ouen's beach, close to the Airport.

The senior man told Mr 'Yellow' stationed there, what was envisaged over the next few days, informed him that the St Brelade's people were coming along to join his group and they were all to congregate down on the beach.

Vacating the airport was necessary to allow the bullion plane to land soon and enable the Island to start functioning again. This had been agreed with Sir James at their recent meeting, as a 'goodwill' gesture, by the leader of the 'Way.'

Meanwhile, back in Room 410 at the Hotel Royale, Stephen Carvell was on the 'phone to Arnold Fleischer. Fearing he might be asked by

Ernesto to make a 'donation' to his 'down and outs' before too long or ask Arnold to deduct such a sum from his share of the gold dealing profits, he wanted to make sure the money due to him was despatched to his bank, without delay.

Arnold was not prepared to do this without Ernesto's permission beforehand. Moreover, as he didn't know what percentage of the money was due to him, apart from Stephen's word for it, that it was 10% of Ernesto's share applicable to him, he couldn't oblige him at this early stage. He'd have to get Ernesto to call him to sanction it.

At this, Stephen terminated the conversation by banging the telephone down. Arnold was concerned about this development; not so much about Stephen's rudeness, nor his haste in trying to get paid out first. It was the reason the man wanted to do so, that really intrigued him.

Was Ernesto beginning to lean on him for a 'donation,' despite him being one of his own men? Now that this Stephen Carvell character was worth a couple of million dollars, did that automatically elevate him into the realm of a target donor? And if it did, with him having only $2.5million to speak of, why not a much wealthier accomplice, like himself?

This possibility troubled Arnold a great deal. It stirred the anxieties he'd felt about this fellow when he first met him. He was sitting in his library, with such thoughts running through his mind, when he looked up at the photo he'd taken of Alvarez, sitting atop his Grand Piano.
'Hmm..., that picture might yet prove its worth; you never know!'

The next few days saw Ernesto, Omah and Stephen visiting the 'troops' at the three location points on the Island. Everybody was now 'up to speed' with the forthcoming ceremony and departure arrangements early the following morning, on the 9th May.

After lunch, on the day before the 'Great Event' to be held in the Royal Square, Ernesto sent Stephen off to check that all the arrangements for it were progressing satisfactorily.

While he was absent, the leader of the 'Way' remembered he hadn't spoken to his cohort in Managua for a while and he wanted to tell him that their quest was close to fruition. It was then that he learnt of Stephen's call to Arnold a few days earlier. The American was happy to pay the man out but needed Ernesto's agreement to do so beforehand, of course.

"Nobody gets paid ahead of us, Arnold; we set all this up a while ago and I'll come over to see you soon and we'll supervise the payouts, then, okay?"

"Sure, sure, Ernesto; that's fine by me. I'll look forward to seeing you soon and let me know when you're due in and I'll arrange for the transport again, alright?"

"Thanks, Arnold, I'll do that -'bye," and he put the 'phone down.

To say Alvarez was stunned by this revelation was a major understatement! Omah had never seen such a look on the Guatemalan's face before and he knew it meant trouble, big trouble, for the mercenary, especially after his boss turned to him and said,

"Omah, this is just too much; the man will have to forfeit everything and I mean everything!"

A few minutes after that telephone call, Stephen breezed back into the room and Ernesto's expression changed in an instant.

"Well, how is it over there, Stephen - all on schedule?"

"Yep, it's all going according to plan, apparently."

"Good, good, that's encouraging news, don't you think, Omah?"

"Yes, that's great to hear, as you say, boss" Omah replied, noting that Ernesto was now addressing Stephen by his first name again.

Not, though, as a 'coming in from the cold' welcome, as Stephen must have assumed, if he'd been bothered at all but a definite *'lulling the man into a false sense of security' tactic,* he felt. He was right.

In the late afternoon, Ernesto got a 'phone call from Mr 'Yellow' on the St Ouen's beach, informing him that a B.A. 737 cargo plane had just touched down at the airport and judging by all the activity around it, it must be the bullion flight. It was.

An hour later, Ernesto was out on his balcony with his binoculars and spotted a small convoy of two armoured security trucks, surrounded by police outriders. They were in front of the leading vehicle and alongside the pair of them, with two police cars at the rear, cruising along the main road into St Helier. The traffic dutifully gave way to the official motorcade, with blue lights flashing and sirens blaring, as it passed along the main thoroughfare into town.

The Guatemalan lowered his binoculars and turned back from the balcony and walked into their hotel room, declaring to his henchmen,

"Hear that, Gentlemen? That's six tons of pure gold passing by; a tithe from Croesus, a compassionate gesture, to assist the helpless and aid the poor. Now that is something to behold, eh?"

Omah beamed at his boss and even Stephen managed to force a smile, of sorts, although he was clearly still pondering what might have been!

"Come on, Stephen, cheer up and know you've done something good for once; something you can be justly proud of!" exhorted Ernesto.

Stephen got out of his chair, still not convinced and moved towards the mini-bar to get another drink, saying,

"If you say so, boss."

Ernesto looked back at Omah again, obviously disillusioned with the response.

The following morning, Ernesto and his cohorts woke up early on this important day - 'Distribution Day' - the 8th May 2000. The leader of 'The Enlightened Way' pulled apart the heavy curtains in their room, as Stephen joined them from next door. The early morning sun filled the room; there wasn't a cloud to be seen, which augured well for the day ahead.

After breakfast, Alvarez received a telephone call from Sir James, just confirming the itinerary for the forthcoming ceremony to be held in the Royal Square. The official presentation of Jersey's 'Maundy Money' equivalent to the needy, the 1 kg gold bar, equating to 32.15 ozs of pure gold, was set for 3pm that afternoon.

A dozen dignitaries, representing the Island's twelve parishes, would hand one of the gold bars to each of the supplicants, as they presented themselves for a share of Jersey's largesse. It was anticipated the award ceremony would take about three hours to complete.

After several 'phone calls to his 'caps' in charge of the black 'army' and a good lunch, the three ringleaders set off for the Royal Square, shortly after 2.00pm.

A large crowd had again gathered outside their hotel but it seemed to be generally good natured, or at least, not so hostile, this time. Their police escort moved along the Promenade with them towards the centre of the town, with little jostling in evidence.

As they approached Royal Square, the trio noticed the modest crowds already there were largely confined to the sides of the quadrangle, behind two rows of barricades. Everything had been properly planned this time; that was self-evident.

Two police officers pulled away a couple of the barriers to allow them to pass through to the centre of the arena. As soon as they had done so, the steel hurdles were quickly brought together again behind them.

At the foot of the steps to the Parliament building was a long dais, draped in a maroon material, which wafted gently in the breeze of the afternoon. Behind this were about a dozen security guards, keeping a close eye on what lay at their feet; sixty five wooden boxes, each containing one hundred of the I kg gold bars.

As he neared the steps to the building, Ernesto noticed a tramp huddled in the corner of an entrance to a jewellers shop, obviously closed for the afternoon. He was clearly a 'down and out' and seemed to be oblivious to his surroundings and what was soon to be taking place.

His belongings consisted solely of a plastic carrier bag, which was gathered tightly to him.

'How incongruous is that?' Ernesto thought to himself, taking a moment to pause at the contrasting spectacle.

'That poor fellow is sitting only a couple of feet away from very expensive items of adornment, gems worth thousands, no doubt, separated from him by a thin pane of glass. Moreover, only fifty yards away, lies more than six tons of pure gold, worth around £43 million; I wonder how he'd react to that, if only he knew!'

Alvarez and his acolytes moved up the steps to be greeted by Sir James Le Marchant, once more. After the exchange of pleasantries, they were introduced to the other 'worthies' most of whom smiled, some awkwardly so and a couple were clearly not enamoured by the situation at all.

Just before 2.30pm there was that hum in the air again, as the sound of tramping feet was heard, softly at first and then growing louder. The black 'army' of journeymen was approaching the Square from the west, marching proudly along the Promenade, without song or speech; the only sound was the melodic 'beat' of marching feet.

The column, consisting of the three beach contingents, was six thousand five hundred men strong and was a mile long. The men, four abreast, marched into the square once again, filing in behind each other, to fill the quadrangle to capacity.

As the last men completed the exercise, a single command from 'Red' cap brought the stomping to a halt and with a military 'stand at ease' order from him, the area fell silent, apart from a rush towards the front steps by the media, for the best viewing positions. It was 3.05pm.

After a short speech of welcome from the elder Statesman, which was accompanied by a battery of cameras clicking and whirring, Ernesto Alvarez was invited to say a few words into the array of microphones on the rostrum. Sir James had to lean forward and call for order, asking for the cat-callers and those intent on jeering to "give the man a chance to speak, to have his say, Ladies and Gentlemen, please; this is not the Jersey way, as you all know."

When the dissent finally fell away, Ernesto opened his address to the Islanders.
"Thank you, thank you very much….Eh, Sir James, parish leaders and to all the good people of Jersey, this is, I tell you now, one of the most important and memorable days in your Island's illustrious history. I say this because….."

The Guatemalan spoke very eloquently and movingly for just over ten minutes to the people who'd congregated in the Square below him. There was silence throughout his short message to them and then when he closed his speech with the upbeat declaration of:-

"And as we all know, God loves those who happily give to others so, my friends, feel his blessing upon you, mirrored in the faces of those who are about to receive your helping hand to them!"

Any doubters or dissenters after that poignant delivery were totally drowned out by the thunderous applause of the crowd. Ernesto waved and muttered softly into the bank of microphones,

"Thank you, thank you again, so much and I salute you, you, the good people of Jersey for your generosity being shown today!"

Ernesto turned away and took a few steps back, enabling Sir James to regain the rostrum and announce to the crowd that the distribution of their gifts would now begin.

At that, six pairs of security guards man-handled half a dozen of the wooden boxes, each containing one hundred of the I Kg bars and weighing some 220 lbs, onto the dais. They were then opened and the contents spread out along the table. Behind each grouping of 100 of the gold bars, stood two of the 'worthies' who would take it in turn to distribute one 'brick' to each member of the 'army' who came up to him.

This carried on for approximately three hours, during which time some background music, by a military band, was played, intermittently.

In the heat of the afternoon sun, many people in the crowd drifted away, being partially replaced by others. Members of the band were also relieved by others, during several of their break periods.

At 6.10pm, the ceremony was all but concluded, with the last member of the black 'army' gratefully receiving his golden gift from the Island of Jersey.

Ernesto noticed, though, as did others, that there was one gleaming bar of the yellow metal left over for some reason. Had the bullion company over delivered by one brick? *'Unlikely, that,'* most of them on the dais must have thought: more likely there were only 6499 'soldiers' who'd come along for the epic journey.

Ernesto stepped forward, picked it up, turned and said to Stephen, "You always wanted one of these, no?" He gave it to him, adding, "You told me you were a poor man, didn't you, Stephen?"

The Guatemalan looked at his greedy 'minder,' seeing him wrestle with himself, as to whether he could get away with holding the heavy, 2.20lbs gold brick in his hand, without pocketing it.

Stephen was conscious of all the 'worthies' looking at him, as they held their breath. They looked aghast, as the burly, ex-marine, clutched it firmly, saying,

"Well, cheers, boss…"

But Ernesto stopped him, gripping his wrist tightly, and replied,

"I was only joking, of course, my friend…You see that man over there?"

"Which man, where?"

Although the people in the Square were drifting away, a good number had spotted the contretemps on the stage and the snap-shot cameras were still clicking and the movie cameras were still whirring, as the drama unfolded.

"That one over there, the one slumped down in the doorway of the jewellers," Ernesto continued, looking in the direction of the expensive establishment.

"You mean that old tramp over there?" Stephen now locating the figure his boss was referring to.

"Yes, that's right, him - he looks very much like one of your 'down and outs' wouldn't you say?"

"Yeah, but…" Alvarez interrupted him,

"Why don't you do something really worthwhile, especially on a day like this? Go over there and give the brick to him. It will give him tremendous hope, given his miserable state. He'll have something really tangible to hang onto and it could well change the rest of his life…unlike yours, my friend."

Stephen now felt distinctly uncomfortable and embarrassed.

Everyone on the stage and those below were looking at him. He had no other choice.

"Okay, boss, good idea; I didn't see him over there, sitting in the corner of the entrance to the shop."

His move down the steps was followed by a million eyes, it seemed. When he got to the unfortunate, the man slowly rose to his feet and was naturally stunned by what the 'heavy' was saying to him.

When Stephen finally handed him the gold object, glinting in the sunlight, the look of disbelief on the man's face was beyond description!

He looked over Stephen's shoulder towards all those on the stage and waved, wildly, at them. The 'windfall' was safely stowed away in the plastic carrier bag and he went around the corner, with a visible spring in his step!

When he got back to the stage, even Stephen had a smile on his face, as he acknowledged, with a wave of his hand, the rapturous applause from those on the dais and from the Square below.

"What did you say to him, then?" Ernesto asked,
"I told him what was happening over here and said here's a gold bar for you, old man. He looked at it in amazement, asked me how much it was worth and I told him, about six thousand five hundred quid. His jaw dropped and he shouted and waved, put it in his bag and legged it round the corner!" Everybody laughed at that.

"Another good deed done today, I think, Gentlemen; what a tremendous day it's been for all concerned, don't you think?" Ernesto intoned.
"I quite agree, Mr Alvarez, I think we've all learnt a lot today," replied Sir James, looking around at the others alongside him for approval, which he got from a unanimous nod of heads.

"Come, Gentlemen, they've laid on some tea for us all; I'm sure we could all do with something to eat after all this, eh?" Sir James told the group on the dais.

He turned to the, now rapidly dispersing, crowd in the Square, waved one final time and led the party back into the Parliament building.

They trio got back to the Hotel Royale around 10 pm, with the 'tea' proving to be a good deal more substantial a meal, than envisaged!

Moreover, the conversation was quite cordial, too, which materially aided enjoyment for all concerned.

Sir James seemed to have convinced the remaining doubters that, although the experience was undoubtedly costly for them, given the 'Rainy Day' Fund had been seriously depleted, there were two major 'plusses' to be borne in mind, too.

The first was, undoubtedly, the beneficial media coverage of the event. The Island was being portrayed in a particularly favourable light and was likely to continue 'basking' in such good publicity, for a few weeks, yet. And on an international basis, as well, by all accounts.

"Tourism should receive a huge boost from all this, for quite some time and the benefit of that to the Island's economy shouldn't be underestimated; it should go a long way in offsetting the 'hit' to the 'Rainy Day' Fund, in the long run, I think," affirmed the politician.

"The other, less tangible, benefit, was the lesson to be learned from all this," he told them.
"The World today is much changed from that of even a decade ago and we need to 'get with it' gentlemen."

When asked to qualify what he meant by that, he looked sternly at the questioner and said,
"There are so many threats out there to a Society like ours and we need to defend ourselves, accordingly. Recent events indicate how vulnerable we are and we need to do something about it and fast! Otherwise, it might happen again, or something similar. Maybe, we were just lucky this time!"

Sir James turned to Ernesto, asking him the $64,000 question,
"So tell us, Mr Alvarez, now all the 'donations' have been distributed to the poor, is there a nuclear device on this Island?"

The 'Way' leader paused for a moment and then simply said, "You'll know tomorrow, gentlemen, I promise you."

Chapter Fifteen

If you play with fire, expect.....

After an exhausting but highly productive day, the Guatemalan and his two cohorts turned in soon after getting back to their rooms in Jersey's Hotel Royale. They knew the next day was going to see the zenith of their efforts and rising early was essential.

Ernesto and Omah awoke just before 6 am and twenty minutes later, Stephen Carvell joined them in Room 410. They had an early breakfast and left the room at 7 o'clock.

As before, the police escorted the trio, once outside the hotel but this time, to the ferry port, where the ferries were to embark with the journeymen back to Agadir, rather than uplift them from the beaches.

This had been arranged with the Port Authorities for safety reasons and the area was closed to normal and commercial traffic until noon. Such arrangements would also facilitate better media coverage, since an official 'send off' would best suit the Island's 'image' it was thought.

It was misty and overcast that morning, with gathering clouds on the horizon threatening a thunderstorm at some stage.

Most of the black 'army' was already lined up on the dockside, with much chattering going on. The obvious talking point was the sudden wealth each had come into and what plans were afoot once they got home.

Ernesto and his 'lieutenants' arrived on the scene, passing a continuous line of journeymen marching towards the embarkation point.

Once the trio were spotted, there was a tremendous roar from the 'army' and Ernesto acknowledged the sea of black, smiling, faces all cheering him, with several waves to them.

He was then greeted by Sir James and a couple of the 'worthies' who'd been on the platform with him at yesterday's ceremony.

"Good Morning, Mr Alvarez, it's just as well we all made an early start, don't you think?" Sir James said, chirpily, looking around at the growing congestion on the quayside as it began to lightly rain.

"Yes, certainly," agreed Ernesto, adding,

"It's a massive turnout by the 'locals' as well as the media, by the look of it," as he surveyed the scene, as well.

A loud blast of the horn from the Makmar Empress made them jump. It signalled the huge car ferry was now ready to take passengers on board and the front ranks of the 'army' started to shuffle forward.

"Shall we go inside, do you think?" Sir James suggested, just as the drizzle started to intensify.

"We can watch and oversee everything from there," he said, pointing to the Harbour Master's office, a few yards further on.

"Yes, good idea," replied Ernesto and they all followed him.

By 9 o'clock, the Makmar Empress had left the port with its cargo of twenty three hundred 'soldiers' and the Makmar Queen had replaced the vessel and was soon taking on board another 2200 odd journeymen.

Around 10.30 am she, too, was leaving the harbour with some two thousand men aboard, destined for the Algerian port and the Makmar Princess began manoeuvring to take her place.

An hour and a half after that, the last of the ferries had collected the remaining two thousand journeymen and Ernesto was waving his final farewell to them.

The last of the trio blew two long blasts on its whistle, as it negotiated the exit from the harbour and twenty minutes later, she was well out to sea, trailing her sister ships in a south westerly, direction towards Agadir.

By 1pm, they were out of sight and the clouds were quite dark now and a thunderstorm threatened.

Sir James turned around to face the man standing next to him, and ask him ***that*** question again,

"Well, Mr Alvarez, was there ever one smuggled onto our Island?"

"One what, Sir James?" The Guatemalan replied, tantalisingly.

"A nuclear dev….."

In that instant, a massive thunderclap cut him short, making them both jump. Ernesto fleetingly saw a look of horror on the old man's face, as he sank to his knees, tearing away the breast pocket of the Guatemalan's jacket, to steady himself. Ernesto helped the old boy up, saying,

"It's alright, Sir James; I doubt if you'd have heard the thunder afterwards, listen."

Never before had that rumble sounded so pleasant and reassuring to him. The terrified look on his face gave way to a much relieved expression, as he got to his feet.

"Some wake up call, that, I must say, eh?" Ernesto quipped.

"Well? Well?!" Sir James insisted, as he steadied himself.

The rain was now teeming down outside but above the noise of it, Ernesto replied,

"No, Sir James…there was never a device brought into Jersey, in the event; I just had to keep you focussed on the 'donations' we were seeking for all those poor people. Their continuing presence would have ruined you all anyway, if you hadn't have bought them off, you know that, don't you?"

"Yes, I did recognise that prospect all too well, I have to say."

Ernesto nodded, adding a cautionary note,

"But the threat of someone trying to really blackmail you on this Island remains a real one, in my opinion. We could have brought one in, quite easily, from what we saw of your woeful security arrangements, though and you need to be mindful of that in the future, I'd suggest."

Sir James, now fully recovered, shook Ernesto's hand and apologised for tearing his jacket pocket. Alvarez thought nothing of it, though and so he enquired about his flight time later that afternoon,

"We depart this lovely Island of yours at 3.30pm; I'm sure you'll be pleased to see us leave at last."

"Well, I,..eh," Ernesto interrupted him,

"Remember the Scouts' motto for the future and you'll be safer for it, I'm sure."

"What is it?...I was never in the Scouts, as a lad."

"Look it up on the internet, after we've gone: If you remember to do that, you'll remember the motto and it'll be worth it, for sure!"

The three visitors flew out of the Island on time and Sir James watched their departure on television, as most of the Islanders must have done, breathing a heavy sigh of relief, as the Boeing 737 disappeared from view.

The old boy remembered his adversary's parting shot to him, though and going 'online,' he punched into a search engine, 'Scouts' Association.' And there it was; their motto - 'Be prepared.'

'That is good advice, very good advice; I'll remember that and make sure the others do, when I'm next in the House,' the elder Statesman thought to himself, as he 'logged off' from the net and poured himself another cup of tea.

Ernesto Alvarez, Omah Djesturi and Stephen Carvell, got through customs at Heathrow, without difficulty, not noticing the officer on the desk had nodded to a large mirror on the wall some twenty feet away. This was a one-way mirror and another officer, seated at a desk behind it, duly noted their arrival.

They got back to Stephen's flat in the Bayswater road shortly after 6.30pm.

As it was a humid evening, they took off their jackets upon arrival and sat down in the lounge to discuss the overall situation. Stephen volunteered to make a pot of coffee and while he was attending to this in the kitchen, one of their mobile 'phones rang.

Ernesto got up to see if it was his, which he'd left in his jacket pocket. He removed the other jackets from the coat rack to get to his and Stephen's slipped off onto the wooden floor, with a resounding 'clunk.'

He got to his mobile and answered it. As he recognised the American voice on the line and started to respond to the caller, he picked up Stephen's jacket to put it back on the coat rack. As he did so, a heavy, gleaming, object fell out of a pocket and crashed back onto the floor.

Ernesto was stunned at what he saw. Omah also looked aghast at what had fallen to the floor with such a thud.

"Eh….Arnold….eh, can I call you back later on?"
"Yeah, sure, no problem; I'm in for most of the afternoon, so get back to me when you're ready, okay?"
"Yes, I'll do that, Arnold, thanks -'bye," replied Ernesto, slowly clicking off, quite mesmerised by what was at his feet.

Still transfixed, he bent down and picked up the object and placed it carefully onto the coffee table in the middle of the room. Omah was still open-mouthed by the sight of it, too, as Ernesto said,
"I don't believe it….I just don't believe it!"

At that moment, Stephen breezed back into the room from the kitchen, with the coffee and biscuits for them on a tray. He immediately saw what was lying on the coffee table, still the centre of attention between Ernesto and Omah and thought to himself,
'Oh, shit,' as he strolled up to them and distributed the fare onto the table, waiting for the outburst from them. It duly arrived.

"And what the hell is this, Stephen?" Ernesto asked him, picking up the 1 Kg gold bar and staring angrily at him. The Guatemalan already knew the answer to his rhetorical question, sadly, so he followed up with,
"You never gave this to the tramp in the Square, did you? Why not? Why didn't you, Stephen?"
"We all saw you give the man the gold bar!" Omah chipped in.

Stephen sat down and started to pour out the coffees for them.

"No, you saw me give the wretched fellow my gold-plated cigarette case; even that would glint in the sunlight, Omah," the ex-marine stated, nonchalantly, with a smirk on his face, as he looked up at him.

"I'm still waiting for an explanation, Stephen!" demanded Ernesto.

Carvell looked up at the 'Way' leader, picked up a cup of coffee, took a sip of it and sat back in his chair. He then responded, condescendingly,

"What would a 'drop out' like him do with £6,500 eh? He'd have spent it on drugs or booze; they're invariably alcoholics, those people, aren't they? They've given up on life in the conventional sense and simply rely on hand-outs from those around them," declared his 'minder'.

His derisive remarks continued, as the other two looked at each other, in disbelief at what they were hearing.

"They're a drain on Society, since they never do any work, don't pay taxes and scrounge all the time. Unlike your journeymen, I have to admit; at least they work damned hard and get little reward for it. Theirs is a much more deserving case, Ernesto; I'd have to admit to that."

Ernesto was still speechless at his outrageous remarks. Omah chipped in again,

"But he jumped up and waved excitedly to us all, after you gave him the gold bar, or so we thought..."

"I told him those people on the dais over there wanted you to have this gold cigarette case. He didn't understand, at first but then I told him he'd have to jump up and wave at them, enthusiastically and then beat it around the corner, otherwise, I'd be after him! He did rather well, I thought!"

Ernesto finally responded to his 'minder.'

"I've known some evil people in my time, Stephen, let me tell you but I've never come across anything as shameful as that. Even Ronaldo Martin wouldn't have stooped as low. Your *love* of money will be the death of you, my friend. I have nothing more to say."

"What do you mean? Is that a threat? Are you threatening me, Ernesto?" The burly 'minder' stood up, as the Guatemalan sat down, picking up his cup of coffee and looking into it, replied softly,

"I have nothing more to say."

Omah knew that Stephen had signed his own 'death warrant' twice over by this latest revelation and it would now be only a matter of time.......

Half an hour later, Ernesto remembered to get back to Arnold in Managua.

"I must return Arnold's call," he said to Omah, ignoring Stephen as he'd done so for the past thirty minutes. He got through swiftly, saying,

"Oh, hello, Arnold; sorry for the delay in getting back to you."

After a short pause, Ernesto spoke again,

"No, no, it's alright…nothing I can't handle."

The conversation continued for another quarter of an hour or so, as Alvarez appraised his gold - dealer of the successful outcome of their experiences in Jersey. He finished off by telling the American he'd fly over to see him again in a few days and promised to let him know the flight details shortly.

He then turned to his comrades and said,

"You two can stay here while I'm away and…." but Stephen interrupted him,

"I'll go with you, too, as you'll need a 'minder' as well, you know, just in case….." Ernesto raised an eyebrow but chose not to make an issue of it,

"Very well, Omah, you should stay here in that case and hold the fort."

"If that's what you want boss?"

"It is, yes."

"Fine, then, I'll stay here and let you know if anything crops up this end, alright?" Ernesto nodded his acknowledgement.

The next couple of days involved the Guatemalan ringing a number of his contacts to let them know about the successful Jersey project, including Stelios Makarios, the Greek shipping magnate, in Piraeus.

He'd been questioned by the Police over there about his ferries being used in the Jersey escapade, apparently. However, having persuaded the Greek Authorities, that his ships were obviously hijacked by this Alvarez character, after he'd leased them to him and he was delighted to get them back again, they believed him.

"I have no case to answer, they told me!" roared Stelios, down the line.

"That's a relief, then, Stelios; I wouldn't have wanted you to get into any trouble over this." Ernesto replied to his jaunty friend.

"No, no, everything's fine over here; we all watched the news reports about it, on TV and we were all cheering you on. You must have heard us, no?!" They both laughed at that.

Finally, when he was alone, he 'phoned the leader of his 'hit' squad, who'd liquidated Ronaldo Martin for him, while he was addressing the crowds in Jersey's Royal Square.

Having brought him up to date, too, with the success of it all, he then lowered his voice as he got on to the final topic - another job for his trusty field commander. He got his response in the affirmative, at the end of the call.

Ernesto and his 'minder,' Stephen Carvell, flew out to Managua on the 18th May. Their plane touched down shortly after 4 o'clock in the afternoon and after passing through customs, without difficulty, they stood outside the airport building. It was raining quite hard but they hadn't long been under the canopy affording them some shelter from the storm, when Ernesto spotted a 'red' pennant, weaving its way through the heavy traffic.

A few moments later, the two-tone, blue, Buick drew up at the kerb alongside them.

"This is ours, I think," said Ernesto, as the front passenger got out of the car and stated,

"Mr Ravel, isn't it?"

"Yes, that's right; nice to see you again, Gentlemen."

Arnold Fleischer's 'flunky' nodded and then opened the near side rear door of the car for them and they got in. He returned to the front passenger seat and closed the door.

They moved off into the heavy traffic but it began to thin out as they sped through the poor part of town, towards central, the more affluent part of Managua.

Twenty minutes later, they were up into the hills overlooking the Nicaraguan Capital. Despite the bumpy ride along the partially made up roads, the passengers marvelled at the wonderful panorama below them. Although Ernesto had seen the view before, he was still captivated by it.

As the rain stopped, the sedan lurched off the 'main road' and along a side road, which gave the suspension a real test, again. The route was now relatively familiar to Ernesto and he quite looked forward to seeing his overweight, finance man, once more.

The car swept past the two iron gates fronting Arnold's substantial property, along the tarmac drive and up to the steps of the impressive building.

The man in the front passenger seat jumped out and opened the rear door for the Guatemalan and his 'minder.' Once out of the car, the four of them walked up the steps, as the two guards on the door moved to either side of it, to let them through onto the portico. Both the 'heavies' eyed Stephen suspiciously.

As before, Salma, Arnold's housekeeper, was on station to open the main door, just as they got to it.

"Ah, Mr Ravel, sir, it is nice to see you again," she said, doing a little curtsy, which Ernesto thought was very sweet.

Having smiled at her courteous greeting, he introduced Stephen as his 'associate' to her and she replied,

"Oh, yes, I see; Mr Fleischer is expecting you, so please come in, gentlemen and follow me."

They walked behind the housekeeper, into the wide hall, turning right into the domed atrium and up the impressive staircase, as previously, as far as Ernesto was concerned.

He sensed Stephen was in awe of what he was seeing; such conspicuous wealth he probably hadn't come across since his days as a bodyguard in the Middle East.

As they got to the huge lounge, a smiling, well dressed, man arose from his chair to greet them.

"Arnold, how are you? It's been a while," said Ernesto, smiling broadly and shaking the American's hand.

"Ernesto, great to see you, too; it seems ages since you were here last, as you say," reciprocating the warm handshake. He continued,

"And who's this?" Arnold asked, looking a little warily at the ex-marine.

"Oh, this is Stephen... Stephen Carvell, my...my..eh., associate."

"Oh, yeah, Mr Carvell, we spoke on the 'phone a couple of weeks back and we got cut off, I seem to recall; nice to meet you, I'm sure," said Arnold, shaking the man's hand, in a perfunctory manner.

"Do come and sit down, gentlemen, please," invited Arnold, as he looked around for Salma, who was standing there behind him, ready to take the drinks order, as usual. She was well used to the routine, of course, although Arnold always seemed a bit uncomfortable without her by his side. She was always, though, unobtrusively, by his side.

After a few minutes, with drinks in their hands, the American invited his South American partner to relay all that had gone on in Jersey to him and he wanted to hear all of it! After that, they'd go into Dinner.

Suddenly, he turned to Stephen and said to him,

"Eh, Stephen...it is Stephen, isn't it? (Arnold deliberately making the 'interloper' be conscious of the distance between them and not waiting for his reply) continued,

"You know all this already, of course, so why don't you have a look around outside, for an hour or so and then come back for Dinner?" Again not waiting for his response, he called out for his trusty housekeeper,

"Salma!" She was by his side in a flash.

"Yes, sir?"

"Oh, there you are...eh Mr ...eh.."

"Carvell, sir," volunteered Stephen, quick off the mark this time.

"Yes, Mr Carvell would like to have a look around the grounds before Dinner, so would you show him to the door and, oh, you might also find him a nice room in the staff quarters, while you're at it, eh?"

"Yes, of course, Mr Fleischer, would you come this way, please, sir?" Salma replied, with a trace of a smile on her face; she also recognised the 'put down,' as did Stephen, as he followed her.

"See you later on, Stephen, okay?" Arnold called after them. Stephen must have heard him but he chose not to respond.

Once out of earshot, the American sat back in his chair and declared,

"I dislike rudeness, especially from a junior member of the team and if he wants accommodation under my roof, then he can stay where he belongs - with the employees!"

Ernesto liked that and replied,

"Yes, it's nice to be free of him for a while; he's only with me for the money, you know, to ensure he gets his share. That's all he cares about. He fears he won't be paid but he will get what's coming to him, of course."

Arnold refreshed their drinks and, being keen to hear all the 'Jersey news' offered the Guatemalan a cigar, which he accepted. Having both lit up, the American said,

"Right, Ernesto, I'm all ears…."

An hour or so later, Ernesto was bringing his summary of the events in Jersey gradually to a close. For most of the time, Arnold sat spellbound listening to the epic tale, only moving a couple of times to refresh their drinks and re-light his cigar.

Salma, the ever vigilant, yet inconspicuous, housekeeper, attended them occasionally to re-charge the coffee pot and, unobtrusively, exchange fresh cups for used, and maintain a steady supply of 'petit fours.'

Just after 7 o'clock, Stephen returned to the spacious lounge to join them again. To minimise any sense of awkwardness the 'minder' might be feeling, Arnold said to him,

"Hi Stephen, did you have a good look around?"

"Yes, sure; it's a very nice place you've got here, I must say."

"Well, thank you; I like it, too. I was just saying to Ernesto that we'll have dinner in half an hour; so would you like a drink beforehand?"

Stephen said that that would be very welcome and after Arnold nodded to Salma, she attended to his request, accordingly.

Towards the end of another of Arnold's sumptuous feasts, Ernesto indicated he'd like to go up North again in the morning, to see his village once more and, more importantly, check on his Mother.

"Okay, that's fine, Ernesto, you can drive up there in one of my cars again, if you like and, in the meantime, I'll draw up all the figures in respect of our gold dealings, so you can see, precisely, the final tally, when you get back. We can then attend to the payouts, with Stephen, here, receiving his 10% cut, at last. I'm sure you'd be in favour, of that, eh?" Arnold stated, with a smile, looking at the ex-marine.

Stephan shifted uneasily in his chair, as he replied,

"Yeah, sounds great, thank you."

"Right gentlemen, as you're up for an early start tomorrow, I think I'll turn in, unless you wish to continue…."

"No, no, I'll retire, too, I think; it's a good idea to be fresh in the morning, don't you agree, Stephen?"

"Yep, that suits me, fine, as well," Carvell replied.

"Until tomorrow, then and sleep well," Arnold said, getting up from his chair, as Salma moved in to show Stephen his room for the night, in the staff quarters and Ernesto, afterwards, to his bedroom.

After breakfast the following morning, Ernesto got permission from Arnold to use the maroon Oldsmobile sedan again; he quite liked the car last time and thought it might be lucky for him, too, after his narrow escape in it, previously!

He found it in one of the garages behind the main house, stowed a hold-all containing a few items in the rear, started her up and drove it around to the front of the house.

Stephen got in beside him and after waving goodbye to the American, saying he'd see him later that evening, they drove away.

Shortly into the journey of some four hundred and fifty miles, Stephen was expressing his annoyance over Arnold's overt snub to him. Ernesto had responded that Arnold didn't know him at all and he was probably a little 'put out' by the earlier request by him to be paid out prematurely.

Since the payout was due to be arranged later that evening, or first thing the following morning, he shouldn't worry any more about it.

Stephen mumbled in acknowledgement, although still a little peeved by Arnold's treatment of him.

Once onto the Inter - American highway, Ernesto picked up the pace to maintain a high cruising speed towards the border.

They crossed into Guatemala at just after 2 o'clock and were on the outskirts of his village, San Luis, forty minutes later. Ernesto slowed down as he drove along the same side street as he'd travelled along a few weeks earlier.

He stopped just short of the corner with the main street, as before and told Stephen to stay in the vehicle to avoid anyone taking a fancy to it. He was going to visit his Mother and would only be twenty minutes or so.

He got out of the car and walked the few yards to the junction. All seemed fairly quiet. Some kids were playing around what was left of the old car wreck opposite him. They didn't seem to have taken any notice of him, nor did the one or two people walking to and fro.

He turned onto the sidewalk, walking as casually as he could to the next junction along and again stopped to assess the environment. There seemed to be a more relaxed atmosphere about the place this time and fewer curtains were drawn, he noticed.

His Mother's place was only fifty yards away on the other side of the street, so he crossed over the road and began walking towards her modest, wooden, property.

The mangy old, ginger, cat was still on the window sill of the shack two doors along from his Mother's house. Although it cowered, ready to spring off the ledge, as he approached its position, it held its ground. A good omen, he thought, as he walked up to his Mother's front door and knocked upon it.

Upon opening the door and recognising her son standing there, the frail old lady threw her arms around him, giving him a big hug and drawing him inside.

"Oh, Ernesto, my son, how are you my boy? Let me have a look at you, then," his Mother said, releasing him, with a beaming smile on her face.
"I'm fine, Mother, fine, thank you; how are you, more to the point?"

"I'm very well, too; it's been much better around here, this past fortnight or so. Come into the kitchen and I'll make us some tea."

Ten minutes later, they were sat around her kitchen table, having a refreshing cup of tea. Both were delighted to see each other; the love between a Mother and her son is the strongest of bonds and that was plain to see.

Ernesto asked his Mother how things had been, since his last visit.

She told him conditions in the village were now much better and especially so since that awful Martin character had been killed and did he know that had happened?

"It happened while you were away, I think, darling, so you might not have heard. Nobody here is saddened by the news, I can tell you!"

"No more visits, then, from those awful men who killed Manuel, you told me about, the last time I was here?"

"No, no, that's what I mean. We all hope they won't come back now, now their boss is no more."

"Well, that's good to know, Mother, I can tell you; I was very concerned about you the last time." His Mother smiled warmly to her son, asking him,

"Have you been up to much since you were last here, Ernesto?"

"Oh, this and that, you know, Mother; I was abroad in Europe for a few weeks and helped with a charitable cash raising effort over there, which was very successful, in the event."

"Ooh, I think somebody told me about that; I think they said they'd seen a picture of you in the paper, or on the television, you know on the news, or something. It made me very proud to hear you were making a name for yourself. My son on the TV, well, well!"

Half an hour later, Ernesto looked at his watch and told his Mother he should go, really, because he had a friend waiting for him in his car down the street.

"Of course, my dear, I quite understand," she said, getting up from the table and putting the tea cups into the sink.

"You take care now, won't you?" She added, smiling concernedly.

He left his Mother, after another big hug and she waved him goodbye, as he walked back along the street, crossed over to the other side and around the corner to his car.

Stephen was tapping his fingers on the dashboard in time with a tune playing on the cars CD player, as Ernesto got back into the driver's seat.

"I thought you were only going to be twenty minutes or so; it's been almost forty five minutes; what took you so long?" Carvell enquired, rather disrespectfully, of his boss.

Alvarez switched off the music, started the engine and turned the car around, as he replied,

"I don't get to see my Mother as often as I'd like and it means a lot to her and to me, too"

"Couldn't you 'phone her, instead of driving the best part of five hundred miles to see the old girl?"

"She's my Mother, not an old girl, Stephen! And anyway, she's not on the telephone; there aren't any cables into the village, yet."

"Well, you could have written a letter to her, then. She can read, can't she?"

"You only have one Mother on this Earth, Stephen and without them, we wouldn't be here….and yes, she can read; she taught me how to, as well, as it happens!"

As the car sped out of the village, little more was said between them.

Thirty minutes later, they had to slow down, owing to some road works being undertaken. Several workers were lounging around a large caterpillar tractor / digger machine, with a huge bucket on the front of it. A sign, indicating a detour to their right, saw them turn off onto a dirt track heading into the hills.

"I didn't see them before, you know, as we came along that road earlier, did you?" Stephen observed.

"No, I didn't either. Perhaps they've just started working; I've no idea where this leads to," Ernesto replied, as the car headed up the side of quite a steep ravine.

A few minutes later, the gradient levelled off and the car picked up some speed, only to come to a sharp bend and an abrupt halt. Around this bend was a gang of armed men, about a dozen in all, some cradling shotguns and others holding Kalashnikov assault rifles.

A cloud of dust overtook the car as it shuddered to a stop, temporarily obscuring the bandits from their view. As it cleared, the menacing group was around them, indicating, with sweeping gestures of their weapons, that they get out of their vehicle. They gingerly did so, neither saying a word to each other, as a dull humming noise was heard in the distance.

They chattered in Spanish and since Ernesto was the only one fluent in the language, he spoke to them.

Stephen Carvell looked anxiously around him, to make an instant assessment of their predicament. *'Twelve, or so, heavily armed, men were confronting them, mostly eyeing him up,'* he thought.

His military training came to him in an instant. *'Without any weaponry ourselves, the only option was to run for it. But where? Continuing up the track they we're on would be arduous and give the gunmen more time to shoot us, certainly. And where would it lead to?*

Straight ahead meant leaping into the unknown; how deep was the ravine they'd journeyed alongside for the past ten minutes? No, if Ernesto can't persuade them to let us go, then the best bet has to be running back the way we came.'

His mind was racing now; survival tactics were kicking in. *'The dirt track led back to the road and would provide a modest safety element, if they could reach it; if not, they could dive off into the bushes, possibly...yes, running downhill was the best bet but what was that noise? It was getting louder, that grinding rumble; whatever it was, it was getting closer, definitely getting closer!'* He thought to himself.

Stephen looked at his boss; *'How was he getting on?'* He wondered.
"How's it going, over there!?" he called out to Ernesto, as his shouting prompted most of the gunmen to greater readiness.

The leader of the 'Way' held up his arm, without turning round to look at him, to quieten him, as he continued talking to one of the bandits. At that moment, the grinding howl reached a crescendo, as the huge, yellow, caterpillar/ digger, machine burst into their clearing from the track leading down to the road.

Stephen noticed only one man was on board the tracked monster, the driver.

'If I can get to that, pull off the guy driving it, raise the bucket to head level to give protection from their fire, I could slam it into reverse and go back down the hill. There's no way they could get us, then!' Stephen calculated. He was right, too, except for one thing; one very important thing. Ernesto was not only in on it, he'd actually arranged the whole event with his field commander. Stephen's end was nigh!

Ernesto Alvarez finally turned around and said, in English, to his, shortly to be, ex-minder,

"Stephen, you shouldn't have taken food out of the mouth of the tramp in Jersey. You denied that poor, poor man, any chance of getting out of the hole he was in. Stealing from anyone is a sin but stealing from anyone much poorer than you is infinitely worse. And to think I'd given the gift to him; you only had to deliver it to him; you stole from him and me and so..."

At this, Stephen knew his time was up and he was about to be executed. He had to get to the digger, by hook or by crook, it was the only chance, however slight the possibility...

As he heard the sound of guns being cocked, he made a dash for the lumbering, yellow, giant. He heard the rat-a-tat-tat of the AK 47's opening up on him and saw numerous spurts of earth in front of him, as he weaved back and forth, getting ever nearer to the mechanical refuge.

The staccato of gunfire seemed endless, with ever more 'pings' of earth spurts around him and he almost got to his quarry, unscathed. Unfortunately, for him, it was truly a case of, *'So near, yet...'* as the saying goes!

He was within ten feet of the huge, tracked vehicle, when a fusillade of rounds hit him from several directions. The bullets spun him around, like a child's top, but he got to the bucket of the digger, somehow, tumbling into it, at last. It started to rise up, he thought and he was right.

Anything to get away from the automatic fire pinging all around him! The metal refuge couldn't have come quicker for him as he looked up at the, still bright, sky.

But then it stopped, the rising scoop, about four feet off the ground, as the shooting ceased, too. He then saw Ernesto looking over the edge of the bucket at him, pistol in hand.

"You had your chance, Stephen; several, in fact but you just couldn't get your mind off money, could you?" I think it's for the best and I'll thank you to think more of my Mother, as you pass over to..."

Two pistol shots rang out as the finale to all the gunfire echoing around the ravine that evening. The huge bucket was raised up to near maximum height on the digger and the tracked monster roared into life. It lumbered forward to the edge of the ravine, stopping a couple of feet from it.

The driver looked towards his leader and Ernesto nodded. At this, the bucket was turned, anti-clockwise, through almost forty five degrees, to empty its contents.

Stephen's corpse tumbled out into space, crashing through numerous shrubs and bushes lining the side of the ravine on its way to the bottom, ending up in the river, some four hundred feet below.

Having peered over the edge at the corpse crashing to the bottom of the valley, Ernesto Alvarez turned back to Emelio, his 'commander,' thanked him for a job well done and returned to his car.

After a smart salute from Emelio, which he acknowledged with a nod, the leader of the 'Way' fired up the Oldsmobile, did a three point turn, narrowly passed the bulldozer /digger, machine and went back the way he'd come.

A few minutes later, he rejoined the main road, smiling as he noticed the 'road works' had been completed, with only a plastic bollard lying on its side, indicating the 'workmen's' presence earlier and he sped off for the border.

Chapter Sixteen

Those who live by the sword......

On his return journey to Arnold's place, Ernesto crossed the border back into Nicaragua and getting rather low on fuel, he decided to 'fill up' at the petrol station he'd visited a few weeks earlier; the one where Ronaldo Martin's men got a right royal soaking.

Having re-fuelled the Oldsmobile, he wandered over to the payment booth and paid for the fill-up with a $50 bill. The young man sitting at the till recognised him.

"Oh, hello, sir, everything alright with you?"

"Yeah, fine and how are things with you, more importantly? The men didn't come back, then?"

"No, not so far, sir; hopefully, they won't!"

"Don't worry; they won't!" Alvarez stated, flatly, to reassure him.

"Goodbye, then."

"Cheerio, sir and thank you."

Ernesto waved to him, as he got back into Arnold's car, started her up and swept out of the forecourt, heading for Managua, whose city lights were now visible in the distance.

He arrived back at the American's luxurious home just after midnight. Having returned the vehicle to the garage at the rear of the property, he walked around to the front steps and the two men at the top stepped aside, having recognised him.

As before, Salma was there to greet him and she told Ernesto that her employer had retired, so he did the same.

The next morning was bright and sunny; the sunlight bursting into Ernesto's room, as he pulled back the heavy drapes. He looked out onto the grounds of the extensive property and beyond to the hills. The early morning mist which often shrouded the hilltops was already dissipating under the warming sun, so he knew this was going to be a fine day.

He recalled the previous evening's execution with modest regret. He disliked having to do such things but was convinced there was no hope for such a greedy and self obsessed man as his former 'minder.' He felt he'd always be trouble for him and for others but not any more!

He heard some activity outside in the corridor, as the household was beginning to stir once again.

He completed his ablutions, got dressed, combed his unruly mop of hair, put on a fresh, white, shirt and blue blazer, with the shirt collar over the jacket and went outside into the corridor.

He was now relatively familiar with the surroundings of his host's house and found the dining room, without difficulty.

Arnold was busily munching away but he got up to greet his house guest,
"Hi, Ernesto, how are you this morning?"
"Fine, fine, thank you," he replied, helping himself to some fruit in a bowl near him and selecting some toast and butter, as he sat down. Salma stood next to him and took his order of scrambled eggs and sausage, with coffee and milk and set off for the kitchen.
"I haven't seen Stephen...eh...what's his name, yet, have you?" Arnold enquired, as he resumed eating his 'Full English.'
"I'm afraid we won't be seeing Stephen anymore; we met some bandits on the road, near the Guatemalan border, yesterday evening. While I was speaking to them, he made a run for it and then he was shot dead."

Arnold's jaw dropped.
"Say that again- Stephen's dead, shot by bandits near the border with Guatemala, you say? Why? What for? I mean..." Ernesto interjected,
"If he hadn't tried to run away, it might have been different; who knows?"

212

"So how did you manage to escape; you know, save your life?" Arnold asked him, still shocked by the news.

"They spoke my language, so I managed to converse with them. I told them I was one of theirs etc., and after Stephen was killed, they let me go."

"Are you going to report it to the Authorities, then?"

"Well, not until I've left here; after all, you don't want the Police crawling all over this place, now do you?"

"Well no, certainly not, that's true, I have to say but what about his things, though?" Arnold enquired, still not having resumed eating his breakfast.

"As the killing took place in the hills…I've no idea where we were…we were diverted off the main road, you see, into the hills, via a fake 'detour' sign and where his body is now, I just don't know."

The big American resumed his breakfast, when Salma returned with Ernesto's scrambled eggs and sausage with coffee order. Having placed the food in front of his guest, she looked across at Arnold, who nodded to her and she left them to it.

After a few minutes, Arnold resumed their conversation,

"It sounds to me, that you had a lucky escape there, my friend."

"Well, yes, I suppose so. He was a very mean and selfish man, though, that's why I don't regret his loss that much, I have to say."

"How so?" Arnold Fleischer asked, now quite intrigued.

Ernesto put down his knife and fork, had a sip of coffee and replied,

"Well, I gave him a spare kilo bar, when we were at the distribution ceremony in Jersey; we found there was one over at the end of it. Well, I'd spied a tramp settled in a shop doorway, obviously out of luck, so I picked up the gold bar and told Stephen to go over and give it to him. He was, after all, just as needy, as the people who were receiving their gifts that day."

"Yes, yes, I'm with you," said Arnold, encouraging the Guatemalan to continue,

"Although he appeared to give the bar to the man, we, Omah and I, that is, subsequently found out that he'd tricked us into thinking he had. He'd given the tramp his gold cigarette case, gold-plated, actually, instead and kept the gold bar for himself."

213

"Wow, what a nerve!" exclaimed the American.

"Well, yes….I mean, he cheated the tramp and us and that's quite unforgivable, in my view! When I tackled him about it, he wasn't bothered at all, saying the tramp wouldn't know what to do with a sum of money like that, whereas, he certainly would!"

Arnold replied, after a short pause,

"I didn't like him, nor his attitude to those around him, as you know but…" Ernesto cut him short at this point,

"He got what he deserved; he cheated us but he couldn't cheat death!"

Arnold was quite taken aback by Ernesto's cold assertion;

'Was there an inference to be drawn here, possibly?' He asked himself. He thought he'd enquire a little more.

"Did you know any of the bandits at all? I mean, if they recognised you that may have been the reason they let you go, do you think?"

"I knew a few of them and I didn't expect them to harm me, for that reason but Stephen got what he deserved, that's for sure," Ernesto replied.

Fleischer thought further about that last remark,

'I heard him use that phrase, 'He got what he deserved' yesterday, didn't I? This fellow exudes a certain menace, in a subtle, cold, sort of way. I need to be still on my guard against him, I reckon.'

Arnold thought he'd persist a little more,

"You didn't ask him for a donation, which he refused to provide, did you, by any chance?"

Ernesto looked up at his host, concernedly,

"Why do you ask that, Arnold?"

The American now sensed he'd put himself on the spot, with the man.

"Well, it's just that some people wind up dead, when they refuse to assist you in your cause; you told me that before, remember? I mean look at what happened to Ronaldo Martin; you had no time for him, because he wouldn't help, as I recall and now Stephen, who's suddenly killed, I mean…"

"Do I frighten you, then, Arnold?"

The American shifted very uneasily in his seat and he began to perspire a little, Ernesto noticed.

"No, no, of course, not; I mean we're friends and business partners after all, are we not?"

Alvarez finished his breakfast and pushed the plates away from him. On cue, Salma then appeared to clear everything away and there was silence between them, as she did so.

After she'd departed, Ernesto resumed the conversation,
"I was thousands of miles away in Jersey when he was killed; you know that, since you watched me on television over there…." Arnold felt strangely emboldened all of a sudden,
"Well, yes, that's true but some people are saying that that was partly staged managed for everybody's benefit, including Ronaldo's, with him being shot after hearing your '*Arrivederci Roma*' gesture to him over the airwaves."
"Oh, that was picked up alright, over here, then?" Ernesto quickly responded, with a wry smile on his face. Arnold retorted,
"Yeah, it sure was, especially as only those who were close to him, or knew him particularly well, knew him by that name."
"Being too close to the man that night must have been very costly for others, too, by all accounts, eh?" quipped Ernesto.
Trying to lighten the atmosphere somewhat, the American replied, with a contrived laugh,
"Yeah, I should say so, too!"
Ernesto smiled obligingly, to lessen the tension, as well.

Arnold got up from the table, wiped his mouth on his serviette and putting it down on the table, said to his guest,
"Well, if you're finished, Ernesto, let's go into the office and take a look at those numbers, I've prepared for us, eh?"
"Good idea, Arnold, let's do that," the Guatemalan replied, leaving the table, too.

In his office, Arnold had all the relevant papers set out for Ernesto's scrutiny. There were three piles of paper on Arnold's desk confronting them. The first, or master schedule, Arnold pointed out to the Guatemalan, summarised their joint trading positions with the overall net profit, shown at the foot of the listing.

Ernesto more than glanced at the important item, the net profit figure of **$51,125,020** overall! Arnold strove to qualify the position,

"That's the aggregate profit, after all deductions, expenses, etc., so, if you look at these other sheets," he said, picking them up off his desk and handing Ernesto one set for him, he added,

"And that's your share; each transaction has been divided equally between us, showing at the bottom, your net profit of **$25,562,510** and I have the same, of course. That's a gain of over 500% on your money; not a bad return over barely ten days, eh?" Arnold said, smiling broadly at his partner in crime!

"That's very good, Arnold and very impressive, I must say," concurred a beaming Alvarez.

"You can keep that copy; it's yours for your records," Arnold stated, handing him a blank envelope, as he gathered up the other papers and placed them tidily onto his desk.

Ernesto started to fold his schedule to put it in the envelope and then into the inside pocket of his blazer, as Salma came into the office, to ask them if they'd like some more coffee? Arnold cautioned his guest, as she waited, respectfully.

"Best keep that safe and out of sight, I'd suggest, eh?"

Ernesto nodded in acknowledgement, as he pocketed the document.

Arnold Fleischer turned towards his loyal housekeeper and said,

"Ah, yes, thank you, Salma...eh, more coffee, Ernesto?" They both looked at him,

"Yes, thank you, that would be very nice," he replied.

"We'll take it in the lounge, I think, Salma, thank you."

"Very good, sir," his housekeeper replied and she turned away.

Arnold and Ernesto strolled into the luxurious lounge to conclude their pleasurable conversation.

"So when is the money from all this profitable activity available, may I ask?" Ernesto enquired, as he sat down in a large and very comfortable, armchair.

"Oh, immediately; option trades are settled the following day. The money's already on call deposit, awaiting our instructions, my friend," Arnold chortled, as he sat down opposite the 'Way' leader.

"Well, that's very efficient and good to know," Ernesto replied, adding,

"I'll donate Stephen's share to the Jersey Welfare Trust, I think. It's a charity over there which caters for all the desperately poor on the Island; there aren't that many destitute souls to care for, fortunately, but enough, as always. I read about their activities in a brochure at the Hotel.

The tramp Stephen defrauded in the Royal Square that day, was probably looked after by them, or a similar organisation, so I think it would be fitting, if they received his share of the money."

"Well, that's for you to decide, of course, my friend and all very laudable, too, I must….."

Ernesto cut him short, with the posing of the question Arnold had long feared would be put to him.

"Would you like to contribute, too, Arnold?"

Thinking it was better to be forthright with such an important response, the American replied,

"No, thank you, Ernesto; I have my own charitable arrangements in place; I will, though, like you, give consideration to such matters."

Ernesto wasn't convinced he was serious about it. He thought Arnold had just said that to fob him off.

"Consideration is never enough, Arnold; everybody gives 'consideration' to such matters at some time in their lives and all too often, that's as far as it gets. One has to do it while it is fresh in the mind; otherwise it's too soon forgotten."

"Well, that's as maybe but I and I alone, am responsible for my actions and how I spend my money," replied the American.

"Come, Arnold, match my offer of $2.5 million to the Charity, so we can make it a really worthwhile donation of $5 million to them, won't you?"

"No, Ernesto, I'm sorry; you do what you want to do with your money and I'll do what I want to do, with mine, okay?"

Alvarez persisted, though, convinced the American was stalling about giving to others,

"Look, Arnold, the money you made came from me and my information; without that you wouldn't have made a penny, now would you?"

Arnold snapped back at him,

"You wouldn't be here at all, if it wasn't for me. Who got you the fresh passport with the new identity? Who had the knowledge to invest our monies for us? Who's provided you with unlimited hospitality while you've been over here?"

Arnold had now lost his temper and standing up, red in the face, he shouted to the Guatemalan,
"Don't you sit in my house and tell me how to spend my own money, dammit!"

Ernesto sat back in his chair, quite taken aback by the American's outburst. He looked at his host with a menacing expression on his face.

Before he could respond, Arnold, now shaking with rage, pointed his finger at him and said,
"Don't you look at me like that, Ernesto! Are you going to murder me, too, just like you did Ronaldo Martin, eh? Just because he didn't agree with your philosophy?"

At that point, Salma came into the lounge with the coffee tray for them and Arnold snapped at her,
"Not now, Salma, out! Out!"

His housekeeper was startled by her employer shouting at her to go away and shocked, more importantly, by his red face and bulging eyes. She'd never seen him so angry and feared he might suffer a heart attack, if this continued.

She dutifully retreated with her fare, put it down, once back in the kitchen and listened at the door to eavesdrop on their argument and thereby determine when it was a better time to re-enter the room.

Alvarez, realising he'd really frightened the overweight money man, decided to calm things down. He leant forward in his armchair and apologised to his host.
"I'm sorry, Arnold. I didn't mean to be rude to you or upset you. It's just that most people think giving to others is laudable and they always intend to do it, at some point but then forget about it.

I mean, here we are, with a 'windfall' so to speak, of what?..., some $50 million profit between us, with providing something for the poor, as the source of our good fortune. Now would be an appropriate opportunity to give something back, don't you think? That's all I'm saying; just 10% of it."

"Well, yes, put like that, of course, I can see where you're coming from but it's not for you to decide who should pay, nor to whom. It has to come from the heart; it's not a perfunctory reaction, no matter how justifiable the need."

"That's true, I suppose but the poor need action not postponement by…" Ernesto started to say but Fleischer interrupted him, not really listening to what he was saying,

"I mean, you murder people who don't comply, don't you? I've never killed anybody in my life and yet you made me an accomplice in the murder of Ronaldo Martin and his men, by getting me to lure him to watch his TV that night, didn't you? I feel really guilty about that now, I can tell you."

Back in the kitchen, Salma had poured away the coffee she'd made for them, and put on some fresh, while listening to most of their argument at the kitchen door.

Ernesto was, for once, finding it difficult to respond. He'd clearly underestimated the sensitivity of this 'hardened' businessman and his reaction to his proposal. Not wishing to continue upsetting him, he said,

"Look, Arnold, you had nothing to do with Martin's execution. You were entirely innocent. I'd have got word to him to watch the television that night, by other means, since he was going to die then, before he got me. You just happened to become available at the time…"

Sensing her boss had sufficiently calmed down, Salma attempted another appearance to deliver their coffee to them. She was relieved to see her employer now sitting down and reaching for a cigar from the humidor on the coffee table. He retrieved one of the two left in the container.

She put the coffee tray down on the coffee table and picked up the cigar lighter to give to him, as he finished clipping off the end of the large Davidoff, he favoured. These Dominican made cigars were the best available, he'd asserted and after five hundred years producing them, Arnold felt the Cubans couldn't teach them anything about the Art!

He took the lighter from Salma and thanked her, apologising for being so rude to her earlier and squeezed her hand, as he did so. She smiled down at him, as he lit up but then looked towards Ernesto, with a stern expression on her face. The Guatemalan noticed.

Salma poured out their coffees, as her boss lit up and Ernesto took a sip of the refreshing drink. As Arnold wafted away the plume of smoke he'd generated, she stood by her employer, with her hand on his shoulder, rather than immediately withdraw.

To lighten the atmosphere, somewhat, Ernesto put down his coffee cup and asked his host if it would be possible to have a horse ride before lunch?

"Yeah, sure, Ernesto," Arnold replied, having finally calmed down and sat back in his armchair, with coffee cup in hand.

His Housekeeper whispered in his ear, stating she needed to go out shortly, to get some provisions and he said to her,
"That's fine, Salma...eh, would you also get me some more cigars; I've only one left, I see?"
"Of course, sir," she replied and left the room.

Half an hour later, Ernesto went outside into the bright sunshine, saddled up the horse he rode before and trotted away from the stables at the back of the house and, breaking into a canter, headed for the hills, at the rear of the property.

A few minutes later, Salma Ramirez, appeared at the front door of the house and briefly spoke to Robert Singleton, Arnold's security chief, who was talking to the guards on the door.

He took her to one side. Once out of earshot of the guards, he listened to her intently and then reached inside his jacket and gave her something, which she put into a shoulder bag she was carrying.

She smiled at him, as she walked down the front steps, went around the back of the property and into the garage block. She got into the 4 x 4 Jeep she always used for her shopping trips and reversed the mauve, converted, 'pick up' into the yard and then drove off towards town.

Ernesto was having an enjoyable ride on the horse he'd borrowed from Arnold; the big chestnut mare seemed full of running that morning and, after an hour or so, he'd stopped to admire the breathtaking view of the canyon below him.

The vista was exceptional; the green gorse on the hilltop around him, gave way to purple heathers, of varying shades, right up to the cliff edge, whilst the dark brown clay of the bridle path he'd cantered along, formed a sharp contrast between the rich colours of the setting.

Beyond the purple 'carpet' and the canyon, lay the light brown cliffs in the distance, with a slight mist in between, hovering above the canyon, somehow. Crowning everything, was the deep blue sky, with just a solitary cloud suspended, motionless, above the distant rock face.

'What a spectacular view that is,' Ernesto thought to himself, as he took it all in. He glanced at his wristwatch, seeing it was just past midday and thought to himself,
'It'll take about half an hour to get back, just in time for lunch at 1 o'clock; I know Arnold likes to be punctual...'

Just then, he heard a car approaching, the engine straining to get up the fairly steep slope of the bridal path to his position. He dismounted, tying the reins of his horse to a small sapling, to avoid it being startled by the approaching vehicle and waited expectantly.

A mauve coloured Jeep suddenly surged onto the flat ground in front of him and braked sharply. The driver got out, a middle aged woman and walked up to him.
"Oh, hello, Salma, it's you; have you finished your shopping? You didn't forget Arnold's cigars, did you?" Ernesto said, with a broad grin.
"No, sir, I didn't forget Mr Fleischer's Davidoffs and I've almost got everything, thank you." she replied, flatly.
"Oh, what do you still need to get then?" Alvarez enquired.

"I need to get rid of you, Mr Ravel or is it Mr Alvarez?" Salma stated, in a very matter of fact sort of way, as she pulled out a pistol from her shoulder bag and pointed it at him.

"What do you...." a single gunshot to the chest interrupted him, as he spun around and fell to the ground. The horse reared up at the sudden crack of the pistol shot and, pulling away from its loose tether, bolted off down the bridal path towards home.

Momentarily distracted by the startled animal, Salma looked away from the Guatemalan but immediately regained her composure and shot him again, fearing he might lunge at her. He didn't.

Ernesto could hardly believe this was happening; through the intense pain he felt, was this woman standing over him, hitherto the epitome of the gentle and courteous housekeeper he'd known only a couple of hours before, about to murder him, in cold blood!

"Mr Fleischer couldn't do what so obviously needs to be done. He wouldn't hurt a fly and yet you terrified him with your implied threats to his life, if he wouldn't obey you. My boss has done so much for me and my family, since he's been here and for the locals, too."

Alvarez sensed he was beginning to lose consciousness, as she continued to explain her presence there.

"You have no right to kill people who will not agree to your demands. Who do you Guatemalans think you are, eh? You're all the same, you people."

Ernesto probably didn't hear the shot which killed him. Salma fired twice more to make sure he was dead; twice into the heart.

"And you'll no longer need this, either," she said to the corpse, as she stooped over his body, reaching into the inside pocket of his blazer and withdrawing the blank envelope. She stood up, looked at the deceased once more and walked back to the Jeep, putting the pistol back into her shoulder bag. She started it up, reversed the vehicle and gently drove down the rutted bridal path, back to her boss's place.

Salma Ramirez returned to the house at 12.45pm, parked the mauve 4 x 4 in the garage, removed her shopping from the front passenger seat (simply the box of cigars) and strode up the front steps of the property.

Robert Singleton was there to greet her and he ushered her away to the side, once again. He smiled, as she reached into her shoulder bag and handed back his pistol to him, which he promptly put inside his jacket. She returned to the front door and smiled to Arnold's security chief, once more, and then breezed inside.

She found Arnold in his library. He looked up from the newspaper he was reading, glanced at his watch and said to her,

"You're late, Salma, that's not like you."

"I know, sir, I'm sorry about that but I had something else to take care of, as well," she replied, handing him his box of twenty five Davidoffs.

"Oh, thank you, my dear…eh, so what was the additional thing you had to do, then?"

His housekeeper moved over to the Grand Piano, picked up the photo of Ernesto Alvarez and took it over to him, saying,

"I took care of him for you; the Guatemalan won't be bothering you any more, so there's no need to keep this reminder of him, is there, sir?"

Arnold's jaw dropped. He was speechless for a moment and then, having regained his composure, he said to her,

"What do you mean, Salma?"

"I killed him on the way back from the tobacconist in the town. I took the country route, around the hills where Mr Alvarez or Mr Ravel or whatever he was calling himself, would be riding. I met up with him and shot him dead. I borrowed Mr Singleton's pistol to do it."

Arnold's mouth was still open in disbelief at what he was hearing.

"It needed to be done, sir, I'm afraid and you couldn't do that, I know you couldn't, so I had to do the job, for your sake and for all of us here."

"I,,..I,,..eh.., don't know quite what to say, I mean…where is the body now, then?"

"He's lying in the gorse, just back from the bluff at Pine Ridge. He was admiring the view when I came along so, at least, he had an enjoyable few moments before he died," his housekeeper stated, flatly.

Arnold was amazed at how resourceful and determined, this diminutive lady of his, was; he thought he knew her really well after all these years but clearly there was a lot more to her than he thought!

"I would never, normally, do anything like that, of course, sir but the way he was treating you, after you'd done so much for him and all; I couldn't bear to see you suffering so much, especially this morning, during coffee…" Her boss interjected,

"Well, then, the least I can do is help with getting him off the property, his body, that is, so no suspicion falls on this household, eh? Ask Mr Singleton to come in and see me, would you? Oh, and I agree we should get rid of this, too," he said to her, giving the photo frame of the late Mr Ernesto Alvarez to her.

"Yes, sir," she said, smiling back at her boss.

Twelve hours later, at just past 3 am, all was quiet in Managua, the Capital of Nicaragua. The stars were out in that cloudless night sky and they shone brightly. The climate was still warm, as the City lights shimmered beneath the heavens.

Nothing stirred; well, almost nothing. Two small dots of light, adjacent to each other, were seen to be on the move. From the top of the hill, overlooking the City, it appeared the lights were getting bigger and they were. A car was moving along the empty road away from Managua, steadily travelling up the hill, well within the speed limit, towards Diriamba.

When it got to the top of the hill, it slowed down and came to a stop, between two street lights, some one hundred yards apart. After a moment or two, a couple of men got out of the vehicle, a mauve coloured, converted, 4 x 4 Jeep, 'pick up.' In the back of the utility vehicle was a step ladder and a long bundle of some kind, like a rolled up carpet.

The men got both items out of the back. One placed the step ladder against the, six feet high, metal, fence and returned to his mate to man-handle the awkward bundle towards it. Having placed the 'carpet' bundle up against the step ladder, it was upended and the bundle slid down the other side of the barrier. The two men walked up the ladder and jumped off it, the second, holding a cord attached to the apparatus, then heaved it up over the obstacle and laid it down inside the fence.

Having looked around to ensure their presence hadn't been discovered, each picked up one end of the bundle and they proceeded to struggle up the hillside with it.

Ten minutes later, they'd reached a clearing of flat ground and gently put the 'carpet roll' down. They moved towards the edge of the hilltop to survey the scene below.

A well lit, two storey, eight bedroomed, house, with a partially repaired roof, was below them. They looked at each other and one nodded. The two of them then moved back to the clearing and picked up the heavy bundle and returned to their vantage point overlooking the substantial property.

With everything quiet down below, they manoeuvred the, trussed up, 'carpet roll' right to the edge of the hillside. Another nod from one of them and a knife cut the three slim ropes binding the bundle. A final nod saw the bundle unwound and something within rolled out down the hillside.

As the body of Ernesto Alvarez, the erstwhile leader of 'The Enlightened Way' crashed through the undergrowth of the steep hillside, gathering speed, it made quite a noise.

Several dogs, in the garden below, started barking, as the corpse neared the bottom of its fall and a number of lights came on in the house.

The two 'depositors' returned quickly to the hilltop and were back down by the foot of the metal fence some three minutes later. They were up and over it, retrieving the step ladder, without difficulty, less than a minute after that.

Having stowed their equipment in the back of the 'pick up,' they jumped into the 4 x 4, started her up, did a smart U turn in the, still deserted, road and sped off down the modest incline, towards Managua.

Three of the guards from the house finally got to the corpse, which was lying approximately fifty yards from the electrified fence surrounding the late Ronaldo Martin's home. Stapled to the chest of the victim was a card, scrawled upon which were the words:-

'An Eye for an Eye' - Arrivederci Ernesto!

Just before 4 am, the mauve coloured, converted, 4 x 4 Jeep, swung into the drive of Arnold Fleischer's home, drove past the front entrance and around the back of the property, to the garages area. Two men got out, after reversing the vehicle into one of the bays, unloaded the step ladder and placed it against a far wall.

They walked around to the front of the house, up the steps to the portico, as their 'buddies' stepped aside for them, all grinning, simultaneously.

Unusually, given the lateness of the hour, Arnold Fleischer was awake and eager to question them.
"Well, how did it go?" He asked the senior man, Robert Singleton.
"A piece of cake, sir, no problem," he confidently reported.
"Did anyone see you?" Arnold asked his security chief, anxiously.
"No, sir, no-one was around, there, during or back," adding,
"They must have found the body by now, given the noise it made, as it crashed down the hillside."
"Phew, well, let's hope so; it seems it couldn't have gone any better, eh?" Arnold said to his men and also to Salma, as she passed around cups of coffee, with a smile, to all present.
"Hopefully, they'll think justice has now been served and that'll put an end to any reprisals, against anybody they suspected might have been involved," Fleischer ventured to suggest.

Ten minutes later, Arnold had finished his coffee and announced that he was going to turn in, at last.
"Thanks Bob," he said to his main man, as he passed by him and then he turned and faced Salma.
"And especially to you, my dear; your loyalty to me is outstanding, I must say and which I fully appreciate."
"Thank you, sir," was the soft response from his housekeeper.

Later that morning, much later, during 'brunch,' Arnold mentioned to his security chief, that there was one item outstanding: What to do about Omah Djesturi? He'd be expecting Ernesto to call him, or Stephen, for that matter, in a day or two, wouldn't he?

After a lengthy conversation with Robert Singleton, Arnold decided to ring Omah and inform him of their deaths. At least this way, the American could gauge his reaction to the news and the likely consequences.

As Arnold made the telephone call to the Deputy of 'The Way' in London, Singleton met Salma in the hall and mentioned to her the expedient nature of their boss's call. She busied herself around him, unobtrusively, as usual and became aware the conversation wasn't going that well.

Arnold finally put the 'phone down, patently hot and bothered, she noticed. He turned to her and said,

"He doesn't believe me that Ernesto was killed by sympathisers of Ronaldo Martin, although he was convinced about Stephen's death. That's something I suppose," he acknowledged, disconsolately.

"What does he plan to do, sir? Did he say, at all?" His devoted servant enquired. Arnold stood up, brushed back his hair and replied,

"He's coming over here next week to collect what's due to him and after making some enquiries of his people up North, I think he said."

"Did he say, when, exactly, sir?" Salma persisted.

"Next Wednesday, I think; yes, next Wednesday, he said. Why do you ask, my dear?"

"Well, it must be helpful to know how long we've got to decide what's best to do. After all, I was the one who killed that awful man, wasn't I?"

"We're all in it together, my dear, so don't feel for one moment, that only you're responsible."

"No, sir, thank you, sir," replied Salma, only partially convinced, if the 'crunch' ever came.

The following Wednesday, Omah Djesturi duly flew into Managua airport, from London, arriving in the early afternoon. He was met outside the terminal building by two men, who escorted him to a waiting car. Not a red - pennanted, blue Buick, though; this one was a black Mercedes 600 Pullman, which speedily whisked him away from the kerbside.

Someone had telephoned Roberto Martin, now back from the U.S and supervising the repairs to his late brother's damaged property that Ernesto's deputy was flying into Managua, from London, that day. He was much appreciative of the anonymous 'tip off' and said to the caller that he'd make arrangements to collect him!

The same caller also telephoned the Managua Post, later on that afternoon and the Police, stating that a 'notorious terrorist' was residing in the home of the late Ronaldo Martin - in the large property on the hill, outside the City and '*No, I'm sorry, I can't give you my name; I'm just trying to do a public service, you understand!*'

The law and the Press arrived, almost together, at the substantial property overlooking the City and, after an extensive search, a dead body had been found in the cellar of the building.

Several arrests followed and the Post ran their 'scoop' with the headline: **'Another death at Drug Baron's house.'**

A couple of days later, two readers of the mass - circulation, tabloid, who were some five hundred miles apart, pondered the sensational story. One was the exiled financier, Arnold Fleischer, still wondering when this 'nightmare' would end and the other, was Emilio Sorca, the 'commander' of the late Ernesto Alvarez's rebel forces, in Guatemala.

The American had read the report of Omah's death in the paper, several times already, but felt it better not to enquire of his staff who they felt might have been the mystery caller. Moreover, he'd reasoned, there was no mention of anybody in his household making such a call and it could have been anyone, of course!

Emilio read the story two days after the American was aware of it. He didn't know any of Ernesto's friends, apart from Omah, of course; only that his former leader had ordered the elimination of the Martin gang and their boss on the evening of the 8th May. They hadn't been aware that the Drug Baron had had a younger brother living in America for quite a while and it was now obvious, he was seeking to avenge Ronaldo's death.

He would have to move against these 'evil doers' once more, to 'cleanse the earth' properly this time and he started making some telephone calls, accordingly.

Back in Managua, Arnold had expressed his relief to his Housekeeper, that the impending threat of Omah's arrival on the scene had been removed by his sudden death at the hands of Roberto Martin, Ronaldo's younger brother. She had smiled, empathetically, to her overweight and congenial boss, as she cleared away his breakfast dishes that morning.

He surprised her, though, when he said to her,

"Whilst I'm sure you know more than me, about these latest developments, my dear, and I wouldn't deign to ask any awkward questions of you, I just want you to know how grateful I am for your unstinting support for me. I'm going to give you a substantial pay rise, in recognition of all the additional, hopefully 'one off,' responsibilities, you've had to shoulder, of late. I'm going to double your salary, forthwith!

"Oh, sir, that's very kind of you and much appreciated," his employee replied, putting down the breakfast tray on a side-table and moving back to her boss. She kissed him on the cheek and added,

"As far as the informant is concerned, I'm sure they did it for the public good; I mean, if there are any more reprisals, then better it be between two evil parties, than innocent folk, wouldn't you agree, sir?"

"Indeed I would, Salma, indeed I would," Arnold replied, reciprocating her affection. She smiled at her employer again, picked up the breakfast tray and withdrew.

Notwithstanding Arnold's more relaxed demeanour, he still had an uneasy feeling about that money, all $52,125,020 of it, which was now, technically at least, all his. He was quite a superstitious fellow, too, despite being a callous money maker and this now got the better of him. He didn't like the notion of the evil influence of it, since he'd never kill anyone over money, unlike some others had done.

'This money is jinxed, I reckon; three people have already died because of it and I think I should get rid of it,' he thought to himself.

'I think I'll give it all to that Charity Ernesto was so keen upon… what was it called, now? Oh, yes, the Jersey Welfare Trust. I'll give them a call shortly and I will then feel better about It,' he further mused.

Just after 11 am, he found the number of the Jersey Charity in a brochure of the Hotel Royale in Ernesto's bedroom and telephoned them, asking to speak to the Senior Trustee there.

At 5.15pm GMT, Sir James Le Marchant was preparing to leave his office for the day, when the telephone rang. He picked up the receiver and said,

"Le Marchant."

"Oh, Sir James, there's an American on the line wanting to speak to the Senior Trustee of the Welfare Trust; I think he wants to make a donation to it," said the chirpy telephonist.

"Well, that sounds promising, doesn't it? You'd best put him through, then," the amiable, Senior Trustee of Jersey's largest welfare charity, suggested.

"Hello, Sir James Le Marchant speaking, can I help you?"

"Ah, yes, I hope so; my name is Fleischer, Arnold Fleischer. I've been seeing a lot of your charitable works on the TV over here and as it's such a laudable cause, I think I'd like to make a donation to it - to boost your reserves, somewhat."

"Well, that's very good of you to consider us, ..eh…Mr Fleischer, might I ask how much you'd like to consider donating to the charity?"

The voice on the other end of the line stated emphatically,

"Something over $50 million; $52,125,020 to be precise. That's about £37million in your currency, with Sterling at $1.40 to the Pound, I think."

There was quite a long pause, before Sir James managed to respond,

"Hello, are you still there, Sir James? Arnold enquired.

Clearing his throat, the Senior Trustee of the charity replied,

"Oh, yes, I'm still here, Mr Fleischer; would you just repeat the figure you had in mind donating to us, please? You know, just in case I misheard you." Arnold Fleischer duly did so.

Sir James wrote down the figures once again and he hadn't misheard the caller. He was stunned!

Half an hour later, after the charity's bank account details had been called over twice to this prospective benefactor, Sir James thanked Arnold Fleischer, yet again, for his extraordinary generosity.

"Not at all, Sir James, we'll all be the better for it, I'm sure and I'll arrange for the money to go off to the bank tomorrow. Goodbye."

Arnold put the 'phone down feeling very much better. Six thousand miles away, on the island of Jersey, Sir James Le Marchant did the same and poured himself a stiff drink to celebrate such a colossal donation.

As he sat back in his chair, he thought to himself, *'That sort of a donor is an extremely rare breed, to be sure. We could all do with some more people like him! Such incredible generosity, I must say. I've certainly got something worthwhile to report to the House tomorrow. Goodness me, that donation represents almost all that that Alvarez fellow cost us recently. Maybe the charity could be persuaded to reimburse the Rainy Day Fund somewhat, since it's heavily subsidised by the States, anyway? Now, wouldn't that be ironic?"*

Sir James finished his whisky, put the glass down on his desk and left his office, with a pronounced spring in his step.

- - - - ooOOoo - - - -

www.ingramcontent.com/pod-product-compliance
Lightning Source LLC
Chambersburg PA
CBHW050510260626
47157CB00004B/1264